TRUTH OR DARE

also by ella monroe

Capital Girls
Secrets and Lies

TRUTH OR DARE
A CAPITAL GIRLS NOVEL

ella monroe

ST. MARTIN'S GRIFFIN ⚞ NEW YORK

This is a work of fiction. All of the characters, organizations, and events portrayed in this novel are either products of the authors' imaginations or are used fictitiously.

www.stmartins.com

Design by Anna Gorovoy

ISBN 978-0-312-62304-3 (trade paperback)
ISBN 978-1-250-03122-8 (e-book)

St. Martin's Griffin books may be purchased for educational, business, or promotional use. For information on bulk purchases, please contact Macmillan Corporate and Premium Sales Department at 1-800-221-7945 extension 5442 or write specialmarkets@macmillan.com.

First Edition: April 2013

10 9 8 7 6 5 4 3 2 1

for my wonderful sister, dee huxtable.

and as always,

for charley, phoebe, and ben.

for my sister, eleanor,

and my brother, stan.

TRUTH OR DARE

ONE

The past month had been hell.

Scratch that. The past *year* had been hell.

And now this?

Jackie Whitman threw herself onto the sofa and glared first at the TV, then at the gold-embossed card in her hand.

Mrs. Elizabeth "Libby" Ballou

Miss Laura Beth Ballou

AND

Senator Jeffrey Ives

KINDLY REQUEST YOUR PRESENCE AT

A CELEBRATION OF THE LIFE OF TAYLOR CANE

1

Jackie could hardly believe a whole year had passed since Taylor was killed in a car wreck. It still seemed unreal. Yet it was also too real. Too raw.

Unreal to think that Taylor—her best friend, the one who taught her that life should be fun and *loyalty* a given—had had sex with Jackie's boyfriend the night she died. Andrew's devastating confession, though, was as real and as raw now as the day she heard it.

A whole year later, and she still hadn't discovered the answer to "Why?" What dark secret had forced Taylor to betray her?

Seething, she reread the surprise invitation to an event she'd known nothing about, then shoved it back in her purse and snapped the clasp. She didn't need this. Not today of all days.

In less than an hour, unless a miracle happened, Senator Jeffrey Ives—Laura Beth's soon-to-be stepfather—would be announcing his candidacy for president of the United States. Running against President Deborah Price, Andrew's mother and the boss and best friend of Jackie's mom.

Throwing Jackie and Laura Beth into enemy camps. Threatening to destroy what was left of the Capital Girls. If Whitney Remick didn't do it first, of course. Jackie shoved away thoughts of the two-faced Cali transplant. She didn't need that worry today, either.

Senator Ives's announcement was why Jackie was sitting in the First Family's private living room in the White House, waiting for President Price and Jackie's mom, Chief of Staff Carolyn Shaw, to arrive. So they could all watch it together. Like one big happy family.

Jackie stared at the TV, where a blond, Botoxed reporter was standing outside the senator's brand-new Iowa campaign head-quarters.

Jackie couldn't believe her ears. The presidential election was almost two years away and Senator Ives hadn't even won the Republican nomination. Yet the reporter was already referring to him as President Price's "worst nightmare" and "her most formidable obstacle to a second term."

"What crap!" she said out loud.

Without warning, Jackie felt a pair of warm hands on her shoulders. She shivered in delight as the strong fingers began to gently yet firmly massage the tense muscles in her neck.

Andrew, she thought, surprised, but also thrilled by his touch.

"Should I stop?" Andrew's brother, Scott, said from behind the sofa. "Or should I see what else needs my magic touch?" he whispered teasingly.

A wave of guilt washed over her. His hands felt so good she didn't *want* him to stop. But what if their mothers walked in on them?

Or Andrew? Though their relationship had hit rock bottom, they were still "a couple" in the eyes of their parents and the public. After all, the Ankie romance, as the media dubbed it, was fodder for the tabloids and great family-values publicity for the president. And as much as she wished it didn't, her stomach still did a little flip whenever she looked at him.

Yet there was also no denying the chemistry between her and Scott. But what if it was more than that? Like Andrew, she'd grown up with Scott. He was a good listener, someone she'd always been able to talk to. Hang with. Trust. The way she used to with Andrew.

Despite her anger toward her best friend, Jackie tried to imagine how Taylor would handle Scott's flirting.

"Maybe we can continue this later," she purred, channeling Taylor's wild, party-girl self.

"I'm down with that. Just name the time and the place." She could hear the smile in his voice.

"Be careful what you wish—"

A voice cut her off.

"Hi!"

Lettie Velasquez walked into the room, beaming.

"I'm here to cheer you up," she declared. "Your mom arranged it. Sorry it took so long. They've really amped up the security around here."

For most of winter break, Jackie had barely moved an inch without a Secret Service tail.

All because some insane person keeps threatening me.

Her skin crawled at the thought of the terrifying note the stalker somehow had smuggled into the White House Christmas party. She felt violated all over again.

"Hi, Scott!" Lettie said. "Where's Andrew?"

"Hey, Lettie! He's helping Dad bake brownies," Scott answered, giving Lettie a quick hug before walking around the sofa and sitting next to Jackie. "Too bad Andrew can't slip some weed in the batter. That'd really cheer us up. But Number One Perfect Son would never do that."

Jackie slapped him lightly on the arm, her hand lingering.

"Behave!" she joked, although she was half-serious.

Scott's fondness for smoking weed had landed him in a Midwestern reform school, sent there by his parents. Now he was on family probation—the Prices having just agreed to let him stay in D.C. for the rest of his senior year.

As for his crack about Andrew, it was anything but true. Actually, Andrew's "perfect" façade had crumbled. At least behind closed doors. He'd been drinking way too much, getting lousy grades at Georgetown University, and generally acting like a jerk. So she wasn't about to defend her so-called boyfriend. Besides, she didn't want to get stuck in the middle of another Andrew-Scott rivalry thing. When they were little kids they'd fought for their mother's attention and argued over stupid things like who got to bat first in a game of T-ball. Instead of growing out of their sibling rivalry, now it was worse than ever.

So she bit her lip. And withdrew her hand from Scott's when she saw Lettie giving her a puzzled look.

"Scott, move over. Lettie, come sit next to me," she said.

"I'm good! You know me, I like to sit on the floor when I watch TV."

Jackie shifted her legs so Lettie could lean against the sofa. She picked up Lettie's long, black ponytail, pulled out the elastic, and started to make a Katniss braid. Lettie, with her dark hair and eyes and olive skin, could have easily passed for the *Hunger Games* heroine.

As she divided the hair into three thick strands, she thought how ironic it was that Lettie was offering to cheer *her* up. When it was Jackie who should be comforting Lettie, whose entire family, apart from her brother, Paz, was trapped in their home country of Paraguay, where civil unrest had broken out.

"Have you heard from your mom and dad?" she asked. Lettie shook her head slowly.

"Not for a while," she said. She was quiet for a moment before continuing. "That's the hardest part. It's so difficult getting letters in and out and the phone lines are down a lot of the time, so it's impossible to call. And of course, the government's shut down the Internet."

"You are so unbelievably brave. I don't know how you do it."

"I don't have any choice," Lettie said simply. "I force myself to focus on my studies and I convince myself that the ambassador will keep them safe as long as Mamá and Papá continue working for him. Besides, most of the clashes are in the countryside, not the capital."

Jackie knew that Lettie followed every single news item about the country and that right now, there seemed to be a little less bloodshed.

"It can't be easy living with Whitney and her mom," Scott said. Jackie had been thinking the exact same thing since the day Lettie moved in with Whitney and her parents, William Remick and Tracey Mills, who were nothing like Lettie's own close-knit family.

"I'm surprised Whitney didn't force you to bring her along today," Jackie said, using both hands to twist the ribbons of hair into a braid.

"Oh, Whitney's not as bad as you think. Anyway, she's still in L.A. Fortunately, her mom didn't know I was coming here otherwise she would have made Whitney fly back early."

"Did you get your invitation yet?" Jackie asked, cutting off Lettie's lame defense of Whitney.

"What invitation?"

Jackie rolled her eyes.

"We've been summoned to a memorial celebration for Taylor. Hosted by Laura Beth and her mom. And Senator Ives.

Tracey Mills probably got to yours first so she could steam it open." Whitney's mom was a gossip columnist who'd do anything for a scoop.

Lettie twisted her head around to look at Jackie, her mouth gaping. "A Taylor celebration? You're not serious."

"I wish."

Not that an event to mark the one-year anniversary of Taylor's death was a bad idea. It was the sneaky way Laura Beth had done it, not even discussing it first with Jackie or Lettie. And why was Senator Ives's name on the invitation? He had never even met Taylor.

The campaign hadn't even started and yet the two Ballou women were already plotting behind Jackie's back to make sure Senator Ives scored political points with the media and Washington's powerful elite. Starting with Taylor's mom. Jennifer Cane. The Fixer. The keeper of Jackie's secrets, who Jackie owed big-time.

My name should be on that invitation, not theirs.

She wrapped the elastic around the end of the braid and Lettie draped it over her shoulder, her Capital Girls charm bracelet jangling. Taylor had come up with the name of their exclusive clique in seventh grade and Libby Ballou had ordered four identical bracelets, adding a charm every year to represent each year of the girls' friendship.

After Andrew's confession, Jackie had thrown her bracelet in a bedroom drawer. And she hadn't worn it since.

Jackie suddenly thought of a whole new reason to be terrified of a Price-Ives election fight. What if someone dug up the secret fact that it was Andrew, not Taylor, who was driving the night of the fatal crash? What if that someone was Laura Beth, who Jackie worried already suspected the truth?

If Taylor was willing to betray me, why wouldn't Laura Beth? Until Sol came along, Laura Beth had harbored a not-so-secret crush on Andrew, obviously fantasizing about one day being his First Lady. But that's all it had been—a deluded dream. Becoming First Daughter in an Ives White House, though, that was a real possibility.

TWO

"Mama, please stop fussin' over my hair. It looks fine," Laura Beth said, ducking out of reach. She'd just spent an hour putting up with the team of stylists that her mama and Senator Ives had kept hidden from the press, in order to prevent any negative stories getting out about the super-rich Ballous.

"Fine just won't do, Laura Beth," her mama chided. "This is our first step on the road to the White House. If all goes as planned, we'll be refurnishing the presidential mansion and presidin' over State Dinners with Kate and Will before you can blink an eye!"

Laura Beth held her tongue. She couldn't blame her mother for being on edge. She knew Mama was so in love with Jeffrey Ives she wanted everything to be just perfect for him. Mama also had a big stake in his success. She'd regain the status she'd had when Daddy was alive and she was the queen bee of the Republican

9

Party. Even so, she'd been extra irritable lately, and Laura Beth wondered if there was something else on her mind.

She forced herself to smile sweetly.

Laura Beth had always envied Jackie's place in the spotlight and never understood why Jackie constantly complained about it. But now she was starting to get it. She was stuck in Iowa for what seemed like forever, rushing from one photo op to the next, practically around the clock and treated like a prop, shoved into the public eye when needed and ignored when the TV cameras turned off.

Obviously, Jeffrey's handlers were incompetent. They didn't seem to understand what an asset she could be to the campaign.

With her political savvy—thank you, Mama and Daddy—her natural acting talent, and her girl-next-door good looks, she'd be the perfect face of the "youth vote for Ives." She pictured her image blasted across social media, from Facebook fan sites to face-to-face interviews with Jon Stewart. She might even be able to swing him Republican.

Yes. She knew *exactly* what her role should be. She just had to come up with a plan to make it happen.

She wished Jeffrey would hurry up and get here so everyone could take their places inside the cavernous Des Moines conference room where the reporters and Ives supporters were waiting for his announcement.

She eyed her two soon-to-be ugly stepsisters, Dina and Frances Ives. They looked like they were actually *into* it—thrilled to be killing time in the middle of freakin' nowhere.

Those two—with their flawless skin, naturally straight black hair, prominent cheekbones, killer bodies, and fake sweetness—truly put her gracious Southern manners to the test.

"Listen! They're chanting his name!" Dina squealed, bouncing up and down on her Mary Janes as the noise filled the hallway. "It's so exciting!"

The only thing the roar did for Laura Beth was give her a headache. Which was fast turning into a migraine when she thought about what she was being forced to wear in front of all those people.

Here she was, about to go on national TV, in a no-brand knit dress that looked like something Lettie would choose if left unsupervised. The beige color totally washed out her delicate complexion and the cut was as shapeless as a sack. When she had a divine, perfectly tailored, turquoise suit hanging in her hotel room.

But the campaign manager had decided all three girls, especially Laura Beth, needed a down-home makeover. To her horror, the three of them had been dragged to dreary Corn Capital Mall, where Ann Taylor passed for high fashion and the only thing French were the fries.

She pulled out her iPhone.

Promise me you won't watch the announcement. They're making me wear a hideous dress. I look like a librarian and not the sexy kind in the movies, she texted her boyfriend, Sol Molla.

She wondered how much this campaign was going to ruin her sizzling love life. It was tough enough with Sol as a full-time student at Columbia in New York City.

"You look very cute, Laura Beth." Frances interrupted her thoughts, giving Laura Beth a condescending glance while also trying to read the text message over her shoulder. "Your frizz is just *adorable.*"

Laura Beth gritted her teeth.

Kill them with kindness, she reminded herself.

Along with being Senator Ives's daughter, Frances was an arrogant congressional aide who worked with First Husband Bob Price on education issues. She was always blabbering on about how great he was, as if he were a hero instead of a two-timing husband and neglectful father.

But Frances's little sister was even worse. A bratty, conniving junior who'd only just started at Excelsior Prep, Dina had quickly become BFFs with Whitney and Angie Meehan, numero unos on the Capital Girls' shit list.

Before she could make nice the way she was supposed to, Laura Beth saw her mama coming at her with the hairbrush again.

"It is not adorable, Frances. It's unruly and she can't walk around looking like she got tossed about in a windstorm."

Nice Southern girls don't sass their mamas, Laura Beth reminded herself.

"Of course not, Mama, thank you," Laura Beth said, flinching as her auburn curls got painfully tangled in the bristles.

She noticed her mother was wearing an antique sapphire instead of her drop-dead-fabulous eight-carat diamond engagement ring.

Surely she couldn't have lost it?

"Mama, where's your ring?" Laura Beth panicked.

"Right here," she said, patting her heart. "Jeffrey says it's so extravagant it sends the wrong message, so I decided to keep it on a chain under my clothes, at least until he wins the nomination."

She held her left hand in front of Laura Beth's face. "This little bitty bauble belonged to his grandmamma. Its value is of the sentimental variety."

Okay. But what kind of message does that four-thousand-dollar Bergdorf

*Goodman handbag send to the voters? Especially if it also turns out to be made
from an endangered species.*

Her mother dropped the brush into her crocodile-skin handbag. "*Now* you look adorable.

"Mercy, I could use a drink right now." She sighed. "Even if it
had to be in a paper cup. Just a teeny bourbon and branch would
do the trick."

Me, too.

Laura Beth remembered the last time Taylor had made them
cocktails. All four girls were sprawled on the deep-pile white rug
in front of the Italian marble fireplace in the Ballous' family room.

*"I fixed a 'Hollywood' for Laura Beth. 'Cuz that's the next step after Broadway,
baby," Taylor said, handing me a glass that looked like it was filled with liquid
gold.*

*"An 'Apple Pie,' natch, for the all-American girl," she joked to Jackie, "who's
gonna be the second female president of the United States, unless I can persuade
her to run off with a Chippendale dancer!"*

*Jackie grinned and sniffed the drink. "Yum. Apple schnapps? With cinna-
mon?"*

Taylor nodded.

*"And for Lettie, a 'Latin Lover' to remind you there's more to life than just
textbooks and law school." Lettie blushed as she took the spiked pineapple juice.*

*"And a 'Sex on the Beach' for moi! What else?" Taylor hooted, shaking her
booty as she drained her glass in one gulp.*

Her mama, plucking imaginary lint off her dress, brought Laura
Beth back to the present.

"Now, remember to smile just the way I told you," she instructed.

"Don't worry, Mama. I'll be a pretty face for you and the senator."

"Laura Beth Ballou, if I've taught you anything, it's that a woman is never *just* a pretty face." Her mother clucked her tongue disapprovingly.

Laura Beth's face got hot.

"Oh, Miss Libby." Dina giggled. "I think Laura Beth only meant that today is my father's show. We don't want to steal his thunder."

"Of course not, sugar." Libby beamed at Dina. "We're a perfect example of the new American blended family. We are all smart, strong women who know how to support their man."

Jeffrey Ives suddenly appeared, flanked by aides, putting an end to the fake love fest.

"Ready, ladies?" He smiled, taking his fiancée's hand.

Laura Beth took a deep breath. Despite the excitement of the moment, all she wanted was to be back home in D.C. with her two best friends.

Who'll probably hate me after today.

"Shit! Shit! Shit! Shit! Shit!" Jackie hissed at the TV as Senator Ives plunged into the crowd outside his campaign headquarters.

A chill ran down Lettie's spine.

If Jackie's already this flipped out, how's she going to survive the next two years?

It didn't help that Senator Ives had given a great speech. He'd hit all the right notes to appeal to his base without sounding like a wacky PAPPie, the breakaway Republican group bent on destroying President Price. From everything Lettie had been reading lately, it looked like the PAPPies were going to pick creepy conservative Senator Hampton Griffin as their presidential candidate.

Lettie studied the TV screen. No Hollywood director could have picked a better-looking cast to play the newly created Ives-Ballou family.

She glanced at Andrew, who was slumped in an armchair at the far end of the room, the Prices' Labradoodle, Leftie, napping at his feet. Unlike Jackie, who'd kept up a scathing running commentary of the speech, Andrew and Scott had traded jokes— until the topic turned to Jackie.

"Well, at least Senator Ives will be the best-dressed man running for president," Andrew said, taking in Senator Ives's immaculately cut gray suit.

"Yeah, but wait till Mom unveils her spring line of pantsuits," Scott joked.

"Doesn't *anyone* care about the issues anymore?" Lettie joined in.

"Sure they do," Scott said. "But it's a lot more convincing when it comes from a handsome knight in shining armor. Not to mention a few cute handmaidens."

"Yeah, and I bet Laura Beth pulls out all the stops for her national debut," Andrew added.

"Laura Beth's no competition next to Jackie," Scott said, throwing her a big smile.

Lettie watched Andrew's face turn into a scowl. "I don't need you to tell me that," he said.

Ouch.

Fortunately Senator Ives wrapped up his speech at that point.

Scott started playing a game on his iPhone, looking up only when the camera zoomed in on Laura Beth.

"That's the ugliest dress I've ever seen," he observed.

"Obviously someone forced her to wear it. No way would she have picked that," Jackie said, studying Laura Beth in amazement.

"Yeah, even I wouldn't wear that," Lettie joked.

"Don't *you* wear clothes like that on the campaign trail, Jackie. Sexy best always gets more votes. Especially your sexy best," said Scott, prompting another glare from Andrew.

Jackie laughed.

Lettie had never flirted in her life but she knew it when she saw it.

What is the deal with Scott? And in front of Andrew?

As if on cue, Andrew snapped, "Jackie would look good in anything."

Jackie didn't answer. Her eyes were fixed on Laura Beth, who was holding hands with Dina and Frances and smiling like there was nobody else she'd rather be with.

"You'd never guess by her little act that Laura Beth hates those two," Jackie said.

"Laura Beth's right where she's always wanted to be, on center stage," Lettie said mildly. "Politics is in her genes."

"Dirty politics, you mean," Jackie said. "Her father was the king of dirty tricks. Let's hope she doesn't follow in his footsteps."

"She hasn't done anything dirty," Lettie said. "She's just smiling. It's typical Laura Beth. Give her a stage and she'll put on a performance."

"Yeah, well, Laura Beth deserves a Tony for this act."

Andrew got out of his chair and bent down to pat Leftie.

"I can't watch any more," he said to no one in particular. "If

16

any of you see Mom or Dad, tell them thanks from me for canceling *another* great family bonding event."

Lettie felt sorry for Andrew. President Price's press secretary, Brian Gillespie, had called to say neither the president nor Jackie's mom could join them after all for Senator Ives's announcement. Bob Price had shown up, but only long enough to pass around a plate of his brownies before disappearing.

Andrew smiled at Lettie, avoided eye contact with his brother and Jackie, and left the room, the Labradoodle trotting behind him. Despite all the flirting between Jackie and Scott, Lettie couldn't help but notice that Jackie eyed Andrew's butt as he walked past her.

Scott got to his feet, yawning. "I'm gonna head out, too. Anyone want to go with?"

"No, thanks. Lettie and I are going to hang for a while," Jackie said.

Scott shrugged and left.

Lettie studied her friend. She was worried about her. First learning about Andrew and Taylor hooking up, then the stalker's threats, and now the possibility of a Price-Ives fight for the White House. At least she was over the panic attacks.

"Do you think you'll be okay going to, uh, this thing Friday?" Lettie asked. Calling it a party didn't feel right.

Jackie was staring at the TV as if she hadn't heard.

"Earth to Jackie . . . Are you going to the memorial thing?"

"What?" Jackie blinked and turned to Lettie.

"Taylor's memorial. Will you be okay going to it?"

"Of course. How can we not go?" Jackie said. She hit the off button on the remote and stood up to stretch.

To celebrate someone we thought we knew inside out but obviously didn't.

One of the things Lettie had most admired about Taylor was her honesty. The way she cut through the crap.

Lettie couldn't believe her luck when she got accepted to Excelsior Prep on a full scholarship. But once there, she felt totally out of place. The girls were way out of her league. They were gorgeous. She felt dull. They were rich. Her family barely got by. They were confident. She was paralyzingly shy. Their parents let them do anything they wanted. Her parents didn't approve of her dating and knew nothing about Daniel, her boyfriend.

Jackie was the first to befriend her at school. Taylor was the first to set her straight.

"Get real, Lets," Taylor lectured me. "You're at Excelsior because of your brains. For what YOU have to offer. The rest of us rode in on our parents' names and the fat checks they write every year." Then she roared laughing. "All I got is my parents' money and my hot body to get me where I wanna go!"

Although it had been several months since Jackie told her about it, Lettie still couldn't wrap her mind around Taylor sleeping with Andrew.

Daniel, who was Taylor's twin, insisted from the start that her death wasn't an accident. Lettie's gut told her nothing about that night made sense. She just didn't know how, what, or why.

"Do you want to come to my place and spend the night?" Jackie asked.

Lettie shook her head. "No, Whitney's flying in from L.A. tonight and I promised I'd be home when she got in."

Jackie raised an eyebrow. "And here I was hoping she'd left and was never coming back."

"Whitney can be . . . difficult sometimes . . . but she's still a person." *And the closest thing I have to a family right now.*

Whitney had confided in Lettie that her father, an economist, was leaving his job at the Washington think tank to work as a campaign policy adviser for President Price. Since he wouldn't have to be based in D.C. anymore, and Whitney's mom could go back to writing Hollywood gossip instead of chasing political sleaze, Whitney had launched a 24/7 campaign to convince her family to move back to L.A.

If the Remicks move back, where will I go?

"How are you getting home?" Jackie asked, tearing Lettie away from her thoughts. "Or are you going to see Daniel for a little fun?"

Lettie knew Jackie was just teasing, but that didn't stop her from turning scarlet.

"Oh Lets, what am I going to do with you?" Jackie hugged her. "You're too cute."

She hugged back, but she thought Jackie was starting to sound almost as patronizing as Laura Beth.

Jackie walked her to the top of the Grand Staircase.

"When Laura Beth gets back, she'll probably want to get together," Jackie said. "Promise me you'll come, too. I can't face her by myself just yet."

Lettie nodded. It was going to be a long campaign and she wasn't sure she was ready for it.

Her heart plunged at her next thought.

At some point, she was going to have to choose sides.

THREE

Laura Beth held the slinky green Alexander McQueen dress against her body and examined her reflection in the full-length mirror, tilting her head and pursing her lips. Sol loved her in this color. He said it made her eyes sparkle.

She sighed and tossed it on top of the pile on her bed. None of them were right. Her mama had insisted the party be black-tie, but Laura Beth felt weird wearing an elaborate gown to commemorate Taylor's death.

She stepped back into her enormous walk-in closet, crammed with couture clothes. But the one outfit that kept drawing her eye was the ugly knit dress from Iowa. It hung there, mocking her.

"I refuse to wear that ugly sack ever again," she huffed as she ran her hand over the next rack of dresses. "I mean, it's bad enough having to wear *anything* twice, but *that* . . ." Still, she didn't

21

have the nerve to throw it in the trash. If the campaign said she had to wear it again, she'd do as she was told for "the cause."

After Jeffrey's announcement, she'd flown home from Des Moines—not on the campaign's private jet, but on a domestic carrier. And only in business class.

It was all so unfair.

She pulled out a violet, strapless number that still had the price tag and marched back to the mirror. This time, she smiled at her reflection.

"Taylor would love this," she said with a grin.

"Laura Beth, no one passed a law saying we have to dress like our mothers," Taylor said as she pulled a dozen designer dresses out of my closet and dumped them on the floor. *"These clothes are gorgeous, but if you ever want to hook up with an actual guy you're gonna need to show more boobs and leg, girl."*

She was right. Taylor was always right about stuff like that. "What do you think I should wear?" I asked. "Mama usually helps me pick my clothes."

"Really?" she teased. "I'd never have guessed. Rule number one. You're starting high school. You gotta dress like you're in college!" She pinched my arm. "You have a sexy little body. Work it!"

I pointed to a pink floral Tracy Reese. "How's this?"

"Perfect!"

I breathed a sigh of relief. Then Taylor frowned and wagged her finger in my face. "If you're going to church!"

We both collapsed on the floor in a fit of uncontrollable giggles. "Tomorrow," Taylor finally gasped. "You, me, and your mama's credit card are hitting Saks. I can't let you go to the ninth grade mixer looking like this."

Laura Beth's heart sank thinking about her friend. It was sad enough remembering Taylor at her best. It was worse discovering that a darkness lurked behind her fun-loving image. No matter how much Laura Beth had daydreamed about Andrew being *her* boyfriend, she would never actually have tried to steal him from Jackie. Yet even knowing the worst about Taylor didn't make her death any easier to accept. The empty place she left behind was still there and Laura Beth wondered if it would ever go away.

I need you more than ever, she thought, blinking away the tears. She wanted to ask Taylor what she thought about Sol. Ask her how to handle her two *ugly stepsisters.* To mediate between her and Jackie when the election campaign got down and dirty.

Laura Beth hadn't been in touch with Jackie or Lettie since returning from Iowa. She'd felt too guilty about organizing the memorial without her best friends, but Mama had insisted. Tonight, there'd be no avoiding them.

Taylor had always been the glue that held the Capital Girls together, and now Laura Beth channeled her dead friend.

She'd say, *"Screw politics. Before anything else, we're friends and don't forget it."* And then she'd raid Mama's liquor cabinet and force them to talk everything through.

A knock on her bedroom door interrupted her thoughts.

"Laura Beth, we need to get movin', sugar." Her mama opened the door without waiting, took one look at her daughter, and frowned. "You're not even dressed yet? What have you been doin'?"

Standing in the doorway, her mother looked fabulous. Her dyed ash-blond hair was twisted into a French roll and her beaded ecru dress flattered her slim figure. Her mother was always immaculately turned out. But since becoming engaged, she glowed.

Laura Beth pouted.

"If you don't stop makin' that face, it'll freeze that way," her mother teased.

Laura Beth removed the violet dress from the hanger and stepped into it. She turned her back to her mother. "I'm almost ready."

Mama zipped her up, prattling on about who would be at the party and which power brokers Laura Beth absolutely needed to charm.

"And don't forget Jennifer Cane," she ordered.

Laura Beth froze, her blood turning to ice water. Of course Taylor's mom would be there. A face-to-face reminder of what Laura Beth had done.

I wasn't trying to hurt Jackie. I was only trying to stop her from making a terrible mistake and ruining her life and Andrew's.

But it had all gone horribly wrong.

If she knew then what she knew now, she would *never* have told Senator Hampton Griffin about Jackie's plan to hook up with his sleazy aide, Eric Moran, at the Kennedy Center.

"Uncle Ham, I need your help," I begged him. He was an old family friend and I thought I could trust him. "You need to do something about Eric Moran. He's preyin' on Jackie Whitman and you have to put a stop to it!"

He promised me he'd forbid Eric to have any contact with Jackie. Ever.

Instead, he'd taken embarrassing photos of Jackie and Eric and then tried to blackmail Jackie. And now poor Jackie owed Jennifer Cane, The Fixer, who did her a favor by destroying the photos.

Laura Beth still felt sick about all of it. Including the fact that she still hadn't fessed up to Jackie. Not to mention that Whitney had somehow discovered Laura Beth's role in the whole mess and had threatened to tell Jackie unless Laura Beth did her bidding.

She tuned in to her mother, who had stopped yammering and was frowning at a text on her cell phone.

"Mama? Is anything wrong?"

Her mama looked up, startled.

"What?" She touched a button on her screen and the text vanished. "Why, no, of course not, Laura Beth. I was just studyin' my to-do list. The most important thing is you must be sure to introduce everyone to Dina and Frances tonight and make them feel part of the family."

After losing the fight with her mother over putting all three Capital Girls on the invitation, they'd argued over whether the Ives sisters, who hadn't even known Taylor, should be invited. Naturally, Mama prevailed.

They've got Mama and Jeffrey wrapped around their manicured little fingers. But they don't fool me.

Laura Beth slipped on a pair of strappy sandals and stood up straight for inspection.

Her mother placed her hand over her heart and smiled. "If you aren't a vision, I don't know what is."

Laura Beth smiled and shook off the bad feelings. There was a party to go to and she had her own role to play.

Libby Ballou sat next to her daughter in the limo. Usually, she reveled in the city's unique sites. But right now she was deep in thought, oblivious to the spectacular view as the limo sailed past the vice president's historic Queen Anne house—with its wraparound porch, white turret, and manicured lawns—and the mansions-turned-embassies lining Embassy Row.

She couldn't imagine losing a daughter. Not that she'd have wanted Taylor for a daughter. Good lord, no. Taylor had run around like a cat in heat. Still, no mother, not even Jennifer Cane, deserved to have her child snatched away.

Libby glanced at Laura Beth, so full of life and promise. Soon she would be leaving home to attend one of those left-wing artsy-type colleges in New York. Certainly not Libby's first choice, but she'd come to accept her daughter's Broadway dreams. *I just hope my connections get her into Juilliard, if her talent can't.*

And then what?

She turned and stared out the window just as the limo eased by the White House. Even from a distance, it glimmered magically under the floodlights.

Her own future was at stake here.

Not just a second chance at happiness with a wonderful man she was madly in love with. But restoring her to her rightful place in this brutal city where the only thing that mattered was, "What have you done for me *today?*"

And it all came down to one thing. Her fiancé winning the presidency. She pictured President-elect and Mrs. Jeffrey Ives pulling up to the White House for the traditional tour led by the departing First Couple. *That's going to be awkward. Having an old friend steal your job and home at the same time.*

As much faith as she had in Jeffrey's talents, nothing could be left to mere chance. And they certainly couldn't afford any scandals. Like the one that she and Jeffrey had managed to keep under wraps so far. They had to find a way to spin it and fast. *And I need to figure out a way to tell Laura Beth.*

Out of the corner of her eye, she watched her daughter's fingers flying over her iPhone. *Probably texting Sol.* Libby was slowly coming around to the idea of Laura Beth dating an Iranian-American Muslim. Thank God the rumors suggesting his family had terrorist ties had been proven wrong. Why, now the campaign could use their romance to its advantage. As proof of a new Republican "big tent" inclusiveness.

Libby reached into her purse and pulled out her own iPhone and scrolled through her new texts. Another one from Jennifer Cane.

Let's hope tonight's gala does what it's meant to—keep Jennifer on our side, Libby thought.

FOUR

The exclusive CityZen restaurant—inside the Mandarin Oriental Hotel overlooking the Jefferson Memorial and the Tidal Basin—was filled with thousands of Taylor's favorite flowers, white gardenias and calla lilies.

Laura Beth's eyes swept across the dining room, taking in the five-piece orchestra and the bevy of bow-tied waiters on standby.

Totally over the top. So Mama. So Taylor.

Her eyes landed on two insanely gorgeous bartenders who were wiping down the marble countertop and arranging glasses. It wasn't only L.A. where the hired help were supplied by a modeling agency. *After all, nobody wants ugly people at their party.*

"Laura Beth, stop starin' at those cute boys and help me find Marco," Mama ordered. "Go look in the lobby."

From the way she was clenching her jaw, Laura Beth knew her

mama was just *this* close to throwing one of her Southern belle hissy fits.

"Yes, Mama."

The lobby was empty but Laura Beth decided to wait and see if Marco emerged from the men's room.

She rearranged the gift bags lined up on a side table. Each held a pocket-size photo album of Taylor and a special Libby-designed paperweight, which featured a hand-painted scene of the Lincoln Memorial—Taylor's favorite monument. The sterling silver bottom was engraved with the words *In loving tribute to Taylor from the Ballou-Ives family.*

Just as she finished, a deep, honeylike voice whispered in her ear.

"Hello, gorgeous."

Laura Beth's breath caught in her throat as Sol pressed himself against her back. His hands slid down her bare arms, leaving a trail of electricity in their wake.

"I've missed you." His breath tickled her ear.

She wished they weren't standing in a restaurant, but somewhere private and alone. Like his parents' pied-à-terre just a few steps from the Capitol.

It had only been two days since she'd seen Sol, but it was two days too long.

"Why, hey," she said, spinning around and pressing her mouth to his. No matter how many times they kissed, she marveled at how he always tasted like perfection.

He nibbled playfully on her bottom lip before releasing her. "Where's Miss Libby?" he asked.

Laura Beth sighed. "Storming the front."

Sol raised his eyebrows. "Why?"

"She got some text message before we left home and it put her in a weird mood. And now she can't find our event planner, Marco, and she's just about havin' a hissy fit."

Sol's eyes grew wide and he backed away jokingly. "Then I better hide." He ducked behind a column and Laura Beth giggled. This is what she loved about Sol. One minute he was so poised and the next, he cracked her up.

"Did someone call for Marco?" a voice boomed from across the room. "There's my favorite girl!" Marco Fabiano said, striding over. "Looking gorgeous as always."

He eyed Sol. "You must be the *boyfriend*."

Laura Beth linked her arm through Sol's and smiled at Marco. "He is indeed! Marco Fabiano, Sol Molla."

The two men shook hands and then Marco narrowed his eyes. "You let me know, Laura Beth, if he misbehaves."

Before she could answer, he spun on his heels and disappeared through the restaurant doors, calling, "Here I am, Ms. Ballou!"

Laura Beth leaned her head on Sol's shoulder.

"Hey, what's wrong?" Sol asked, wrapping his arms around her.

She shook her head, her eyes moist. "I wish you'd met Taylor. You would have loved her."

Sol kissed the top of her head. "I'm sure I would have."

It was comforting to hear him say that, but it didn't make her feel any less nervous about the evening ahead. She desperately wanted this party to be not just a success, but also a reminder to the Capital Girls of how important their friendship was.

She knew perfectly well what her mother's motive was. And it would have taken Jackie about two seconds to figure it out, too. She now regretted waiting until tonight to reach out to Jackie. To explain how it was all Mama's idea. Even Jackie knew there was no stopping Libby Ballou, the Velvet Steamroller.

Laura Beth was dying to move into the White House, but she hated what it was going to take to get there.

Hidden behind the SUV's tinted windows, Jackie watched the guests filter into the luxurious hotel, where one night in the Oriental suite cost six grand. "Taylor didn't even know half these people," she hissed under her breath.

Typical Washington function. Most of the adults were there to kowtow to Jennifer Cane, chat up anyone else who might do them a favor now or in the future, or show support for Senator Ives's presidential bid. How many would give Taylor even a passing thought?

Laura Beth, Lettie, and I should be celebrating Taylor's life with a flask of Jack at the Lincoln Memorial. Not here.

"It's not right."

"Are you okay, Miss Whitman?" Secret Service agent Ellen Fellows asked from the front passenger seat.

Jackie wanted to scream, "Hell no! I'm not all right! My life's a freakin' circus. First the media stalks me, then the stalker stalks me, and now all of you are following my every move."

Just hurry up and catch him. How hard can it be?

But she just nodded. She wasn't about to confide in her gatekeeper.

On top of everything, she dreaded putting on another public performance with Andrew, especially when he'd look totally gorgeous in a tux. Not to mention the whole Scott complication. Aunt Deborah was too busy to make a personal appearance at the party, but she had ordered both sons to be there. She'd also arranged for the White House photographer to take a shot of Jackie and Andrew honoring Taylor. Once again, Jackie would have to pretend they were still together, still Ankie in the eyes of the world, while spending the rest of the night avoiding Scott's flirting.

So far senior year sucks. What's the point of being the It Girl if I can't enjoy it?

She pictured the scene inside. Laura Beth and Miss Libby, and their new blended family, all at the center of attention.

Tracey Mills—with insider details supplied by Whitney—had probably already written the story: *"I don't know about you, but I'm voting for Senator Jeffrey Ives for president if last night's blowout party at CityZen, hosted by his fiancée, Libby Ballou, is a prelude to White House entertaining in an Ives administration."* Followed by a rundown on who was there and what they wore. Taylor would be a postscript, if anything at all.

Jackie walked through the hotel lobby, her head held high. Inside the restaurant, she brushed past the crowd of teenagers clamoring for her attention. A small group was standing in front of a giant TV screen, which was showing a photo loop of Taylor's life.

She scanned the faces, looking for Lettie or Laura Beth, but saw only Daniel, standing by himself near the bar.

When he spotted her walking toward him, he raised the glass in his hand as if to toast her. It was such a Taylor gesture that Jackie's heart skipped a beat.

"Hi," she said, planting a kiss on his cheek. "How are you coping?"

Daniel swirled the amber liquid in his glass. "The free drinks help."

Being a skateboard champion and a fitness fanatic, he usually didn't drink much. But Jackie figured this was one night he needed lots of help to get through.

She just hoped Andrew wasn't going to get drunk. The two guys had been at each other's throats ever since Daniel decided that Andrew somehow was to blame for Taylor's death. No one needed a replay of his and Daniel's fistfight at the Homecoming dance.

"Where's Lettie?" she asked him.

"She texted me that she's stuck at the Watergate waiting for Whitney. I guess that means they'll be late."

"I don't know how Lettie puts up with her."

"Lettie's the only one with the patience to do it," he said with a sweet smile.

"Hi, Jackie," came a throaty voice from behind her.

She whirled around. Jennifer Cane and her husband, Aaron, stood hand in hand. She gave Jackie an air kiss then whispered something in her husband's ear. "Daniel, can you come with me for a second?" Aaron Cane said to his son after nodding hello to Jackie.

Jackie felt the hair on the back of her neck rise. *What does she want?*

"Thank you for being here tonight," Jennifer said. "Taylor loved you like a sister."

"I felt the same," Jackie answered, relieved. "I miss her so much."

Jennifer nodded. "I'll never stop missing her."

She stepped a little closer and her eyes hardened. "So, tell me, how have you been?"

It was an innocent question. But Jennifer Cane made it sound ominous.

How does she do that? Go from mommy to menacing in the blink of an eye?

"Fine."

"No need for me to pay Hampton Griffin another call?" she asked, arching her eyebrows.

Just as Jackie was about to utter a polite version of *No, I just want you to forget about it and go away. Forever* . . . someone grabbed her from behind.

"Jackie! It's so great to see you! You look fantastic!" A lanky guy with dark blond hair and a deep California tan was grinning at her. It was Taylor's older brother, Sam.

"Hey, Mom, quit hogging the most awesome girl in the room," he joked, waving Jennifer Cane away. "Besides, Dad needs you. He's over by the bar."

No sooner had Jennifer turned away, than Sam pulled Jackie into a tight embrace and kissed her lightly on the lips.

"Sam, I haven't seen you in ages," Jackie answered, trying to pull away. Aside from Taylor's funeral, the last time was when he came on to her at a Thanksgiving party just before Taylor died.

"Aren't you glad I rescued you from my monster mommy?" He laughed bitterly. "She's one of the reasons I hardly ever come home. But no way would I have missed Taylor's anniversary."

His face was sad for a second. Then he shrugged. "As Tay would say, the party must go on! Let me get you a drink."

Still holding her close with one arm, he grabbed a waiter to swap his empty glass for a full one. "Is champagne okay?"

She stepped out of his grasp and shook her head. "No, thanks." She needed to keep her wits about her.

"How's college?" she asked to change the subject.

"Boring. But hey, I'm not complaining. Just another year and I'm done. And living in L.A. beats D.C. any day."

He moved in close to her again and was stroking her arm when Daniel came back.

"Hey, bro. Down, boy. Give Jackie some breathing space," Daniel interrupted.

"We're just catching up," Sam said, smirking. He dropped his hand. Only to put his arm around her shoulder. "Jackie and I go way back, dude."

Um, no, we don't.

Sam, who was three years older than his twin siblings, rarely hung out with the Capital Girls even when he'd lived in D.C. And Taylor had acted real jumpy whenever he had shown up.

When Lettie got a crush on him years ago, Taylor quickly nixed it.

"I told Lettie he's gay," Taylor said to me, admitting it was a total lie.

"But what if Lettie really likes him?" I argued, shocked.

Taylor just shrugged and told me to drop it.

Daniel moved between them and Jackie shot him a grateful smile.

"Sam was telling me how much he loves L.A.," she said.

"I'm glad to be out of L.A. and back in D.C.," Daniel answered. "What's so great about it?"

While Sam boasted about his nonstop Cali party life, Jackie studied the scene. Libby Ballou, her arm linked with Senator Ives, was feverishly working the crowd, moving from one VIP to the next and pushing the senator's two daughters up front and center. There was no sign of Laura Beth.

I wonder how she managed to escape.

Someone put a hand on her back.

"Jackie, it's time." Andrew pressed his lips to her hair.

He stroked her back tenderly before moving away to shake hands with Sam. Jackie held her breath, waiting to see if he would shake Daniel's hand, too. Both of them took a step toward each other and shook hands soberly.

"Sam, Daniel, I know tonight must be difficult for you," Andrew said. The two brothers nodded. "Sam, I haven't seen you since . . ." He paused. It was obvious he was about to say "the funeral." "It's good to see you," he added instead.

"You too, Andrew," Sam answered.

"I'm sorry, but I need to steal Jackie away for a few minutes," Andrew said, turning back to her.

He looked as incredible as she'd expected. His bow tie had a touch of green that brought out the color of his eyes and his hair had that tousled, just-out-of-bed look that always turned her legs to jelly.

And he didn't just look hot. He also seemed sober.

"See you two later," she told the two brothers. Andrew guided her through the crowd.

"You're the most beautiful girl in the room, as usual," he murmured, taking her hand. Her heart fluttered. "And not just because of that awesome dress."

As much as she'd dreaded coming to the party, she'd chosen her dress carefully—a white, gauzy, strapless Rachel Zoe—out of respect for Taylor. And to prove a point to Andrew: *See what you're missing. See what you screwed up.*

"Thanks," she said coolly, though against her will, her heart still raced.

"The photographer's outside. We're supposed to pretend we're arriving together," he said. "Mom's issued her instructions. We have to look romantic but sad. But not too sad."

He's still Mommy's boy obeying orders. "Let's get this over with," she said sharply.

He looked hurt by her curtness.

"I know tonight's really hard on both of us," he said softly. "Dredging everything up."

She nodded mutely.

"Listen, I'm not going to stay long," Andrew continued. "As soon as the speeches are over, I'm going to slip out. I just wanted you to know."

"Yes, I think that's a good idea," she replied, relieved. "I wish I could do the same."

Fortunately, the White House photographer was a pro at snapping Ankie. When Andrew held her hand to pose for the shots, her skin tingled at his touch. She stole a look at him, but his face was impassive. *He's a hot guy. Of course, it's going to feel good touching him,* she thought, *but this is just us doing our political duty. That's it.*

Five minutes later she made her way, alone, to the buffet table. It was decorated with exotic, brilliantly colored orchids and laden with rich lobster salad, buttery-smooth foie gras, and succulent bite-size slices of bacon-wrapped quail.

Not even Whitney, who never eats any damn thing, could resist this feast.

A familiar figure was biting into a toast point spread with foie gras.

"Mom!" Jackie exclaimed, happy to see a friendly face. "When did you get here?"

Her mother brushed a few crumbs off the front of her little black cocktail dress. She had at least a half-dozen identical outfits, suitable for any occasion—weddings, funerals, parties, fund-raisers, or entertaining heads of state.

"I'm not telling." She grinned. "I'm the consummate Washington mingler. You never see me arrive and most importantly, you never see me leave."

Which means she's only staying long enough to be seen by the principal players.

The orchestra suddenly stopped playing and everyone turned to the front of the room, where Libby Ballou stood arm in arm with her new BFFs, Jennifer and Aaron Cane. They were flanked by Laura Beth, the Cane brothers, the senator, and his daughters.

Jackie scooped a spoonful of lobster onto a plate before realizing she felt sick to her stomach.

I'll throw up if I take a single bite.

Jackie and her mother put down their plates and moved toward Miss Libby.

"My dear friends," the hostess began. "From the bottom of my heart, I want to thank y'all for gracin' us with your presence tonight.

"The good Lord, in his wisdom, has called the Canes' precious angel to heaven. I know at this very moment dear, sweet, little Taylor is lookin' down on us tonight . . ."

Yes, and thinking, Who are all these self-inflated suck-ups I hardly even knew?

". . . and seein' how much so many of us loved her so. Aside from her devoted family, Taylor had a circle of very special friends. I'd like y'all to come on up here with us, too."

Jackie's stomach twisted into a knot.

"Jackie Whitman, Laetitia Velasquez, Andrew and Scott Price, y'all come join us."

Jackie grabbed her mom's hand for reassurance.

"You'll be fine," her mother whispered. "Taylor would want you up there." She squeezed Jackie's hand and gave her a gentle push.

Jackie looked around for Lettie. A grim-faced Andrew, trailed by Scott—who appeared out of nowhere—were making their way toward the front of the room. She felt a flash of sympathy for Andrew.

This has got to be hell, knowing he was the driver that night and feeling the guilt of keeping it secret.

Jackie kissed her mom's cheek, walked up alone, and stood next to Andrew, who briefly brushed against her.

As she silently rehearsed her own speech, which she'd prepared just in case, Miss Libby's voice became a faint drone.

By the time she refocused, both Miss Libby's and Jennifer Cane's speeches were over, the crowd was in tears, and Laura Beth was stepping up to the microphone.

"No more tears!" Laura Beth said, wiping her eyes. "As you know, Taylor Cane was one of my best friends."

A few cheers erupted and she paused, waiting for silence.

"And even though she's no longer with us," she continued, "Mama and I felt it was important to celebrate the anniversary of her passing with what made her happiest—a party."

There were a few whoops.

"So after our tributes, the staff is going to clear a dance floor and bring in a rock band. So we can party the way Taylor would want us to."

Laura Beth turned to Jackie.

Beads of sweat trickled down her back. The moment she'd been dreading was here. She was used to standing in front of a crowd and faking it. But this was different. This was too close to her heart. She had to sing Taylor's praises, reminisce about their friendship, and pretend nothing bad had happened.

But she *could* swallow her anger at Taylor and Laura Beth and pull it together when she had to. That's what made her Jackie Whitman, D.C.'s It Girl.

Both she and Laura Beth instinctively moved toward each other to hold hands.

Laura Beth leaned in and whispered, "I've missed you."

"Me, too." It was true, she realized, as their heads touched. Out of the corner of her eye, she saw Andrew slip through the restaurant doors.

"And I know my dear friend Jackie Whitman would like to say somethin' about Taylor, too," Laura Beth said into the microphone, sounding absolutely sincere.

A million of Taylor's crazy pranks ran through Jackie's head as everyone—her friends, the political power brokers, the Canes' and Ballous' friends—waited. Like the one about Taylor persuading the president of the United States to go midnight skinny-dipping with the Capital Girls in the White House pool. Or the time Taylor baked pot brownies in the First Family kitchen and fed them to an unsuspecting Bob Price. Or when Taylor got practically the entire student body drunk by substituting vodka for bottled water in the Excelsior cafeteria.

Not that she could share those stories with this crowd.

Nor could she say out loud what haunted her night and day. Taylor's bewildering betrayal with Andrew and the mystery of why, why, why.

Every word of Andrew's confession was seared into her brain.

"Taylor started crying, saying something about how nothing would ever be the same," Andrew said. "So I put my arms around her, just to try to calm her down, to comfort her. The next thing I knew, we were kissing. And then it just happened."

They had sex. My boyfriend and my best friend.

I just wanted Andrew to shut up but he wouldn't.

"She kept telling me to drive faster and get her back to the party," he said. "Saying she only slept with me because she had to."

Laura Beth squeezed her hand, bringing her back to the present.

Jackie straightened her back and started her speech, the one with only *good* thoughts about Taylor.

First came a little suck-up to Jennifer Cane, and then a nod to her future nemesis, Libby Ballou. (As Miss Libby herself liked to say, keep your friends close and your enemies closer.)

Then—the grande finale—the reminder of why they were all there. How Taylor had taught the Capital Girls the most important lesson ever: Be true to yourself and the friends you love. Period. No excuses.

Which was why Jackie was still haunted by her betrayal. And wouldn't give up until she got to the truth.

FIVE

Lettie glanced at her iPhone—an unexpected gift from Tracey Mills—and checked the time again. One hour late and counting.

"Whitney, we're going to miss the entire party if you don't hurry up," Lettie said for the millionth time, banging on the bathroom door.

The door flung open and Lettie jumped out of the way.

"What's the hurry?" She paused to squirt breath freshener in her mouth. "It's not like parties ever start on time."

"Memorials do," Lettie said, eyeing Whitney's choice—or lack—of clothing. Her skinny body was squeezed into a tight, black, strapless dress that hit midthigh. But what really pushed it over the top were the sheer, horizontal rows of "nude illusion." If it was an illusion.

Lettie gave up arguing. Whitney did what Whitney wanted to do. And right now, she was tugging the top of her dress so it barely covered her tiny, caramel-colored breasts and shaking her wild hair so it fanned out like a halo.

"Then maybe it's not a party worth going to," she griped, screwing up her nose. "I know Taylor was your friend and all. But seriously? LB and her mom throwing a *party*? Like, to celebrate the fact that she's dead? Weird."

"No, we're celebrating Taylor's *life*."

"What, with a bunch of old people making sad speeches? From everything you've said about Taylor, she would have hated that."

True, but that wasn't the point.

"We still have to go. Or at least I do."

"Nah, I'll come. You said there'd be free booze, right?" She wiggled her hips. "And maybe I can get me some free l-o-o-o-ve, too. 'Specially if I can ditch Franklin."

Lettie frowned at the mention of Whitney's boyfriend. So far as she was concerned, Franklin Johnson, despite being St. Thomas Episcopal's star football player and the son of a powerful D.C. council member, was a steroid-addicted loser who supplied Whitney with weed, speed, and sleeping pills. He wasn't even particularly nice to Whitney, always criticizing her sticklike legs and flat chest.

Lettie had tried to convince Whitney to dump him but she shouldn't have wasted her breath. It was just one more example of Whitney refusing to take any advice.

I bet Taylor could have convinced her. Taylor might have smoked his weed and popped his pills, but she would've seen through him in a second, and never, ever would she have taken his crap.

"Let's go! Now!" she said, pushing Whitney toward the door. "And Whit, promise you'll behave. It's a memorial service, not a rave. Do it for me."

Whitney threw back her head and laughed. She picked up the keys to her yellow Mini Cooper and jangled them at Lettie. "I'll try, Lets. But I can't promise. You know me."

Yeah, I do. That's the problem.

The bass thumped hard against Whitney's chest as she shimmied to the song and tossed down a vodka shot. She hadn't managed to shake Franklin yet, but if the party turned boring, at least there'd be weed.

Her eyes darted around the restaurant to see which St. Thomas guys were watching her.

Just about every guy in the room. Including a few pathetic, middle-aged pervs huddled by the bar. *Gross.*

She'd made a beeline for the open bar as soon as they arrived. *Gotta get my fun fast before Lettie Square Pants shuts me down.*

Both Jackie and Laura Beth seemed to be going out of their way to avoid her. Which was fine with Whitney. She needed the *Crapital* Girls for feeding gossip to her mom—for her one-way ticket back to L.A.—and getting her into the right parties while she was stuck here. But definitely not for the *partying* part.

"Oh my God, Whit! You look ah-maz-ing!" Angie Meehan and Dina Ives were charging toward her.

Whitney posed with her hand on her hip. "I don't watch what I eat for nothing."

"I *want* that dress," Angie said enviously.

"Where's Aamina?"

Angie rolled her eyes. "She had to leave. Her parents were making her show up at some Saudi embassy thing."

The best thing about being a Saudi diplomat's daughter was

the police couldn't raid your parties. The worst was having to attend a bunch of stuffy embassy crap.

Whitney ran her eyes over Dina.

"Is that a Libby-approved dress, or what?" she scoffed. The cutesy, ruffled, high neck and short sleeves looked like something a little kid would wear.

Suddenly a sharp pain shot through her heart. It took her a second to realize why. Dina's ruffled dress reminded her of one Mara was wearing in a birthday picture that Whitney kept stashed in a photo album under her bed. She quickly shut down the memory.

"Shut up. I've gotta play the role of Daddy's Little Girl until Election Day," Dina was saying. "Soon as he's president, it's bye-bye Little Miss Perfect."

"I think your sister's getting a head start," Angie cracked. "I just saw Frances sneak out with Daniel's brother Sam and a bottle of champagne. Too bad, cuz I was checkin' him out earlier."

"Frances is a fast mover." Dina grinned. "And she usually has more than one guy going at a time."

"Yeah? Well, soon as you move into the White House, you better snag the hottest, hunkiest Secret Service agent for yourself before she does. Emphasis on 'servicing,'" Whitney leered.

"Yeah, and make sure Laura Beth gets assigned a fat old agent with bad breath and stinky armpits." Angie giggled.

Dina nodded gleefully. "Serve her right. She's already acting like First Daughter."

"More like First Freak," added Angie. "She's such a tool. You should've seen her earlier. She was hanging on to the microphone just like the way she clings to Sol. Like she's afraid to let go."

"I don't get what he sees in her," Dina said. "He's super hot."

"Really. I bet he's not even getting any," Angie added.

"He's *totally* wasted on her. Take it from me." The two friends looked questioningly at Whitney. She just winked and started dancing again.

Until now, she'd never even hinted about her onetime hookup with Sol last summer. As far as she knew, neither Laura Beth nor anyone else had found out about it. Well, almost no one. With a pang, she remembered the anonymous e-mail telling her to stay away from Sol. For a split second, she wondered if she'd just made a huge blunder by almost spilling to Angie and Dina.

Whatever.

"Take a look at Scott," Daniel whispered in Lettie's ear as they danced. His breath was tinged with whiskey, but Lettie didn't mind. She knew how tough tonight was for him.

He motioned to the other end of the room, where Scott was huddled with Franklin. Nearby, Whitney stood with Dina and Angie.

"Scott's crazy to be hanging in public with a pusher," Daniel said.

"He's just being friendly," Lettie protested. "He's been gone so long he needs to catch up and get to know people all over again. He's been really sweet to me whenever I've seen him." She didn't mention Scott's flirting with Jackie. Not at a party, where anyone could overhear.

Lettie was more worried about Whitney and what she was plotting with the other two.

She still hadn't forgiven Angie, Excelsior's meanest Mean Girl, for trying to humiliate her at the start of seventh grade.

Lettie tensed as Daniel put his arms around her. It was a

reflex, left over from when she was trying to hide their relationship from her traditional parents. She forced herself to relax into his arms.

Daniel held her close and leaned in for a long, deep kiss. The whiskey tasted unfamiliar, but sweet, on his lips.

Their kiss slowly ended and Lettie wondered if she should make the next move. *Another kiss? Wrap my arms around his neck? Pull him in closer? Why am I overthinking this? It's supposed to be spontaneous, isn't it?*

Just then a shrill whistle pierced her ears, followed by Whitney's drunken laugh.

Oh no. Here it comes. What's she doing?

SIX

To Lettie's relief, it was Dina who had the microphone.

Good, Whitney is keeping her promise to behave. So far.

"Hey, guys," Dina said. "I know Mrs. Ballou already thanked you for coming tonight. You being here means a lot to us."

"What does she mean, 'us'?" Laura Beth appeared at Lettie's side. "She never even met Taylor." Lettie shrugged.

"Now it's our turn to thank *her* and my father, Senator Jeffrey Ives, for putting together this amazing event to honor Taylor Cane." Dina practically cooed into the mike.

"She's toasting *my* mama. *My* mama," Laura Beth repeated. "She's acting like she's *family*."

Lettie wondered what was coming next. Perhaps a direct plea to vote for Senator Ives?

Angie sidled up to them. "What's wrong, girls? Someone steal your stage?"

"This is none of your business, Angie," Laura Beth snapped.

"Looks like your *mama* has a new favorite daughter. You better be careful." She sneered.

Laura Beth's face was red with fury. Jackie, who'd kept silent, moved between her and Angie.

"She's just trying to upset you, Laura Beth," Jackie said soothingly. "Ignore her."

Angie, a satisfied smile on her face, moved away and Sol leaned down and whispered in Laura Beth's ear. The tension deflated slightly, and Lettie felt her heart slow back down.

Everyone in the room cheered.

Then Whitney grabbed the microphone.

"In case you hadn't noticed, most of the adults have left!" she yelled, prancing back and forth in her skimpy dress. "But the bar's still open and the band's still rockin'. So let's party! And in Taylor's honor . . . the wilder the better!"

Lettie couldn't believe it.

It was worse than her worst nightmare.

But Whitney wasn't finished.

"But first, Dina and I have a surprise for you." She beamed. "We didn't get to meet Taylor. But we feel like we know her. So we've decided to set up the Taylor Cane Memorial Scholarship Fund for disadvantaged kids to attend Excelsior."

Dina took back the microphone.

"Yeah, like Lettie Velasquez over there," she said, pointing. "Who knows where she'd be today without the generosity of others?"

Lettie felt the breath sucked out of her lungs.

There was dead silence and the eyes of every person in the room bore into her like a thousand sharp cuts.

She felt as if she was soaring through the air, then hovering, looking down on the scene below, seeing herself frozen in time and place, expressionless, watching Daniel move behind her and pull her close.

Then she was back in her own skin.

"Oh, Lettie, I'm so sorry," Jackie whispered. She and Laura Beth surrounded her, as if to block her from view.

"Don't give them the satisfaction of seeing you upset," Laura Beth said softly. "Try to be brave."

For a moment, Lettie was too stunned to speak.

She turned to face Daniel, who'd been squeezing her shoulders so tightly it almost hurt. "Why would they do that? I don't understand."

"Because they're thoughtless and selfish and rude," he answered. "You don't understand because you're nothing like them."

"That's all you can expect from someone like Whitney." Jackie fumed.

"And that bitch Dina," added Laura Beth.

"Whitney can't be trusted," Jackie continued. "Ever. She double-crossed Laura Beth and she's double-crossed me. Now, apparently it's your turn."

I might be naïve but I'm not stupid.

Everybody thought Lettie was all sweet innocence. But you couldn't survive at a place like Excelsior or in a city like Washington if you didn't have a steely inner core.

Lettie recalled the time she sent that threatening anonymous e-mail to Whitney after she saw her and Sol sneaking off at Aamina's party. It had been a surprisingly easy way to stop Whitney in her tracks.

And the calculated decision Lettie made in choosing to live

with Whitney and not Laura Beth, not wanting to become the Ballous' latest pet project to remold her in their image.

But she'd dropped her guard with Whitney. She thought they were becoming *real* friends. Not like Jackie and Laura Beth, but still . . .

It looks like Whitney's been playing me all along, to get in with the Capital Girls. Just like she plays everybody else. Maybe I am stupid as well as naïve.

Libby Ballou rushed over to hug Whitney, nearly knocking her off her seven-inch heels. "Gosh, honey. You're nothin' but skin and bone."

Whitney tried to wriggle away but Libby grabbed her hands.

"That was so sweet of you girls! And completely unexpected."

Dina smoothed down her hair. "I've pledged five thousand dollars from my trust account, Miss Libby, to start things off. You know, Dad raised us to help the less fortunate."

"Well, I think you're wonderful. I'm going to make sure Laura Beth gives the second pledge," Miss Libby burbled.

She lowered her voice. "And Whitney, I'm so glad you convinced Lettie to let us use her name. She's such a marvelous example of charity. But she's always been so embarrassed about havin' to depend on the generosity of others. Until now."

Whitney looked over to where Lettie was wrapped in Daniel's arms. She seemed to be crying.

It had been Dina's idea to create the scholarship and it had seemed a perfect way to show up Jackie and Laura Beth. But Whitney hadn't known that Dina had also planned to single out Lettie. *Bad idea, seeing as I have to live with Lettie.*

They should have just stuck with her idea for a prank: secretly stuffing fake "Taylor-made" condoms and recipes from the *Cannabis Cookbook* into Mrs. Ballou's goody bags.

"Can we leave?" Dina said impatiently as soon as Libby Ballou disappeared into the crowd.

"Soon." Whitney was trying to decide whether to kiss up to Lettie now in front of everyone or in private at home.

I'll do it later. No way am I gonna give Jackie and LB the pleasure of watching me grovel.

"I wanna go to the after-party," Dina whined. "Scott and Franklin are probably already there."

"Yeah, so?" Whitney muttered.

The truth was Whitney was getting bored with Franklin. Sure, he was hot. But he was s-o-o-o immature, especially compared to Lettie's brother, Paz. Who she'd tried to seduce at the White House Christmas party until LB rudely interrupted. For some reason, Paz hadn't tried to contact her since.

And he probably won't once Lets tells him what just happened.

"So, go get Angie and we can split," Whitney ordered. "She's here somewhere."

She looked around and saw Angie right up in Jackie's face.

"Where's Andrew?" Angie was saying.

"I have no idea," Jackie said calmly.

Angie scoffed. "You two haven't been together all night. Did the little Ankie lovebirds break up?"

Everyone within earshot stopped talking.

Whitney edged closer. If Angie was gonna take down Jackie in front of every Excelsior and St. Thomas senior, she wanted a bird's-eye view.

"I hate to disappoint you, Angie, but we're fine." Jackie smiled serenely.

Whitney felt a grudging admiration for Jackie. *How does she keep it together like that? I mean, I know the truth.*

The bile rose in her throat whenever she thought about her mom's refusal to run Whitney's scoop about Andrew having sex with Taylor. Her mother hadn't even been impressed that Whitney had followed the *Crapital* Girls to the Lincoln Memorial, overheard their conversation, and secretly recorded it on her cell.

Ever since Jackie and Andrew planted their fake "engagement" story with her months ago, her mom expected her to triple verify everything. Another reason to hate Jackie.

"You and Andrew are so fine that you've been hooking up with his brother?" Angie pressed.

No way she knows that. She's gotta just be fishing for a reaction.

"Jackie is not two-timing anyone, unlike some of your friends!" Laura Beth hissed, trying to keep her voice low. She was addressing Angie, but her eyes were locked on Whitney.

Whitney closed the six-foot gap between them.

"Be careful who you're calling names, you backstabbing liar!" Whitney sneered. "Or did you think I'd forgotten you're a fake friend?"

Whitney let her threat hang in the air. *She looks terrified. Jackie obviously still doesn't know LB blabbed to Eric's boss.*

Before anyone could stop her, Angie lunged at Laura Beth and grabbed the front of her Jason Wu.

Laura Beth stared at her in shock, not seeming to realize the delicate silk had ripped, exposing most of her boobs. Jackie and Lettie also looked too stunned to move or speak. Sol quickly stepped forward to shield his girlfriend.

Whitney stifled a giggle. *Wish I had my cell on me.*

"You need to leave. Right now," Sol said firmly to Angie, without raising his voice.

Dina instantly appeared at Whitney's side.

"You should see the shots I got on my phone," she boasted in Whitney's ear. "One down. Two to go."

"No. One down, one to go. Lettie's off-limits," Whitney snapped. "At least until she moves out of my condo."

Then she grinned. With allies like Angie and Dina, taking down the *Crapital* Girls actually seemed possible. "Jackie's next. And the sooner the better."

"Yeah, and I just thought of a great way to do it," Dina said giddily.

SEVEN

Bang! Bang! Bang!

Jackie shot up in bed, her heart pounding in her ears.

The stalker!

She broke into a cold, panicky sweat as she frantically groped around in the dark for something to arm herself with. Her hand landed on one of her Ugg boots. Useless.

Groggy, she stumbled out of bed, her feet tangled in the sheets. The door opened and she screamed.

"Oh my God, Jackie! It's just me."

Her mom, juggling a breakfast tray in both hands, turned on the light with an elbow.

Jackie sank back down on the bed.

"I was sound asleep. I thought it was the stalker or something. What was all the pounding?"

Carolyn Shaw put the tray at the foot of the bed and sat down.

She smoothed the hair off of her daughter's face. "Sorry, I had my hands full and I was trying to kick open the door."

She reached for the tray. "Look, I made your favorite breakfast. Banana pancakes and hot chocolate. But the way you look maybe I should've mixed you a Bloody Mary. That was a joke, by the way." She grinned.

"Wow." Jackie smiled back, eyeing the food. "Thanks, Mom. What a nice surprise." *She hasn't brought me breakfast in bed since I had my wisdom teeth out.*

While Jackie smothered the pancakes with syrup her mother flipped open a magazine lying on the tray.

"There's something you need to see," she said, handing Jackie the hot chocolate and stirring sugar into her own mug of strong, black coffee.

Hell. She's found out about the thing with Angie last night. And somehow it's all my fault and this is the Last Meal before my execution.

Her mother held up an advance copy of Sunday's *Parade* magazine for Jackie to see. Jackie put down her drink and closed her eyes. She imagined the headline: "Jackie Whitman Caught in Cat Spat at Socialite's Party."

Instead, her mom pointed to a two-page spread on the Ballou-Ives romance: "Political Powerhouse Couple Eye White House Love Nest."

Jackie's eyes moved from the headline to an enormous photo of Miss Libby embracing the senator.

As relief washed over her, she couldn't help herself. She dissolved into laughter.

"It's not funny, Jackie," her mom snapped. "Do you know how many people read this magazine? Sixty-five million. We're talking everyone from New York City to Nowheresville, Texas."

Yeah, it's the D.C. equivalent of a wannabe starlet landing the Playboy *centerfold.*

"I'm sorry." Jackie stifled another laugh as she scanned the first few lines of the story.

Senator Jeffrey Ives has a dream. To carry his soon-to-be bride, Republican uberhostess Libby Ballou, over the threshold of 1600 Pennsylvania. If his dream comes true, they'll be the first newlyweds since Grover Cleveland to set up a love nest in the White House.

"Poor Laura Beth. This is so embarrassing," Jackie murmured, studying each photo of the "picture-perfect twenty-first-century blended family," which included all three daughters doling out lunch at a local shelter and shopping for bargains at Walmart.

Walmart? Laura Beth's never even stepped inside a Macy's.

"I suppose it is. But she's a pro. She knows it's a small price to pay for this kind of free publicity," her mom said.

Jackie handed back the magazine.

"Deborah is beside herself." Her mom took a big gulp of coffee. "And of course she wants to know why I didn't think of it first."

"A spread on her and Bob? Give me a break! They barely even talk anymore."

Her mom frowned. "That's enough, Jackie."

Yeah, but you didn't deny it. The Price marriage is as big a joke as Andrew and me. The difference is, everyone knows it.

Her mother straightened her back as if to steel herself.

"So, speaking of embarrassing . . . What I wanted to talk to you about is . . . The president wants Ike Sawyer and me to pretend that we're a couple so the media will chase us around, too.

You know, a cute office romance between the vice president and the chief of staff." Her mother gave Jackie a sheepish smile. "You have Ankie, and Ike and I will have 'Carolike.'"

"You have to be joking," Jackie choked out. "Is the president *that* desperate?"

Two fake romances in one family is two too many. Her mom knew she and Andrew were having a rough time. She just didn't know how bad it was.

Her mother's cell rang, abruptly ending the conversation.

"Yes, Deborah?" Her mom, instantly back in chief-of-staff mode, stood up, motioned for Jackie not to speak, and slipped out the door.

Jackie picked up the iPhone on her bedside table and scrolled through her texts.

There was a brief one from Laura Beth: *Yeah! No mention in the media about the fight!*

The second was from Daniel's brother, Sam: *It was great seeing you last night. Are you free one night to get together before I go back to Cali?*

What's up with that? she thought. *The guy's been in L.A. for years and suddenly he's acting like my long-lost best bud? That's a complication I don't need now.*

She deleted his text and her mind went back to her mom and Ike Sawyer.

Maybe it wasn't such a bad idea after all. Because if Aunt Deborah had Carolike, she wouldn't need Ankie.

This could be the perfect "out."

Whitney walked into her mom's study, nibbling on a rice cake.

"Yo, Tracey! You're alive!"

Her mom hated it whenever Whitney called her by her first name. It was useful, though, when you needed to get her attention or piss her off.

"I thought you must be dead, cuz I couldn't find anything about the fight on your blog." She elbowed her mother in the arm. "Last night you couldn't wait to download Dina's photos."

That wasn't totally true. Her mom recently had made it pretty clear she was more interested in campaign gossip now that the presidential race was starting. But Whitney had persuaded her it was a "twofer." Spoiled D.C. brats acting out *and* an embarrassment for Libby Ballou and Senator Ives.

I come through for you big-time. Names. Details. Pictures . . . I risk pissing off the Crapital *Girls forever and you blow it off.*

Her mother shoved away her laptop so hard it almost sailed off the edge of her desk.

"Do you want the long version or the short version?" she snapped, spinning around in her chair.

"Whoa!" Whitney put her hands up, backing away. "Short version, thanks."

"I've dealt with irate Hollywood publicists screaming down the phone, egomaniacal actors throwing temper tantrums, and studio bosses threatening to run me out of town. But they were pussycats compared to that superbitch Jennifer Cane."

"You must be getting soft," Whitney scoffed. "Don't tell me you fell for her teary-eyed mourning mommy act?"

Tracey snorted.

"Hardly. No, she just happened to mention that little plagiarism misunderstanding back in L.A. Oh, and she also congratulated me on your father's new job with the Price campaign. I don't know how she found out about it. It's not even official yet. And how she hoped the background check into our family won't dredge it up."

Whitney knew all about the "plagiarism misunderstanding." When they were still living in L.A., her mom got caught "accidentally" lifting a gossip item from one of the British tabloids and "forgetting" to credit the newspaper.

She yawned. "Kids plagiarize all the time. What's the big deal?"

Her mother glared at her.

"I'm new here. I have to establish a solid reputation so all these Washington politicians will come to me with—"

. . . All the shit they've got on their enemies.

"—useful insider information. They have to know they can trust me."

Like the way I trust you to break every single promise you ever make to me? Like the other day when you crapped out of our movie date and never even called to let me know?

Whitney felt the familiar cramps clawing at her stomach.

"But I still get paid, right, Mom?"

Her mother shrugged.

"Last night I was ready to pay you. But now that I can't use it, it's worthless."

"Jeez, Mom. I need the money." *Even if it is going straight into Franklin's pocket for the speed he gave me last week.*

"Okay, okay. Your whiny voice is the last thing I want to deal with this morning. You're either pestering about moving back to L.A.—and that's not happening—or bugging me for money. Go take a hundred . . . no, a fifty . . . out of my wallet. It's on my bed."

Whitney was seized with anger. *Keep treating me like shit and I'll put that audio file about Taylor and Andrew on your blog and watch while Jennifer Cane destroys you and your stupid career.*

As the stomach cramps took over, she looked at the half-eaten rice cake in her hand and tossed it in the trash can on her way out of the room.

EIGHT

The three girls sat around Jackie's kitchen table, their eyes fixed on Taylor's cell phone spinning around and around on the lazy Susan.

"Jackie, you're making me dizzy," Laura Beth complained. "Just go ahead and play the messages for us. Now, please?"

Jackie had finally decided to share what was on Taylor's cell, praying that if all three of them put their heads together they could make sense of it. She sure couldn't.

But first they'd rehashed the previous night's events.

Laura Beth apologized again to Jackie and Lettie for springing the party on them.

"Mama made me keep it a secret," she insisted. Jackie wasn't sure whether to believe her, but she didn't press it.

Jackie was just about to ask Lettie how she was dealing with

Dina's singling her out at the party when Laura Beth brought it up in her usual well-meaning but clumsy way.

"I know you must be frettin' about facing everyone at school on Monday, Lettie," Laura Beth said. "But don't you worry. Jackie and I will be right by your side to support you. Besides, you're not the only one gettin' a free ride at Excelsior."

Before Jackie could jump in and do her usual, "What Laura Beth means is . . ." Lettie spoke up.

"I was really upset last night when it happened. It was incredibly humiliating. But after talking to Daniel and thinking it over, I've decided it's unimportant. I mean, here I am, separated from my parents and siblings who are living in danger every single day and unable to even communicate with me most of the time. So who cares about some silly insult from some ignorant girl?"

Laura Beth looked chagrined.

"You are so *right*, Lettie. It's not important what those awful girls think or say."

Lettie never ceased to amaze Jackie. *Here I am, freaked out about Taylor and Andrew and how I feel about Scott. And yet Lettie manages to cope with whatever life dishes out with incredible grace.*

"As strong as you are, Lettie, you know we're here for you whenever you want to talk about it or need a shoulder to cry on," Jackie said.

Lettie smiled sadly and nodded.

"Of course we are," Laura Beth agreed. "You know, I think after what happened, you really should come live with Mama and me. That way, you only have to see Whitney at school and you never have to talk to her."

Lettie shook her head.

"No, thank you, Laura Beth. I'm going to stay where I am. Whitney says she had no idea what Dina was going to say and I've decided to believe her. But I'm putting my guard back up."

"I understand," Laura Beth answered, though she didn't look as though she did. "It's probably just as well right now, anyway. Mama's been acting very on edge lately."

"It's probably stress over the campaign," Jackie said.

"It's not just that." Laura Beth shook her head. "There's something else goin' on, but she won't say what."

Jackie couldn't help but wonder if Miss Libby was cooking up some campaign mischief. But she couldn't very well ask Laura Beth.

"Oh, come on, Laura Beth," she said instead. "Your mother loves drama. It's probably nothing more than her hairdresser used the wrong shade of blond."

The girls laughed, remembering the fit she'd once pitched after her masseuse insisted on trying a new line of body oils and she ended up smelling like sickly sweet apple blossoms.

"Speaking of embarrassing, thank the Lord—and Sol, too—that no one saw my wardrobe malfunction," Laura Beth said.

Jackie wasn't too sure about that but she didn't press the point.

Laura Beth lowered her voice despite the fact that the Capital Girls were alone in the Foggy Bottom town house. Jackie's mom had left for the White House immediately after taking the president's call.

"Between you and me, I think Sol found it a turn-on. He couldn't keep his hands off me on the ride home."

"Oh, gross, Laura Beth," Lettie interrupted.

"And you didn't get hell from your mother when you got home?" Jackie asked, surprised. It seemed to her that their mothers were always blaming them for anything and everything that went wrong.

"She barely even mentioned it except to tell me she'd get the Jason Wu mended and drop it off as a charity donation at Inga's."

Lettie rolled her eyes but Laura Beth was oblivious.

"It also helped that I plied her with bourbon and branch. Well, let's just say I skipped the branch. I just kept pouring her another and another and telling her sorry for Angie's ugly behavior. She just waved it off. She seemed distracted."

It was Lettie who raised the unspoken issue of how the girls were going to handle the presidential campaign.

"We haven't talked about Senator Ives's announcement," Lettie began. "I think . . . Maybe we should discuss what . . . It's possible things are going to be said that . . ."

She stopped and gave them both a help-me-out-here look.

Usually Jackie knew the right thing to say and when to say it. But an election in which both she and Laura Beth had a personal stake was something else. She didn't want to make it worse by saying the wrong thing.

Laura Beth must have felt the same way because for once she was speechless, too.

"What I'm saying is, we need to stay friends no matter what happens." Lettie stumbled on. "It's just politics. No matter how bad it gets, it's not personal. It's not more important than *us*. We can't ever forget that."

"We won't," Jackie said, her voice sounding more confident than she felt.

"Of course not," Laura Beth answered faintly.

Jackie stopped turning the lazy Susan and picked up Taylor's cell. Laura Beth was right. She'd stalled long enough.

"Maybe one of you two will recognize the voice. I certainly didn't," she said, not even trying to hide the fear in her voice.

Lettie reached over and took Jackie's free hand and grabbed Laura Beth's with her other.

With a trembling finger, Jackie hit the play button.

"Taylor, sweetheart, it's me. Don't tell Daniel. Please."

Lettie gasped at the sound of Daniel's name.

"Shh," Laura Beth hissed.

There was a second message: *"Taylor, please call me, honey. Please, I'm begging you."*

Then a third. Even more ominous.

"Taylor, we have to talk. This is not just about you. This could be dangerous if they find out."

And the fourth and final message was from the same woman, crying so hard that her words were unintelligible.

Jackie had played the recordings alone in her room so many times she'd memorized them. But it wasn't just the words that struck dread in her heart. It was the voice. The voice of a desperate woman. As if her life hung in the balance. As if she was at Taylor's mercy.

Jackie fought an urge to run from the room, to race out the front door and never come back. But where would she go? And what good would that do?

If her mom had taught her anything, it was to tackle your problems head on, *"so they don't come back to haunt you, Jackie."*

"Is there anything else?" Laura Beth asked.

"Taylor made some calls to her mom in the last few days before she died. And she also called a couple of numbers I didn't recognize."

Any hopes that Laura Beth or Lettie could solve the phone

riddle were quickly dashed. Neither girl had a clue to the mystery voice or the mystery numbers.

"That woman sounds terrified. Like there was a murder or something," Laura Beth said breathlessly. "Maybe Taylor saw it happen."

"You're not helping by getting all dramatic, Laura Beth," Jackie snapped. "We need to stay focused and work through this thing step by step."

She ignored the offended look Laura Beth gave her and focused on Lettie, whose white face was streaked with tears.

"Why is she talking about Daniel?" Lettie asked in a hollow voice. "What's he got to do with it?"

"None of this makes any sense," Jackie answered.

"Maybe we should just leave it alone," Lettie said softly. "Daniel doesn't need any more hurt."

Neither do I. But answers are better than questions.

"I don't think we have any choice, Lettie," she said gently, hiding her impatience. "We have to call this woman and those other numbers."

"I agree," Laura Beth said. "But what do we say?"

Jackie shrugged. "We'll have to play it by ear."

The three girls looked at each other in silence. Then Jackie picked up her iPhone.

"Don't use that. It'll show who's calling. The murderer might come after us next," Laura Beth said frantically.

"Will you cut it out about murder?" Lettie said in an angry voice. Or as angry as Lettie ever got, which wasn't very much or very often.

"All right. But no matter what it's about, we don't want our call to be traced," Laura Beth said sulkily. "I think we should call from a pay phone. We should wear hats and sunglasses so nobody recognizes us."

"Yeah, and we could speak in a bad French accent," Jackie joked, trying to cut the tension.

Even Lettie giggled then. "And wear trench coats," she added.

The last time Jackie had used a pay phone was when she called that blackmailing scumbag, Eric Moran. It sickened her to think of it. Raiding her mom's desk at the White House and feeding the information to Eric over the phone—so his boss, Senator Griffin, could try to block the president's proposed immigration reforms. Thank God it backfired.

She shuddered.

"I hate pay phones," she said. "We have a secure landline that you can't trace calls on."

She dialed one of the numbers. "Disconnected," she announced.

She dialed the second number and hung up without speaking. "That was the main number for the Virginia Hospital Center," she said, puzzled.

She took a deep breath.

"Okay. I'm going to call our mystery woman now."

Lettie's knees were bouncing up and down nervously. Laura Beth twisted a curl around her finger so tightly the flesh was turning blue.

"Shit." Jackie slammed down the phone in frustration.

"Voice mail's full," she explained. "I guess I'll just have to keep trying."

She didn't say it out loud but she knew the other girls were thinking it, too.

It looks like Daniel was right about one thing. This was no simple car wreck.

NINE

Lettie shut the SAT prep book and patted Tanya Wilson's arm.

"You're doing great," she reassured Tanya, who pushed her wheelchair away from the table and smiled hopefully.

She'd been visiting Tanya at the veterans' rehab hospital for weeks now, trying to get her ready for the SATs.

Before Tanya could respond, there was a light tap on the door and Private Vic Hazelton walked in. He nodded at them, without saying hello.

"Tanya, Dr. Rosen wants to know if you can come over tomorrow morning so he can brief you on your new job," he said in a quiet monotone.

Lettie studied him while he filled Tanya in on the details. He was slightly built to begin with, but he'd lost more weight since she last saw him. His uniform seemed to hang off his narrow shoulders. The scar at the back of his head was fading, though, and his light brown hair was starting to grow back where it had been shaved for surgery.

He looked at Lettie. "Is Jackie here today, too?" he asked eagerly.

"She comes on Thursdays, remember?" Lettie answered.

All the wounded veterans seemed to look forward to the girls' weekly volunteer visits, especially Laura Beth's dance therapy and Whitney's self-named "slut-apy," which was basically just flirting and flaunting her body. "Guaranteed to cure whatever ails 'em," she'd told the girls.

But Vic, more than anyone, enjoyed being with Jackie. His face lit up whenever she appeared. She'd confided in Lettie that he'd started sending pages of his therapeutic diary, in which he recorded his problems adjusting to civilian life.

Both Jackie and Vic worked alongside Dr. Paul Rosen, the veterans' rights activist who'd taken Vic under his wing and given him a job while he recovered from his traumatic brain injury.

Lettie worried that Jackie's lending her name to Dr. Rosen's cause would lead to more and more trouble, especially if he kept up his attacks on the Price administration for not doing enough for war veterans. Jackie's mom had already warned her to be careful.

"My memory's still not back to normal. I was thinking it was Thursday, Jackie's volunteer day," Vic said disappointedly. He turned and left.

"Poor Vic," Tanya said after the door closed and his footsteps faded. "Jackie seems to be the only person he feels comfortable with."

"Well, maybe you can befriend him, too, now that you'll be working with him," Lettie said. "I'm really proud of you."

"Thanks to you, Lettie," Tanya said gratefully. She ran a hand through her tight black curls. "It's only part-time, but it's a start. Speaking of jobs, how's your brother? Is he liking his new job?"

Lettie hadn't seen much of Paz since he'd started as an assistant to President Price's body man—really, he was just a glorified gofer. But Jackie said she occasionally saw him at the White House.

"I think he's doing well," Lettie said. "He's keeping busy with work and his classes at Montgomery College."

As far as Lettie was concerned, busy was better for Paz. It kept him away from the gang he used to hang with and from falling back into his old habits. And it kept him away from Whitney.

"How's the rest of your family? What's the latest?" Tanya asked.

"You know, you and Daniel are the only ones who *always* ask me about my family," Lettie told her. Jackie was a lot better about it than Laura Beth, but Lettie still had the feeling it was something on her to-do list rather than genuine interest.

Sometimes Lettie literally ached for Christa and Maribel. She'd wake up in the middle of the night, imagining for a second that they were back in their old apartment in Mount Pleasant, all snuggled together in her bed. She wasn't sure that Jackie and Laura Beth, not having any siblings, would understand the emptiness she felt. She'd once tried to talk to Whitney about it. Even though Whitney was an only child, too, Lettie thought it would be a way for the two of them, living under the same roof, to get closer. But Whitney had visibly flinched, as if Lettie had punched her, and cut her off cold.

Lettie had recently pasted photos of her family into her journal to make sure she didn't forget a single detail of what they looked like.

"I write to Mamá and Papá all the time, but I don't know how much mail gets through," she told Tanya sadly. "I get a letter now and then. And sometimes Papá can call me from the ambassador's office but it's usually a bad connection."

"At least your father calls you." Tanya scowled. "My folks are only in Detroit but I never hear from them. At least I don't have to depend on them for college. Thank God for free college on the GI Bill."

Thinking about family turned Lettie's thoughts to Daniel.

It had only been two hours since she'd listened to the voice mails from Taylor's phone, and she longed to confide in somebody. But she couldn't share this with anyone and especially not him. She needed to protect him from bad news, not bring him more.

"How's Daniel?" Tanya asked suddenly, as if reading Lettie's mind. "I really like him. He seems like such a nice guy. And you two are great together."

Lettie thought about that last sentence.

She and Daniel *were* "great" together. He was sweet and funny and smart. He was interested in world politics, just like she was— she'd even shown him parts of her journal, where she clipped interesting articles and wrote her comments. But he also was teaching her how to loosen up and have fun. Relaxing didn't come naturally to her.

"Lettie? Hello? You look worried. Are you and Daniel okay?"

Lettie pulled her chair closer to Tanya.

"Yeah, we're good. I don't know. When I'm not around him, I can't wait to be with him. But sometimes . . ."

She felt strangled by shyness.

"You don't have to say anything, Lettie, if you don't want to."

"I know."

Tanya leaned forward.

"Let me tell you something. It's perfectly normal to blow hot and cold sometimes. Like, one minute, you're totally into the person and then, wham, it's like you can't get away fast enough."

It wasn't that exactly. Lettie *did* want to be with Daniel. She loved being with him. It was just that she wasn't sure if she should feel . . . well, more . . . giddy like Laura Beth. Or intense like Jackie. Or exhilarated like Taylor.

When she still didn't say anything, Tanya filled the silence.

"Can wise old Auntie Tanya give you a piece of advice?" They grinned at each other. At twenty-two, Tanya was only about four years older than Lettie. But so much more experienced when it came to romance.

"Sometimes the best way to sort out your feelings is to throw yourself totally into the relationship," Tanya said. "Sort of committing yourself to test your true commitment. Does that make any sense?"

"Yes, it does. Thanks, Tanya."

She's right. Maybe I've been holding back. I don't have any experience at this. He's my first boyfriend ever. I owe it to him to throw myself into it. And I owe it to myself.

TEN

Whitney let out a loud, lewd wolf whistle.

"Wow. Impressive," she said, grinning at the photos posted on Excelsior Prep's home page. "You got serious criminal potential, here. How'd you break into the school Web site?"

"Let's just say five years of computer classes at boarding school finally paid off," Dina said smugly.

"This is my favorite," Angie said, pointing to a doctored photo of Jackie's head on Laura Beth's body—to make it look as if it was Jackie who'd had the near nip slip at Taylor's memorial. She closed her laptop.

"I didn't think Laura Beth's boobs were that big," Whitney sniped.

Dina laughed.

"They're not. I borrowed them from Kelly Osbourne. You'd be amazed what you can do with Photoshop."

"This thing's going viral!" Whitney hooted.

At first Whitney had been pissed. Not because it wasn't a great idea, but because *she* hadn't thought of it first.

She'd known Dina and Angie were planning to do something with Dina's catfight photos. Just not exactly what or when.

But the more she mulled over it, the better she liked it this way.

The It Girl was going to be the laughingstock of the entire school—even when it became obvious the photos were fake.

And if anyone found out who was behind it, Dina and Angie would be the ones taking the rap. Not Whitney.

And I can honestly say I had nothing to do with it. What's that expression those dumb politicians are always saying? Plausible deniability. Yeah.

Something else occurred to Whitney. She frowned.

This'll be the first and last time I let those two amateurs go rogue. I'm the one who runs this little clique and the sooner they realize it, the better for them.

Whitney had quickly realized Dina could be useful to her on the first day Angie introduced them at school. Certainly more useful than Aamina Al-Kazaz, who'd started hanging with her and Angie, but was too scared to take on the *Crapital* Girls. It was like she had one foot in each camp. *She better be careful, that's how you get injured.*

Dina, on the other hand, was psyched from day one.

"Hey, Whitney, I don't think you've met Dina Ives," Angie said, shoving the newbie under my nose.

Like I care? The kid was a loser junior and even newer to Excelsior than I was.

"Dina's dad is dating Laura Beth's mom. She's my new BFF and my go-to girl for Capital Girls dirt." Angie smirked.

Hmm. My interest level suddenly rose a notch.

"Yeah?" *I answered, deliberately sounding bored.* "Well, Dina, tell me *something I don't know about the* Crapital Girls." *I made a point of raising my eyebrows and checking my cell to let her know I was not impressed.*

Dina snorted. "Only that Libby won't shut up about how perfect Laura Beth and her friends are. How I can learn just by hanging with Laura Beth."

"Like, who doesn't know that?" *I gave her one of my cold stares but the little bitch stared right back without flinching.*

"Give me a break. I just got here," *she snapped.*

Her ballsy attitude was impressive.

"You'll see," *Dina went on.* "By the time Dad marries Libby-the-Lush I'll know every dirty little secret there is to know about the* Crapital Girls *and their parents."*

I gave her one of my fake buddy smiles and draped my arm over her shoulder.

"Why stop there? Why not show them there's a new group of 'It Girls' in town?" *I suggested.*

"Whitney? Can you come over here for a minute?" Jackie, standing with Laura Beth and Lettie, called out to her.

"Listen and learn, ladies," she called over her shoulder as she sauntered, extra slowly, over to the other side of the quad. "And get your cameras out. It's not often that Jackie Whitman loses it."

Jackie smiled at the Cali girl, although every nerve in her body was on fire and the blood pounded in her head. She folded her arms casually, hiding her hands, which were clenched into fists.

Take a deep breath. Don't lose it.

"Your pathetic attempt to embarrass me?" Jackie said calmly.

"Everyone knows it wasn't me in those photos. I'm surprised you pulled such a childish little prank. Such a waste of time."

Whitney looked her up and down, as if considering her next move.

"Calm down, Jackie!" she said in a loud, patronizing voice for everyone to hear.

Don't let the bitch provoke you.

Jackie laughed just as loudly.

"I'm perfectly calm, Whitney. Laura Beth was just pointing out how lame it was, putting something on the *school Web site*."

She looked over at Laura Beth, who looked shocked that Jackie was dragging her into the fight. "Right, Laura Beth?"

"Wha— Oh yeah, Whitney, totally lame," Laura Beth said, sounding lame herself.

"I had nothing to do with those stupid photos," Whitney snapped. "When I want to make you look bad, Jackie, you'll know it. My advice to you is: Watch your back!"

Whitney turned and walked off.

Laura Beth tugged on Jackie's arm. "She's a bitch and all, but it's possible she really didn't do it. She flunked computer class last semester, remember? I don't think she'd know how to do it."

Lettie nodded. "Yeah, and even if she got someone else to Photoshop the pictures, you'd think she would have given them to her mom for her blog."

"Yeah, I think it was someone else," Laura Beth added. "Like my ugly stepsister and Angie *Meanhan*."

The bell sounded for the next class, but Jackie ignored it, her anger finally erupting.

"When are you going to realize Whitney's no good?" she demanded. "She's given up trying to worm her way into the Capital Girls and now she's determined to do anything to take us down."

Before either Laura Beth or Lettie could make any more excuses, Jackie asked them flat out, "Why are you two always defending that bitch?"

The answer was pretty obvious. Lettie depended on Whitney for a roof over her head. And Laura Beth *had* to be under Libby's orders to do *nothing* to antagonize Whitney. Or more to the point, her gossip-mother.

"That's not fair, Jackie. We're on your side, not hers," Laura Beth said.

"Yes, of course we're on your side! But we better get to class. We'll be late," Lettie fretted.

"You go ahead," Jackie answered, giving them a dismissive wave. She punched in a number on her iPhone.

"Scott?"

ELEVEN

Scott pulled up in a black convertible she didn't recognize.

"What happened to your brother's Prius?" she asked, climbing in.

He grinned.

"The campaign happened," he quipped. "Mom wants us to start driving made-in-America again. It's a Chrysler. Watch this."

He turned the heat up full blast and with the push of a button the retractable hardtop disappeared in seconds.

"Cool. I want one," Jackie gushed.

As Scott maneuvered the car into the traffic, she studied him out of the corner of her eye. He'd thrown his school blazer and tie on the backseat and had undone enough shirt buttons that she could see the top of his smooth, muscular chest. His chocolate-brown eyes—so different from Andrew's brilliant green—were hidden behind dark Ray-Bans. But he smelled just like Andrew. Delicious.

Funny, I never noticed that before. They must use the same cologne.

"Thanks for ditching class with me. You're a lifesaver."

She eyed the Secret Service tail in the rearview mirror. Her agent, Ellen Fellows, had left her car at Excelsior and was in the passenger seat next to Scott's agent, Luke Forsythe.

"Aw, don't they make a cute couple?" Jackie joked.

"Not as cute as us," Scott said mischievously. "Anyway, you're the lifesaver. I was just about to take an AP physics test I didn't study for. But don't tell Frances."

Frances Ives was tutoring Scott in physics, which seemed pretty bizarre to Jackie. Why would Aunt Deborah allow her chief rival's daughter to snoop around the First Family quarters? Or leave her alone with Scott, a horny guy with a secret drug bust in his past? Scott said his father had insisted on hiring Frances, claiming there was no one smarter or more up-to-date on teaching tools. Blah, blah, blah. That was weird, too.

"Is she as big a bitch as her little sister?" Jackie asked.

"Not to me. But I have that effect on women." Scott laughed. He reached over and playfully squeezed her knee. The electric jolt of his touch made her jump.

She answered him with a flirty smile.

God, Jackie, what are you doing? You shouldn't be here—bailing on school, flirting with Scott, risking getting caught.

Get real, she told herself. *You know what you're doing. You're trying to have it both ways. Hiding behind Ankie means you don't have to confront Mom and Aunt Deborah. And it lets you postpone making a final, fatal break with Andrew. While keeping Scott interested without having to figure out your true feelings for him.*

Screw it. It's senior year and I deserve some me time. What's the big deal?

"I'm all yours. What do you want to do?" Scott asked. Both his hands were back on the wheel, but his voice was loaded with suggestion.

"Let's just crank up the music and drive."

Scott headed north for a couple of miles and turned into Rock Creek Park. This time of year, the national park that cut through the city was a sparse forest of brown, leafless trees, the creek a fast-running gush of water that threatened to overflow its banks.

It was only midmorning but dark clouds were already moving over the winter sun.

"It looks like rain," Scott said, taking off his Ray-Bans and putting up the roof. He turned on the headlights and wipers as a drizzle smeared the windshield. "Too bad."

Stifled by the heat now trapped in the car, Jackie stripped off her crimson, double-breasted Burberry trench, unwrapped the cream and navy Excelsior scarf, and tossed them in the back.

She wished she were wearing something other than her school uniform. It was so much easier for guys. They could be wearing school-issue khakis and still look hot. *And so do I. I'm the It Girl, aren't I?*

Scott steered the car with one hand, the other stroking her arm. They passed the National Zoo, famous for its pandas, and historic Pierce Mill, where the CIA installed surveillance gear to spy on nearby communist embassies during the Cold War.

"There's a place up here where we can pull over for some privacy," Scott shouted above the music. The tires squealed as he took the next curve a little too fast. "Want to?"

He started to turn his head toward her as he sped around another bend, even as the rain got harder.

Nervous about his one-handed driving on the slick road, she removed his hand from her arm.

"You need to slow down!" she answered, frowning at him.

Scott threw her a confused look. "What do you mean?"

"Slow down!" she repeated hotly. Ever since Taylor's death, she'd been—not scared exactly—but extra cautious riding in cars. Especially in the rain. With someone else driving.

"I don't get it, Jackie! One minute you come on to me and the next you're telling me to stop!" He was still shouting to be heard above the music and the rain.

She suddenly realized he'd misunderstood. She was talking about his driving. *He's talking about us.*

Before she could explain, he frowned at her, his face flushed. "Are you just using me to get back at Andrew?"

"No, you don't understand—" Jackie tried to explain, fumbling with the knobs on the radio to turn it down.

The sentence hung in the air, unfinished, as the car hit a wet patch and slid off the road.

She shut her eyes tightly. But instead of blackness, she saw that rainy January night. The wet surface of the road. Taylor trying to grab the wheel from Andrew. The car slamming into the tree. Andrew's words, the day of his confession, pounded through her head.

"Taylor was lying near the tree and she didn't have a pulse."

"No!" Jackie screamed.

Andrew stood at the top of the Grand Staircase and yelled down at his brother, who was ambling up the stairs.

"Yo, Scott! Frances is looking for you. She says you're late. She's pacing the floor of your study."

Andrew had bumped into her wandering along the hallway outside his bedroom. She was wearing a clingy, low-cut dress and stilettos. Her lips were painted dark red to match her fingernails. Definitely not your standard congressional aide attire.

She's gotta be teaching him more than physics.

Scott looked up, shrugging. "Frances needs to chill 'cause I'm in no hurry. She only wants to grill me on the physics test I skipped today."

Andrew met him halfway down and stopped. "Dude, what are you doing cutting class like that? Do Mom and Dad know?"

"No. Why? You planning on telling them?"

"Gimme a break. Believe it or not, I'm trying to help you out here. Colleges are still going to check your grades, even after you're accepted."

"You're always quick with the brotherly advice, aren't you?" Scott snapped. "Look what happened the last time you handed it out. I ended up in Midwestern Siberia for two years."

Andrew winced. "I've told you over and over how bad I feel about that and—"

Scott cut him off. "Yeah, well when you figure out a way to give me my two years back, I'll figure out a way to forgive you."

Andrew exploded. "Look, I don't give a shit where you were or why you missed school. I've got too many problems of my own without dealing with yours."

Andrew regretted the words as soon as they left his mouth. He *did* care what happened to Scott. But right now the two of them couldn't be in the same room without being at each other's throats.

It wasn't just Scott's resentment and Andrew's guilt over Scott being banished from D.C. after ninth grade. It was also Scott's jealousy—Andrew knew what Scott called him behind his back, *Number One Perfect Son*.

And then there was Jackie. Or more to the point, Scott's flirting with Jackie. Right under his nose. It drove Andrew insane. It was bad enough that she was barely speaking to him right now. But it was unthinkable that Scott would try to take advantage of that. And especially if Scott's main motive was just to get back at him.

Just thinking about Jackie sent a stab of longing through his body. Every day they were apart just made him want her more. He'd tried to convince himself that it was only because he couldn't have her. But he knew in his heart, despite everything wrong between them right now, they *were* meant to be.

Scott bounded up the stairs, two at a time. At the top, he turned around and looked down on Andrew.

"Oh by the way, you should know I was with Jackie." Scott grinned. "We both ditched. Together."

Andrew was consumed with anger, wanting to wipe the cocky smile off Scott's face with his fist. He shoved his hands in his pockets and forced himself to turn away and walk down the stairs.

"Hey! I *said* I was with Jackie!"

Keep walking. Just keep walking.

"Do you even know how to fight?" Scott yelled. "You ran away from her and you're running away from me! You are pathetic!"

The truth of the words stung. He *had* let Scott down when his brother had needed him most. And he'd virtually thrust Jackie into Scott's arms by giving up so easily. He *was* pathetic.

TWELVE

Laura Beth had no choice. She *had* to come clean with Jackie. Fess up that she was the one who told Senator Griffin about Jackie's disastrous hookup with Eric Moran.

Jackie would understand. Maybe not immediately, but surely eventually. Yes, it was a betrayal. But not in a mean way like Taylor's. It was a betrayal with *good* intentions that just happened to go bad.

There were two reasons she couldn't put it off any longer. She wanted to be free of that blackmailing bitch Whitney *and* she didn't want any BFF drama disrupting the presidential race.

Laura Beth decided to do it in an empty classroom near the end of lunch hour. It was neutral turf with controlled conditions, and most importantly, Jackie couldn't very well yell at her for half the school to hear.

Like all professional actresses, she'd carefully memorized her lines. Not that she was putting on an act or anything. She just didn't want to go off-script.

It was an unusually mild winter day and the Capital Girls took their lunch outside to eat.

"I'm really excited to go to the president's State of the Union speech to Congress next week," Lettie said happily. "I hope she brings up Paraguay. She could really pressure the government into backing down or calling new elections."

Jackie shook her head. "I wish she would, too, Lettie. But don't get your hopes up. I don't think Aunt Deborah wants to wade into another country's domestic politics."

Lettie's eyes flashed with anger. "That's never stopped the United States before."

Laura Beth was just about to launch into a hot defense of the Bush wars in Iraq when she remembered now was not the time to piss off Jackie by arguing about politics.

Fortunately, Jackie changed the subject.

"I wish Aunt Deborah would announce a new program for returned veterans," she said. "That would get Dr. Rosen off the administration's back and make my job with him a lot easier if he thought Aunt Deborah was adopting his ideas."

Laura Beth and Lettie looked at her hopefully.

"But when I asked Mom, she said there was no money in the budget for any big new spending program," Jackie added glumly.

Just as Laura Beth was thinking up ways to get Jackie alone, Lettie stood up. "I'm headed to the library, guys. I'll see you later."

As soon as Lettie disappeared, Laura Beth turned to Jackie. "I need to talk to you about something. In private. Let's go find an empty classroom."

She led Jackie to one of the English Lit rooms, knowing it was bound to be empty.

"What is it? Is something wrong?" Jackie asked with a worried frown.

"Not exactly wrong," Laura Beth answered. "Let's sit down."

She grabbed a chair and they sat across from each other at the teacher's desk.

"What I'm about to tell you isn't going to sound like something one best friend does to another," Laura Beth said, reciting her opening line. "But try to remember, Jackie, please, that I did it only because I love you and I wanted to save you."

Jackie rubbed her arms as if she was cold. She raised her eyebrows and gave Laura Beth one of her cut-the-crap looks. "Just tell me."

"Well . . ." She launched into her speech, reminding Jackie of that day last year when all three girls and Whitney were hanging at Laura Beth's house.

"Quit stalling," Jackie interrupted.

Laura Beth realized if she had any hope of retaining control over her confession, she'd need to do an abbreviated version.

So she quickly explained how it was she, not Whitney, who had eavesdropped on Jackie's phone call with Eric, the one in which they'd planned a secret rendezvous at the Kennedy Center.

At first Jackie looked puzzled, like she didn't get it. "And you told Whitney?" she asked, incredulous. "The very person who would be sure to leak it?"

"No," Laura Beth said hesitantly. She swallowed. "I didn't tell Whitney. I told Uncle Ham."

Jackie shook her head slowly as if trying to absorb each word. "No. No. You couldn't have. I don't understand."

"It was the only thing I knew to do to stop you from making a *huge* mistake," Laura Beth said. Then, feeling desperate, she went off-script. "You were going to make a fool of yourself."

She could practically see the steam coming out of Jackie's ears. She wished she could eat her words.

"That came out wrong. I didn't mean 'fool.' I meant I didn't want you to get hurt by that sleazebag.

"Uncle Ham promised he'd make Eric stay away from you. I had no idea he was lyin' through his teeth. That he was goin' to take total advantage of me!"

"Take advantage of *you*?" Jackie seethed.

"No, no. Not just me. You, too. He took horrible advantage of both of us. Please, Jackie, just hear me out."

Jackie nodded.

"I was so horrified by what I'd caused to happen, I let you think the leak must have been Whitney," Laura Beth said. "Then somehow Whitney found out what I'd done and threatened to tell you unless I brought her into our group. I didn't know what to do. I didn't want you to hate me."

Throwing out her script, Laura Beth practically squealed, "Jackie, please forgive me. I was so wrong. I don't know what else to say." Just for a second, until she regained her senses, she thought of walking around the table, getting down on her knees, and outright pleading.

I want her to forgive me. But Ballous don't beg.

Finally, she ran out of ways to say sorry.

There was a very long silence.

When Jackie spoke, her voice was so soft Laura Beth had to lean across the table to hear.

"Laura Beth, I can't even begin to process any of this," she said, without any emotion at all. "I need time to think this through and figure out where we go from here. But you were right about one thing. It doesn't sound like anything 'one best friend does to another.'"

Then she got up from the table and walked out. She closed the door quietly behind her but it was like she'd slammed it in Laura Beth's face.

Even though Laura Beth didn't want the whole school knowing their business, she almost would have preferred Jackie to have screamed hysterically about how it was all Laura Beth's fault that Jackie had had to ask Jennifer Cane to destroy those wicked pictures. That it was all Laura Beth's fault that Jackie was now forever in The Fixer's debt.

Laura Beth sat at the desk until the bell rang.

Jackie made her way down the hall, which was crowded with kids heading to class, barely registering their *Hi, Jackie!* chirps as she pushed her way past them.

The numbness she felt after listening to Laura Beth was slowly lifting. Waves of anger rose and crashed over her instead. She recognized the first familiar pangs of panic, the tingling in her fingers and the unbearable chill. She walked faster, just trying to make it to the bathroom in time.

"Hey, Jackie! Wanna walk with me to Bio?" asked Denise Collins, who was drying her hands under the blower. "I can wait for you."

"That's okay. I'll see you there," Jackie mumbled, disappearing into the first empty stall and locking the door.

She sank down on the toilet seat, sucking in big gulps of air, desperately trying to block the pain burning through her heart and silence the words hammering in her head. *"I told Uncle Ham. I told Uncle Ham. I told Uncle Ham."*

She forced her breathing to slow down and even out.

One more betrayal. One more friend turned traitor.

She counted off Laura Beth's sins: *She spied on me. She told on me. She lied to me. And she waited till now to tell me.*

Jackie listened for sounds in the bathroom. It was deathly quiet. She stood up, opened the stall door, and walked over to the washstand.

There was nothing in her reflection to show how she felt inside. Her makeup still looked fresh and her hair was only a little mussed. She pulled a brush out of her brown Longchamp tote and ran it quickly through her hair.

Staring at the mirror, applying a coat of lipstick, she had an instant flashback. She and Dr. Rosen were standing on the Capitol steps surrounded by reporters as she deftly and confidently fielded their hostile questions.

She thought of a Nietzsche quote, one of her mother's favorites: *"He who has a why to live can bear almost any how."*

Jackie wasn't sure what her future held, but she knew she had a role to play. And the strength to overcome the hurdles along the way.

Laura Beth had inadvertently set up one of those hurdles. She'd not only let Jackie down, but her meddling had forced Jackie to be forever in debt to Jennifer Cane.

But we've been a part of each other's lives forever. We owe it to each other to try to resolve this.

Her mother's voice rang in her ear. It was another quote from Nietzsche. *"That which does not kill us makes us stronger."*

THIRTEEN

Jackie paced the First Family's empty living room as she waited for Andrew to show up. Once again, here she was, back playing her part in the Ankie farce. Tonight it was an appearance at Aunt Deborah's State of the Union address to Congress.

The president had decided that Bob Price and Scott should go ahead so as not to detract from the Happy Young Couple's staged entrance for the media.

At the thought of Scott, Jackie sighed. She'd put the car "accident" in perspective. Now all she felt was embarrassed that she'd overreacted to what was a minor mishap. They'd missed hitting any trees and there was no damage to the convertible. Not even their agents thought it was a big deal, especially after Scott lied and told them he'd swerved to avoid a deer. "I can't afford any infractions," he'd told Jackie, half-seriously. "Mom might revoke my parental probation."

As to the bigger issue—what to do about her attraction to Scott—she'd shoved it right back in its box and slammed the lid shut. A Pandora's box with DO NOT OPEN!! written in bright red letters.

Her cell rang.

"Hi, Dad," Jackie answered suspiciously. "What's up?"

"Does your dear old dad need a particular reason to call?"

Yes.

Harry Whitman and Carolyn Shaw had been divorced forever and lived totally separate lives. The one thing they had in common, apart from Jackie, was that they were both workaholics. His job was lobbying Congress for tax breaks and other perks for renewable energy firms.

Aside from major celebrations like birthdays, Jackie hardly saw him, though they kept in touch via e-mail.

Like, *Just got your grades. Keep up the good work! Dad xox* or *Turn on CNN. My hit is at 6:15 P.M. Dad xox.*

"I just wanted to check that you were going to the State of the Union," her father was saying a bit defensively, "so I can boast about you to one of my clients who's meeting me at the office tonight."

Client? That's one word for it. Her dad was a serial dater who often mixed business with pleasure.

"Yes, I'll be there, Dad. I'm at the White House now, waiting to get a ride with Andrew."

Her father chuckled. "Ankie still going strong?"

"Yeah, sure," she lied.

"So, is your mom driving over with you?"

"No, she's already over there. She rode over with Ike."

There was a slight pause. "Oh. Er, I see where Tracey Mills

had a small item about your mother and Ike attending a lot of events together. And a photo of them all decked out at some charity ball."

So that's why he called. He wants to know if they're hooking up. She decided to make him work for it.

"Oh, yeah, I saw that. I guess they're busy on some project because he's *always* in her office." She waited for him to take the bait. He jumped.

"Really? How so?"

"Yep. And they have a lot of evening meetings, too." She added, teasing, "Mom won't say what it's about."

"So, uh, on the weekends, too?"

She laughed. "Okay, Dad, what's going on? Are you jealous or something?"

For years after her parents split up, Jackie dreamed they would get back together. She knew all kids did that. But she'd given up that idea a long time ago. What was more important to her now was that the three of them got along okay. Which they did. And that her dad at least showed up for her birthdays and major holidays. Which he usually did.

"Jealous? Don't be silly!" her father protested. "Just curious. So, where will you be sitting tonight?"

What a lame attempt to change the subject.

"I'll be sitting next to Andrew, Dad, duh."

"Yes, of course you will. Okay, sweetie, I better let you go!"

That was her dad's way of saying he wanted to hang up. But she wasn't going to let him off that easily.

"Okay, Dad. Oh, by the way, I thought the photo of Mom and Ike that Tracey Mills ran was really cute. Would you like me to get a copy from the White House and have them sign it for you?"

"Very funny, Jackie—"

Aunt Deborah stuck her head in the door.

"Jackie, I haven't seen enough of you lately," she said. "Come talk to me while I finish getting ready."

"Gotta go, Dad. Bye," she said hastily.

Aunt Deborah led her into the presidential bedroom suite.

Jackie braced for a lecture about hanging out more with Andrew.

But Aunt Deborah just seemed to want to catch up about school and going off to college, while tentatively probing her about how much campaigning she'd be willing to do.

It was another of those Washington moments. The TV anchors were probably reporting that the president, at this very moment, was holed up in the Oval Office making last-minute changes to her big speech. But, in fact, she was just hanging out in her bedroom, chatting with Jackie.

"You and my two handsome boys will just wow the youth vote. You three will outshine Laura Beth and those two Ives girls every time," she said, checking her hair in the antique gilt wall mirror.

Or we could just stage our own Hunger Games and let the best teen team win.

"Uh, thanks. I just hope my friendship with Laura Beth doesn't suffer," Jackie answered vaguely. *If there's any friendship left after the heart-to-heart we're going to have.*

Aunt Deborah smiled. "Libby and I have weathered our differences. I'm sure you and Laura Beth can, as well. Just remember, hurtful things are always said in the heat of the campaign but it's all soon forgotten."

A Tiffany box on the bed caught Jackie's eye.

"Did you get something special to wear tonight?" she asked.

Aunt Deborah giggled. Jackie had *never* heard her do that before.

"Shh," she joked. "It's a diamond tennis bracelet. I found it in Bob's dressing room. It must be his Valentine's present to me. I should put it back right now so he doesn't know I saw it."

Maybe I'm wrong. Maybe their marriage isn't dead after all.

Andrew appeared in the bedroom doorway.

"What secrets are you two plotting?" he joked, pointing at the telltale Tiffany blue box in his mother's hand.

"Never you mind," Aunt Deborah shushed him, quickly closing the lid. She looked her son up and down. "Your tie's crooked. Jackie, fix it for him, will you?"

She vanished inside Bob Price's dressing room. Andrew walked over to Jackie and stood at mock-attention, so close to her she could feel the heat of his body.

He was wearing a midnight-blue wool suit she'd never seen before and it fit him perfectly. But his mom was right. The silk tie, in gradated shades of bright blue, was slightly askew. She hesitated.

"Try not to strangle me." He grinned.

"It's tempting, but I'll try not to."

She raised her arms and fiddled with the knot. "Did you remember your belt? You're always forgetting it." The words were out of her mouth before she could take them back.

What the hell, Jackie? You just slipped into girlfriend mode.

She stepped back abruptly, her heel catching on the Oriental rug, and Andrew lunged to catch her, both of them falling onto the bed. For a second he lay on top of her. His eyes burned into hers and she could feel his racing heart, matching hers, beat for beat.

"We've never done it in the presidential suite," Andrew whispered, moving his mouth to her ear.

"We've never done it anywhere," she snapped, breaking the spell.

Aunt Deborah marched back into the room. "I can't leave you two alone for five seconds," she kidded. "You can make out in the car on the way over to the Capitol. Scoot, both of you."

Like that's gonna happen.

Laura Beth had never felt so left out.

This night last year she was sitting with Jackie, Lettie, and the Price family in the VIP gallery overlooking the House chamber, waiting for Deborah Price to give her first State of the Union address.

She remembered exactly what she'd been wearing: a cream-and-gold Proenza Schouler suit and Mama's favorite double strand of Mikimoto pearls. She'd even managed to grab a seat next to Andrew, though with Jackie on his other side, he'd barely noticed Laura Beth was there.

And now, a year later, here she was in her flannel Nick and Noras, forced to watch the State of the Union on TV—just like the rest of the country who bothered to tune in.

"Not fair," she grumbled.

Of course, with the campaign and all, Mama wouldn't have let her go under any circumstances. Not that she'd been invited.

Even Mama had abandoned her tonight. She'd decided to watch from Jeffrey's apartment at the Four Seasons so they could discuss it when he got back from the Capitol. But Laura Beth suspected her mother really wanted to be alone with Jeffrey so she could unload something big on him. There was definitely something brewing. Furtive phone calls, secret texts, the way Mama was acting . . . None of that had let up.

She couldn't even Skype or text Sol, who was at some New York function for his parents' foundation, to raise money for a cardiac wing in a hospital in Iran.

The camera panned briefly over the president's guests.

Jackie was sitting between Andrew and Scott. Lettie was in the second row, behind Bob Price and Carolyn Shaw.

Although she only got a quick glimpse of Jackie, Laura Beth knew her well enough to see she was stressed.

For one thing, she was wearing the *same* navy blue Alice and Olivia suit she had on when *People* magazine photographed her at the British Embassy Christmas party.

She's definitely not thinking straight.

She was sitting stiffly as if deliberately avoiding touching either brother and she seemed to be staring into space, not paying attention to what was going on.

Laura Beth hoped like crazy she and her confession weren't responsible for Jackie's funk.

Maybe she's had another fight with Andrew. Or the stalker's contacted her again. Not that I'm wishing either of those things on her.

The relief of telling Jackie the truth—and getting Whitney off her back—had been almost worth risking the end of their friendship. Especially after Jackie had texted her and they'd arranged to "talk it out some more."

It was ironic, really. Just as Jackie seemed to be losing it—her weirdly calm reaction to the classroom confession, her hysterical overreaction to the teeny tiny car mishap with Scott—Laura Beth's own star was rising.

Yes, the ugliness at Taylor's memorial was an unfortunate detour. But thankfully, her mama had barely noticed it *and* she'd promised to talk to Jeffrey about her youth vote idea. Not that she was taking any chances. She already had a plan in the works to prove her value to the campaign.

Who knew? It might not be long before D.C. had *two* It Girls.

From her seat overlooking the House chamber, Lettie soaked up every detail of the scene below.

A smiling President Price was walking down the blue-and-gold-carpeted center aisle. She'd swapped her trademark pantsuit for a royal-blue skirt-suit. Lettie guessed it was a nod to conservative congressmen who still didn't approve of women wearing trousers in the chamber and who made a big fuss over Michelle Obama's bare arms at her husband's speech.

Lettie wished Daniel was sitting next to her, soaking up the experience.

Members of Congress from both parties rose from their seats, applauding the president. Dozens pressed in, eager to shake her hand or kiss her cheek. The camera paused briefly on Senator Ives, who was standing and clapping politely, his face expressionless.

You'd never know that a couple of hours ago, half of these politicians, including him, were fighting her on every issue.

But that was the great thing about a *real* democracy. You could openly oppose your president without reprisal.

It seemed to take forever for President Price to reach the massive, three-tiered rostrum. The applause died down and she began to speak.

Almost immediately her words were drowned out by shouts from the other end of the public gallery. A group of spectators were on their feet, opening their coats to reveal THANK GOD FOR PRICELESS PAPPIES emblazoned across their T-shirts.

"Impeach President Price!" they screamed. "Hampton Griffin for president!"

Out of nowhere, a dozen Capitol Police rushed in, grabbed the protesters, and roughly herded them out the door.

Without thinking, Lettie jumped to her feet.

This is America! They have a right to speak out!

"Don't!" she said. Before she knew what hit her, a police officer grabbed her.

She heard Jackie call out her name. She, Andrew, and Scott were out of their seats.

"Sit down," Bob Price hissed under his breath, yanking on Scott's jacket. Andrew hesitated, then slowly sat back down, his eyes staying fixed on Lettie. Scott shook off his father's hand and made a move as if to leap over his chair to jump the cop.

Jackie, ignoring the First Husband and her mother's glare, reached out her hand toward Lettie.

"Officer, this young woman is our guest," Bob Price said in a low but authoritative voice. "Please unhand her. Lettie, sit down. Jackie, Scott, return to your seats. Now."

The officer let go of Lettie. Her legs were so shaky she almost fell back in her seat. Her face burned and she gritted her teeth to keep from crying.

What have I done? she thought frantically. *If only Daniel were here.*

"I'm so sorry. I'm so sorry," she whispered to Bob Price. "I didn't mean any harm."

He turned around and shrugged. "It was just a misunderstanding."

Carolyn Shaw reached behind her and patted Lettie's arm. "Everything's fine, Lettie. Don't worry."

Below them, President Price regained control of the chamber.

"They must not be aware of the House dress code," the president joked. "No T-shirts."

Everyone burst out laughing.

Except Lettie. She just wanted to curl up and die.

"Shut up, Dina!" Whitney snarled.

Dina raised her eyebrows in surprise. "What? You don't think Lettie practically getting arrested on national TV is funny?"

She giggled and nudged Angie and Aamina, who were sitting next to her on the white leather sofa in Whitney's living room.

"Yeah, for someone who's supposed to be so-o-o smart, Lettie sure looked stupid," Angie said.

"Everyone knows you can't pull a stunt like that when the president's anywhere nearby," Aamina added.

"Yeah and if she was gonna get herself arrested, you'd think she'd wanna look better for her mug shot," Dina said. "What's she wearing, anyway?"

"Probably some thrift store hand-me-down," Angie answered, downing another shot of vodka. "How come your mom didn't buy her something nice to wear, Whitney?"

Whitney just shrugged. *Mom offered to get her something new, but Lets wouldn't let her.*

"Daniel could've paid for a new dress. The Canes are loaded," Aamina mused, tugging on the legs of her 7 jeans.

"I think she looks fine," Whitney said testily.

She wasn't sure why she was getting worked up about this. Until a brief but powerful memory flooded her mind.

———

I was wearing my favorite outfit, my Barbie bride's dress and veil. We were at a family picnic and all the kids in the park were teasing me and their parents were laughing at me. I was crying and Mara came over and yelled at them, even the grown-ups, and hugged me and told me I looked beautiful.

"I've got the munchies bad. Whitney, where are the snacks?" Angie looked around and slapped her forehead in an exaggerated way. "Oh yeah, what was I thinking? You never have any food."

"Shut the fuck up, all of you," Whitney said.

Whitney was sorry she'd agreed to have them over to watch the State of the Union address.

She didn't get why anyone with a pulse would want to waste their free time listening to a stupid speech by the stupid president. But Angie and Dina had promised to bring Purple Chronic and a bottle of Absolut and Aamina had offered them all a limo ride afterward to the 9:30 Club downtown. Whitney figured they'd all have a good laugh watching Jackie play Little Miss It Girl. It'd also be a chance to look for chinks in the Ankie armor.

The last thing she expected was for Lettie to flip out. Watching her getting manhandled by the cop was just plain shocking. Then listening to these three putting her down was pissing her off, especially after what they'd done to her at Taylor's memorial.

"Here, chill," Angie said, handing Whitney a half-smoked joint.

She took a long drag, hoping it would mellow her out. It had the opposite effect.

A few minutes later, she stood up. "Okay. Party's over."

"Whaddya mean?" Dina protested. "It's not over yet. Lettie

might do something else stupid. Or maybe Jackie will start kissing Scott and then Andrew will punch him and . . ."

". . . Jackie'll try to break it up, and she'll lose her balance and fall headfirst off the balcony . . ." added Angie.

". . . and flatten President Price. That'd make Dad's run for the White House a whole lot easier," Dina said, like she actually believed it could happen.

It's too bad "Crapital Girls" is taken cuz that name fits these losers perfectly.

The three of them dissolved into another bout of juvenile giggling that made Whitney want to smack them. She stared at the TV, where the camera was back on Lettie, who looked utterly shattered.

Whitney's eyes started to burn and to her surprise, she felt a tear spill down her cheek. She quickly brushed it away before the others noticed.

What the hell? I must be really stoned.

Then the tears started falling faster than her hand could make them disappear.

"I gotta go to the bathroom," she mumbled. "I think the pot made me feel sick. You guys gotta go. I mean it. Now. Let yourselves out."

She ran to her bedroom and flopped on the bed, feeling dizzy.

She thought about Lettie being humiliated at Taylor's party and now on national TV.

Although Whitney wasn't used to saying sorry, she'd apologized several times to Lettie—even teared up a little bit without faking it—about the Excelsior scholarship fund. Lettie had accepted her apology but Whitney still felt bad. She wasn't sure why and it bothered her.

A face flashed before her eyes. Mara's. Then the picture in her mind began to blur and fade.

Her body convulsed with sobs and she buried her face in her pillow, trying to smother the noise.

FOURTEEN

Jackie hated feeling nervous like this. But how else could you feel when you're about to try to convince someone you're not a tease—yet you know that's exactly what you are? A tease for stringing along Scott and making Andrew jealous, without knowing how she really felt about either brother.

She'd arrived at the White House a few minutes early so she and Scott could be alone before their meeting with Andrew and Monica O'Connor, their event planner.

They were getting together to finalize plans for a fund-raiser for Dr. Rosen's Veterans Rights Activist Group (VRAG). It was Aunt Deborah's idea that the two boys help Jackie host it, obviously hoping Dr. Rosen would be so grateful he would quit publicly criticizing her policies.

Jackie wasn't sure the president's ploy was going to work. Dr. Rosen, unlike the rest of D.C., wasn't into deal making, spoken or unspoken. So Jackie had organized to have Monica rush on-stage and shut him down at the first sign of trouble.

But first Jackie wanted to address her misunderstanding with Scott just before they ran off the road the other day.

"Great, Jackie, you're here. You wanna talk?" Scott said, walking into the First Family's private kitchen and pulling out a chair.

She nodded and tried not to stare. He looked cute. No, he looked totally hot in jeans and a soft North Face pullover, the sleeves pushed up to his elbows. Even his hair, which had grown out of the reform-school buzz cut, looked sexy.

"I just wanted to say I'm sorry if you thought I was jerking you around the other day in the car," she answered, trying to focus on her message.

"It sounded like you were."

She flushed.

"I wasn't. The music was really loud, so it was hard to hear, and our signals got crossed."

"What do you mean?"

"I just wanted you to put both hands on the wheel. The rain and the windy road were making me nervous, but I overreacted."

She sucked in her breath. *This is awkward.*

"I was talking about your driving," she repeated. "And you thought I meant I didn't want you to touch me."

He grinned. "So now you're saying you *do*?"

She smiled back, fighting an urge to grab him in her arms.

"I've been skittish, you know, since Taylor's accident. Then when we drove off the road, I must have freaked out because I had some sort of weird flashback."

"A flashback?"

"Can you have a flashback if you weren't there? Whatever you call it, it had to do with Taylor's accident."

If this was Andrew—the old Andrew—he'd put his arms around me, she thought. That's what they did whenever they had a problem. They held each other and talked it out. Making up was even better. Warmth crept up her body as she remembered their incredible hunger for each other. How he'd nibble her earlobe before moving his lips over to her mouth. *Stop it,* she told herself. *It's over. You've got to move on.*

Scott nodded sympathetically and got up. But to her disappointment, it was only to pour a cup of coffee.

"I'm still not sure what it is you want, Jackie," he said, sitting back down. "Are you interested in *us*?"

"It's complicated. Our parents want Andrew and me to stay together, especially with the election campaign starting and—"

He interrupted, "You sound like Andrew. He lets Mom dictate his life, but you have *got* to have more guts than that."

"Don't pretend to be naïve," she shot back, annoyed. "It's politics. You of all people know that. They sent you away for two years because of politics. Even now, you're on probation. If you screw up, you'll be on the next plane out of here."

"Yeah, you're right. But could you just give me a straight answer? Do you like me or not?"

"You're rushing me," she said. "I know we talked on the phone now and then while you were away. But you've only just come back."

Scott frowned.

Before he could answer, Frances Ives stuck her head in the door.

"Whoops. Hi, you two. Looks like I'm interrupting something."

"Yeah, it's called a coffee break," Scott said, pulling his gaze away from Jackie. "What are you doing here, Frances? We don't meet till tomorrow."

She stepped into the room and handed Scott a book. "I just wanted to drop off another sample test."

Jackie had to admit she was gorgeous. Her black hair was pulled into one of those loose buns with a few strands framing her heart-shaped face and her long, thick eyelashes looked real.

Frances's sleeve fell back, exposing a string of diamonds encircling her slender wrist.

"It's from Tiffany's," Frances said, seeing Jackie's stare.

Since when are congressional aides that well paid?

"A gift from your father?" Jackie asked.

She studied it closer. It was identical to the one that Aunt Deborah had shown her the night of the State of the Union address. The tennis bracelet supposedly meant as a surprise Valentine's Day gift from her husband.

Frances coyly pulled down her sleeve. "No, it's from a secret admirer."

She threw Jackie a triumphant smile. "See you guys later."

Jackie felt sick to her stomach.

Frances, she realized, was either a jewelry thief or a husband thief.

As soon as she was gone, Scott shook his head. "Man, she's always hanging around. I don't get it."

She toyed with telling Scott her suspicions about the bracelet, but sanity won out. *No way am I getting entangled in that little domestic drama.*

"I don't trust her and you shouldn't, either," was all she said.

"Whatever. Let's get back to talking about us." He gave her one of his seductive smiles that made him so irresistible. "I'm sorry if I seem to be rushing you. It's just that I think about you all the time. And it's driving me crazy, not knowing where I stand. Not knowing whether you want to be with me."

She hesitated before deciding to go with honesty. It was one of Taylor's few rules for the Capital Girls. *Until she broke it.*

"You know I like you," she said bluntly, meeting his eyes. "I just don't know what to do about it."

"Come on, Lettie, you *know* in your heart that Andrew had something to do with Taylor's death," Daniel repeated. "All you have to do is look at how he's behaving. He obviously feels incredibly guilty about something. What else could it be but Taylor?"

Lettie sighed. They'd been over this so many times. *Let it go.*

They were sitting on the floor of Lettie's bedroom, something that would never, ever have happened if Lettie were still living with her strict parents. But Tracey didn't seem to care what either she or Whitney did. Not where they went or what time they got home or who they brought with them. Not that Lettie had anything to hide. It was a big step for her just to let Daniel hang out in her room.

"Well of course he feels guilty," Lettie replied wearily. She drained her mug of hot chocolate and put it back on the tray between them.

"He was there in the car and probably feels bad that he hadn't insisted on driving. You've got to move on."

"I can't. I've tried, I really have, but it's eating me up," he said in a strangled voice. He paused, then looked up and held her gaze.

"I have to tell you something," he said, his eyes pained. He hesitated again. "It was me who tipped off Senator Hampton Griffin."

Lettie had no idea what he was talking about. "What do you mean?"

"Remember Senator Griffin's press conference just before Christmas?"

She nodded. How could she forget? The girls had been hanging decorations at the veterans' hospital when the TV station broke into regular programming for the senator's press conference. Surrounded by reporters, Senator Griffin had hinted at a White House cover-up involving Taylor's accident. Jackie had gone ballistic and rushed home.

Lettie dreaded what Daniel was about to say.

"I called his aide, Eric Moran, and told him they should look into the accident," Daniel said, his eyes still locked on hers. "I said that Andrew was acting like he had something to hide but I had no proof."

Lettie was speechless. *Jackie can't ever find out it was Daniel. She'd never forgive him.*

It took her a second to find her words.

"How could you do that? You know Senator Griffin wants to be president. He and the PAPPies would do anything to discredit President Price and get her out of the race."

"I know you think I shouldn't have done it, Lettie. I don't want to hurt you or Jackie. But I *know* Andrew's hiding something. If anyone can dig it up, it's Senator Griffin."

When she didn't answer, he continued. "I can't ask Taylor and Andrew's never going to tell me. I'm truly sorry that you're upset, but I'm not sorry I did it."

Lettie recalled Homecoming, when Andrew, totally out of control, started screaming something about lies and cover-ups and punched Daniel. How could she blame Taylor's twin for wanting answers?

But since hearing the mystery woman's voice pleading, *"Don't tell Daniel,"* she had no doubt that the truth would be more painful than the frustration of not knowing.

"Daniel, you've got to stop all this," she begged. "You're the one who's going to end up getting hurt."

He ran his hands through his beautiful blond hair and shook his head as if to banish his thoughts.

"Please," she added. "For my sake. I care about you *so* much."

She moved sideways until her face was just inches from his. She took his head in her hands and met his eyes. He broke into a wide smile.

She pressed her mouth against his, exploring with her tongue. His response was strong and immediate and she felt a surge of confidence. He folded her in his arms and they kissed long and hard.

At some point they lost their balance and toppled over. They both burst out laughing as Lettie fell on top of him.

But instead of untangling themselves, they kissed again. And again. Daniel slid his hands under her shirt and stroked her bare skin. She heard herself moan.

Was that me?

She felt his hands effortlessly unhook her bra.

Where did he learn that? she wondered.

Don't think. Just enjoy. Remember what Tanya said. You can't know if you don't commit.

She sat up, slipped her shirt over her head, and shyly held her bra in place.

"Are you sure?" Daniel's face was flushed with the passion of wanting her, but his questioning eyes were filled with tenderness.

Instead of answering, she unfolded her arms and let her bra drop. This time, he was the one who moaned. He pulled her down and gently shifted her body under his.

She lost all sense of time and place.

Until Whitney burst into the room.

"Lettie, are you okay? I heard moaning!"

Her voice went from concern to shock. Her jaw practically hit the floor.

"Whoops. My bad," she chortled. "Way to go, guys."

Lettie was mortified. Whitney of all people barging in on the most intimate moment of her life. Whitney, who was sure to blab it all over school. *I can't take any more humiliation.* Though she'd more or less accepted Whitney's explanation for the Taylor scene, she'd vowed not to trust her again.

"Whitney, if you breathe a word of this . . ." she began.

Whitney shook her head and shut the door.

"Don't worry, Lets. For once my lips are sealed. But next time you might wanna put a sign up. Or just lock the door!" she called from the hallway.

Lettie pushed away from Daniel and struggled to her feet.

"I'm so sorry, Lettie. This was so beautiful and Whitney had to . . ."

"It's okay. Really."

And for some reason she didn't understand, it *was* okay.

She walked over to the door and locked it.

"Come here," she whispered shyly.

FIFTEEN

Laura Beth dumped her gray Kooba satchel on the marble floor of the foyer. She paused for a second, savoring the smell of roasted sesame seeds wafting from the kitchen. Her mouth watered just thinking about fresh-baked benne wafers, a favorite Southern cookie.

"Mama? I'm home!" she called out.

Maria, the maid, appeared in the foyer.

"Miss Laura Beth, your mama's in the sunroom. She asked to see you the minute you got home from school," she said.

Maria lowered her voice to a whisper. "She's having one of her spells. But I'm sure you can cheer her up."

It must be one of her "sick headaches" again, Laura Beth thought. It always happened the day after she'd had one too many bourbons.

Laura Beth sighed. She barely had enough time to change out of her uniform before driving to Jackie's for their "talk."

But she plastered a broad smile on her face and headed for the sunroom at the rear of the house.

Her mama was sitting on the chintz sofa, staring out the huge Palladian window that overlooked the covered pool.

"Mama? Are you feelin' poorly?" Laura Beth asked, walking over to her.

Her mother turned around and took her daughter's hand. She smiled but Laura Beth could see it didn't reach her eyes.

"Come sit on the davenport with your mama," she said, patting the seat next to her. "I have somethin' to tell you that will be a shock. But I believe eventually you will come to see this as a beautiful gift to our family."

That's almost exactly how I began my confession to Jackie. This can't be good.

Mama took a deep breath, hesitating.

"Mama, just tell me. Quick," Laura Beth pleaded.

The news was more dreadful than any of the possibilities that had flashed through Laura Beth's mind: that Mama was pregnant; or she and Jeffrey were splitting up; or Jeffrey had banned Laura Beth from the campaign for some reason.

The second her mother finished speaking, the room started spinning. Laura Beth leaned over and put her head between her legs. *Too bad smelling salts have gone the way of whalebone corsets,* she thought wryly.

How am I goin' to tell my friends? How can I look anyone in the eye ever again? My life is ruined.

She tried to process the bombshell, fact by fact:

Her beloved dead daddy was a cad, no better than that two-timin' Bob Price.

Her daddy—*her* daddy—had knocked up some intern at his office years ago. *At least Bob had the good sense not to get anybody pregnant.*

Then he and Mama had hushed it up by sending the young woman back home to Alabama to raise the baby.

And horror of horrors, her parents had turned to Jennifer Cane as the go-between to send the mother and child monthly support payments. *No, make that thirteen years' worth of hush money.*

"Laura Beth, are you all right? Are you fixin' to be ill?" Her mother reached over to pat her back gently, but Laura Beth recoiled.

Her mother called out for the maid: "Maria, please fetch me a glass of water! And a mess of tissues! Quickly now."

Laura Beth sat up straight, tears streaming down her cheeks. She stared wordlessly at her mother, who still looked the same— the blunt-cut, dyed ash-blond hair, the thin lips plumped slightly by Botox, the tiny mole on her left temple, the eyebrows dyed a soft brown and plucked into a gentle arch.

But she was not the mama Laura Beth recognized. Not *her* mama, whom she thought she knew inside and out.

Maria knocked softly and came in carrying a cut crystal pitcher of water, two matching glasses, and a box of tissues on a silver tray, which she placed on the coffee table in front of them.

"Why didn't you just fix her up with an abortion and be done with it? Then I would never have had to know," Laura Beth hissed as soon as Maria was out of earshot.

Her mother's face drained of color. "Laura Beth, how dare you say that to me?" Her voice shook with outrage. "You know perfectly well that I've devoted a good chunk of my life crusadin' against such things."

Laura Beth sank back against the cushions.

"Why are you tellin' me any of this, Mama?" she whispered. "Why are you doin' this to me?"

Her mother poured two glasses of water, and handed one to Laura Beth. She set down the pitcher, gave her daughter a tender look, and took a sip from her own glass before answering.

"Let me finish, Laura Beth. Then I think you'll understand."

There's more? *What more could there be?* She bit her lip to stop from screaming.

"There's been a dreadful tragedy," her mama continued. "The child's mama, Hollis Oliver, suddenly took ill and passed, and the child has no other relatives."

Suddenly Laura Beth knew what was coming next. If she hadn't felt so weak, she would have leapt up, stamped her foot, and yelled, "I forbid it!"

Her mama tried to take her hand again but Laura Beth snatched it away.

"Jeffrey and I have decided the *right* thing to do is make Arden— that's her name—part of *our* family. We are planning on adoptin' her as our own as soon as we're wed."

Laura Beth stood up, hands on her hips, trying not to sway on her feet so she could stare down her mother.

"And what about the right thing for *me,* Mama?"

Her mother smiled at her. "Why, Laura Beth, it *is* the right thing for you. At long last, you're going to be a big sister."

If you're looking for big sisters for this girl, try Frances and Dina. But count me out.

Jackie was adamant that she and Laura Beth meet at her Foggy Bottom town house. On her turf. Not Laura Beth's.

She'd decided her bedroom was too informal, too comfortable, and too full of girlfriend memories for such an important talk.

She needed to keep Laura Beth focused and a little intimidated.

She arranged a pair of chairs in the living room so that they faced each other, put a low table between them with a coffee thermos and mugs, and sat down to wait.

The ticking of the wall clock seemed extra loud. Laura Beth was already ten minutes late.

Just then the doorbell rang and a key turned in the lock. Jackie heard her Secret Service agent, who was stationed outside, ushering Laura Beth in.

Jackie walked into the hall. Laura Beth was just standing there, her eyes red and moist from crying.

So, my strategy is keep it businesslike and yours is "poor little misunderstood me."

She had no intention of letting Laura Beth control the agenda.

"Hi, Laura Beth, you're late. Come on in," she said matter-of-factly, deliberately ignoring the tears.

"Sorry, something came up." Laura Beth slipped off her coat, draped it over the newel post, and started up the stairs.

"No, Laura Beth. We should talk in the living room. I made some coffee."

Her friend looked surprised but meekly followed Jackie into the formal parlor.

They'd barely sat down when Jackie started talking.

"Laura Beth, you're my oldest friend and I know you would never do anything to deliberately hurt me. But how can I trust you when I can't be sure you'll think before you act?"

"But I did think, Jackie. I was thinking of you," Laura Beth protested in a hurt voice.

"You didn't think it *through*. You know as well as I do that Senator Griffin is a conniving, self-serving bastard who'd sell out his own mother if it suited his purposes. What you *should* have done was come directly to me."

"But I couldn't, Jackie. You didn't want to hear anything bad I had to say about Eric."

Jackie couldn't deny it. She'd had an all-consuming crush on him. He was an older, good-looking guy who'd made her feel wanted at a time when Andrew was acting like he did not want or need her.

"Yeah, you're right," Jackie admitted. "But you should have tried. You can't go rogue like that. Ever again. You just can't."

"Well, you should have come to *me*, instead of Jennifer Cane," Laura Beth shot back. "You know Mama loves you and that she has a direct line to Uncle Ham. She'd do anything to get you out of a fix like that."

Jackie had to admit Laura Beth had another good point. She poured the coffee to give herself time to think.

"I made a horrible mistake," Laura Beth said, accepting a mug. "I know I did. I'm so, so sorry."

She looked kind of pathetic.

"I know you are," Jackie said. "But what I'm worried about is the campaign. We have to promise to be honest with each other."

Laura Beth nodded so hard Jackie thought her head was going to fly off.

"I don't mean revealing campaign secrets or anything like that," Jackie added. "Just that we be as up-front as possible. And not do anything behind each other's back."

Laura Beth nodded again, but not as enthusiastically.

"I agree. But you know it's going to be rough and a lot of things are going to happen that are out of our control . . ." Her voice died away.

"Yeah, of course. All we can do is make sure *we* play fair."

There was one more thing they hadn't discussed.

"What should we do about Lettie? Should we tell her?"

Laura Beth's face turned white. "Please don't tell her. There's no reason to. I'm so ashamed, Jackie."

One more secret, Jackie thought. But sometimes that was the best way to go.

"Then let's not," she decided. "Lettie's got enough to worry about as it is. Really, this just concerns the two of us, anyway."

They both stood up and hugged tightly. Then Laura Beth's body began to shake and she buried her head in Jackie's neck, sobbing.

Jackie's heart softened. *Poor thing. She's really beating herself up about this.*

"It's okay, Laura Beth. We'll be fine."

Laura Beth pulled away. "No, no. I'm not crying about us. I'm crying about *me*. You'll never believe what Mama just told me. My life is over!"

Here comes the me, me, me part.

They sat back down and Laura Beth filled her in on her newly discovered, definitely not wanted, half sister, Arden Oliver.

A dozen reactions bounced around Jackie's head. Poor Laura Beth. Sleazy parents. Selfish Laura Beth. Poor Arden. Campaign scandal.

"All they're thinking about is the campaign," Laura Beth fumed. "If Jeffrey wasn't running for president, they'd just increase the hush money and farm her out to an adoption agency or foster care."

Jackie secretly agreed but she didn't want to be unkind.

"Laura Beth, I'm sure it's more than that. Miss Libby is a compassionate person. I bet she really believes it's wrong to deprive you of your own sister."

"Well, why did she wait thirteen years?"

"The circumstances changed. Arden's mother might not have wanted her to have anything to do with your family." Jackie took her hand. "I'm so sorry. I know this a lot for you to take in."

She wondered how she would handle it if she suddenly discovered a brother or sister out there somewhere.

As it was, she didn't much like sharing her mom with Ike Sawyer. Even though it was a fake romance, it still meant her mother was spending more time with him and less time with her.

Laura Beth was being forced to share her mother with a stepfather with presidential ambitions, two bitchy stepsisters who hated her, and now a surprise thirteen-year-old love-child sibling.

"This is my last year living at home and no one seems to care. It's like I'm at the bottom of Mama's list. I should be at the top, shouldn't I?"

"Yeah, you should. It sucks."

Laura Beth left a half hour later. Jackie flung herself on her bed, emotionally exhausted. She was happy they'd had a long talk to try to clear the air. She hoped the whole horrible episode had taught Laura Beth to rein herself in. Even if, as usual, the conversation had ended up all about Laura Beth.

Some things you just can't change, Jackie thought.

SIXTEEN

First Wale did his D.C. "Chillin'" thing. Then Soldier Hard, the war veteran rapper, roared on stage straddling his Harley-Davidson.

Next up was Citizen Cope, who ambled over to the microphone, his acoustic guitar strung over his chest.

"Hello, D.C.! It's great to be back in my hometown," he shouted, his voice echoing across the enormous, columned great hall of the National Building Museum.

Hundreds of red, white, and blue balloons dropped from the ceiling and hundreds of teens, all dressed in camouflage VRAG T-shirts, went wild. Vic Hazelton, Tanya Wilson, and dozens of other wounded, uniformed soldiers sitting in a single line of front-row seats clapped.

"Look what kids can do when they want to make a difference," Jackie murmured to Andrew and Scott. They were standing offstage, watching from the wings as Citizen Cope sang one of his bluesy laid-back rock hits. "*We* should be running the country," she added.

"Let Andrew do it. I'd rather be onstage with those guys, fighting off all these hot babes," Scott joked.

"I nominate Jackie for president," Andrew said. "After all, Mom might have come up with the idea for the fund-raiser, but she did all the work. Scott and I are mere eye candy." He laughed and threw an arm around Jackie, absentmindedly massaging her shoulder the way he used to. Without even realizing, she draped her arm around the small of his back, resting her hand on his hip.

They fit each other like a glove, warm and snug and safe. It was only when Scott raised his eyebrows that she was aware of what they were doing. Flustered, she quickly dropped her arm and moved away.

How did that happen?

It had been utterly spontaneous. At least on her part. She sneaked a look at Andrew, whose mouth was curled up in a tiny smile, which made her suspect that his hug had been a very deliberate hands-off signal to Scott.

Why does it all have to be so complicated? Why can't it be like it was when we were little and the three of us played together all the time? Although she knew the answer. There were too many sides to this triangle— she and Scott hanging out in ninth grade, Scott leaving D.C., her falling in love with Andrew, then Andrew and Taylor, and now Scott returning . . .

Monica, the event planner, appeared at her side, interrupted her thoughts. She handed Jackie a sheet of paper.

"Dr. Rosen says we've probably raised three hundred thousand dollars this afternoon," Jackie read out loud. *But that's probably not enough to buy his loyalty.* They'd decided to charge one hundred dollars a ticket, and all the music, food, and sodas were donated. A lot of parents had written checks, probably to get on Aunt Deborah's good side. And a couple of anonymous donors, apparently with no ulterior motive, had picked up the tab for renting the museum, creating the free tees handed out at the door, and the raffle prizes.

"Great," Andrew said gruffly. Scott just nodded.

"Hey, guys," Monica called to them from the edge of the stage. "Citizen Cope's act is over." Jackie and the two brothers walked onstage without speaking.

"That was amazing!" Jackie shouted into the mike. "Thank you, Citizen Cope!" She waited for the applause to die down. "Don't go anywhere! The fun's not over yet."

"We have to draw the ten lucky raffle winners, who'll each go home with the latest iPad," Andrew yelled on cue.

"It's not even in the stores yet, guys," Scott added.

"And then Excelsior's own Laura Beth Ballou will close the event with her original arrangement of 'America the Beautiful,'" Jackie announced. "I promise you, this'll be better than Miranda Lambert and Blake Shelton."

As she waited again for the cheering to end, she noticed Vic staring at her from the front row. She smiled at him and he blushed.

She hoped he was having fun. He'd sounded so depressed in the last diary entry he'd let her read.

She waved to Tanya, Lettie, and Daniel, who were standing behind him, then grabbed the mike again. "But first, I have the privilege of introducing the head of VRAG, Dr. Paul Rosen. He's worked tirelessly to get returning soldiers better health care, better housing, better jobs, and a better future."

She glanced offstage to make sure Monica was on hand and ready to gag Dr. Rosen if he tried to bad-mouth the Price administration.

The audience broke into polite applause. Jackie, Andrew, and Scott took a step back as Dr. Rosen strolled onstage, his salt-and-pepper hair and tall frame giving him an authoritative air.

"I don't know if any of you noticed but there is a frieze along the front of this historic building depicting Civil War soldiers," Dr. Rosen began. "This was not originally a museum. It was built by a grateful nation for the sole purpose of distributing military pensions to our deserving war veterans and the families of those who died on the battlefield."

He gestured to the soldiers at the foot of the stage.

"So this is a fitting venue to honor those who risked their lives fighting for our freedom and now find themselves fighting for survival back home."

He pointed at Vic Hazelton. "Vic—Private Hazelton—can you come up here, please? I want everyone to see my right-hand man."

That's sweet of him to acknowledge Vic.

The soldier came up and stood quietly next to him, staring at his shoes, as Dr. Rosen explained VRAG's mission.

Everything seemed to be going so smoothly, Jackie couldn't help but feel pleased and proud of what she and everyone there had achieved. But just as Dr. Rosen appeared to be wrapping it up, he half turned to Jackie, Andrew, and Scott.

"You three need to stand next to me, too," he said. "I want to publicly thank these three kids—you all know who they are—for their wholehearted support of my organization and everything it stands for."

Jackie felt uneasy. *Where's he headed with this?* She tried to make eye contact with Monica, who was deep in conversation with Citizen Cope.

"It can't be easy, if your last name's Price, or you're dating the president's son, to stand up here with someone who's willing to take on the president for not doing everything she can to support our vets."

Oh my God.

Her breath quickened and a sharp pain ripped through her heart. *Not another panic attack. Not now. Not up here.*

She swayed and Andrew moved in to steady her. He held onto her arm and whispered through his teeth, "Jackie, we've got to get him off the stage right now."

Her eyes searched frantically for Monica. But now there was no sign of her.

Vic stepped over to Jackie. "Are you all right?"

She nodded once, trying to will away the panic. She pulled the microphone stand toward her.

"Oh, Dr. Rosen, you're exaggerating," she said, trying to sound unfazed. "We just wanted to show our support for the soldiers and—"

"You're being modest, Jackie. You're my best ambassador," Dr. Rosen cut her off. He suddenly made a grab for Scott and Andrew's hands and raised their arms in a sign of victory, like they'd all just won the marathon. The boys looked tense and uneasy, obviously resenting the forced show of support but not wanting to draw attention to themselves by dropping their arms.

Finally, Monica rushed across the stage to rescue them.

"Okay! Thank you, Dr. Rosen!" she said, wresting control of the microphone. "Now it's time for Ms. Laura Beth Ballou."

Andrew and Scott walked off the stage stiffly, followed by Jackie and Vic. Dr. Rosen sauntered off in the opposite direction.

"Well that was awkward," Scott said at the top of the stage stairs.

Andrew didn't answer. He took Jackie by the arm. "Did you know Rosen was going to say that?"

"Keep your voice down," Jackie hissed, jerking away. "Of course I didn't."

Vic, who'd been standing on the sidelines, stepped between them.

"Do you need any help, Jackie?" he asked quietly.

"No, Vic, thanks. Andrew and I need to talk in private."

The soldier moved a few feet away and stood at ease, military style, with his feet apart, his thumbs interlocked behind his back, his eyes fixed on her as if she were his commander.

"Where the hell was Monica?" Andrew raged. "I thought she was supposed to shut him down if he went off-message."

"Yes, you heard me tell her. But she got sidetracked flirting with Citizen Cope."

"Well, it was one gigantic screwup and God knows what Mom's gonna say."

Jackie was beyond fed up.

Just when she thought he'd started to pull himself together—staying sober at Taylor's memorial, hugging her before they went onstage—here he was, acting like it was all her fault. Just like he tried to blame her for Senator Griffin's ludicrous press conference late last year.

Hot tears of anger blinded her.

"I'm so sick of this," she shot back.

She wanted to scream and beat his chest with her fists.

Then just as quickly, all her anger dissolved and she just felt horribly, overwhelmingly sad.

"It really is over, isn't it, Andrew?"

His shoulders sagged as his anger evaporated as well. "I'm sorry."

She turned her back. *Sorry? That's all you can say? Sorry for what? For not trusting me? For betraying me? For throwing us away?*

Andrew turned on his heels and Vic was suddenly back at Jackie's side. She sank against the wall and he moved in closer and took her hand gently.

"Did you and Andrew just break up?" he asked.

We did that months ago. You just witnessed the death of Ankie.

"No," she lied. She straightened up and forced out a light-hearted laugh. "We're always having silly little fights. It's nothing."

"Oh, okay." He gave her a quizzical look.

"Excuse me, Vic." Jackie ran down the stage steps and submerged herself in the hushed crowd. She didn't want to talk to anyone.

Fortunately, no one was looking at her. Every eye was on the stage, where Laura Beth stood alone, in a pale blue organza gown that seemed to float around her in gentle waves. Her sweet, pure voice, unaccompanied, rang out through the great hall.

Beautiful, Jackie thought. Some of her despair rolled away.

The song ended to raucous applause.

But instead of bowing graciously and walking offstage, Laura Beth did a little shimmy. The gown dropped to the floor, revealing a red, white, and blue sequined leotard, red tights, and red tap shoes.

Three identically dressed girls appeared behind her, one of them holding a top hat and a cane, which she threw to Laura Beth.

133

Oh my God, Jackie thought for the second time that afternoon.

Jackie thought—wished—she was hallucinating as canned music started up from somewhere and Laura Beth and her back-ups took their cue, singing and dancing their way around the stage in a rap-and-tap version of "Yankee Doodle Dandy."

The fact that no one was laughing was a testament to Laura Beth's talent. Somehow she'd managed to take a ridiculous song and make it fun and sexy. By the end, everyone was dancing and Wale, Citizen Cope, and Soldier Hard were rapping right alongside her.

The song ended and the four girls ran off.

It's a miracle it didn't turn into a disaster like everything else.

Jackie waited for Monica to walk on and thank everyone for coming. But it was Laura Beth and her three dancing cohorts who reappeared, each holding a large white basket.

"Remember, we're the generation that can make a difference. If you want change, you gotta vote!" Laura Beth yelled to the crowd.

The four girls started throwing candies into the audience.

That's kind of cute.

Jackie picked up one of the candies at her feet. To her horror, the hard caramel was wrapped in red, white, and blue and emblazoned with the words *IVES CHANGES LIVES.*

Screw you, Laura Beth. Screw you.

Jackie ran back up the stage steps, ready to strangle Laura Beth over yet another double cross.

Laura Beth was standing in the wings, waving a candy in Dina Ives's face.

"I can't believe you did this!" she was yelling.

"I thought you'd like it. I just changed one word," Dina said sulkily.

As soon as Laura Beth saw Jackie, she turned her back on Dina and ran over. "Jackie, I didn't do it," she babbled. "I promise it wasn't me. You have to believe me. I just had this great idea to throw out candies that said, VOTING CHANGES LIVES." Laura Beth looked as if she was about to cry. She pointed a finger at Dina, who was smirking.

"That little two-timin' brat offered to handle everything. You know, ordering the candies and placing them in the baskets. But when she put in the order she changed the message on the candies without telling me."

Laura Beth looked so distraught, Jackie was pretty sure she was telling the truth. "Think before acting, Laura Beth, remember?" Jackie sighed.

This was like playing a never-ending game of Whac-A-Mole.

Just as I whop the Laura Beth mole on the head, the Dina mole pops up. Or the Angie mole. Or the Whitney mole.

SEVENTEEN

"Jackie said the president was angrier than she'd ever seen her. Worse than when the tabloids ran those photos that made it look like Jackie was hooking up with that guy in the Princeton bar."

Lettie, bracing herself against the icy wind, was on the phone with Daniel, filling him in as she walked to the Capitol South metro station. Ahead of her, a group of Japanese tourists, their guide holding a bright yellow umbrella high in the air, were blocking the sidewalk, madly snapping photos of the Capitol. She dodged around them, forced to walk in the gutter.

"What about Jackie and Laura Beth? Are they even speaking?" Daniel asked.

"Apparently it was Dina, not Laura Beth, who pulled the candy stunt. Dina didn't even deny it."

"Poor Laura Beth. She's going to have her hands full dealing with Dina during the campaign. Although I bet she's planning some stunts of her own, too. Think she might dress up as Scarlett O'Hara to win the Southern vote?"

Lettie giggled. "Whatever you do, don't suggest it."

She could just see Laura Beth emerging from the campaign plane in a hoop skirt and bonnet and busting out of a low-cut bustier with a swashbuckling Sol in a fake mustache and a cravat.

"First you and now Jackie," Daniel mused. "Angie better watch her back if she wants to keep her Mean Girl status at Excelsior."

"Let's not talk about her any more," Lettie said, her stomach churning. "Oh, I forgot to tell you . . . President Price and Jackie's mom are making her quit VRAG."

"Surprise, surprise."

"Yeah, really. But she would have anyway—she's so mad at Dr. Rosen. Tanya told me that Vic Hazelton—that soldier Jackie's become friends with?—was so upset, he left a note on Dr. Rosen's desk telling him off for publicly embarrassing Jackie."

"That was gutsy. Isn't Dr. Rosen his boss?"

"Yep. But I guess when you've fought in a war, you have a different definition of 'brave.'"

Like Vic and Paz, who had faced death daily.

"Thank God he and Paz are home safe," Daniel said gently.

They'd both been thinking the same thing.

"Yes."

"So, Jackie survived the wrath of the president and her mom," Daniel joked, trying to lighten the mood.

"Jackie said it was kind of funny. The whole time President Price was raking her over the coals, she forgot to mention the fund-raiser was all *her* idea. Then just when Jackie thought she could escape, the president went on a rant about Tracey Mills's latest blog post."

"What's Whitney done now?"

"Daniel!" Lettie protested feebly.

"Just kidding! What's Whitney's *mom* dug up now?"

"Somebody leaked her receipts showing Bob Price had bought a bunch of really expensive Tiffany jewelry."

Just like Daniel, she assumed Whitney was behind the leak. And she was worried that Whitney had somehow conned Paz into snooping in the White House for her.

Surely Paz would never do something like that. Unless he needed money. For drugs.

But Paz was always telling her he loved his new job and his new life and his new friends. And that he had zero interest in drugs or Whitney. As for the embarrassing scene at the White House Christmas party—where Laura Beth saw him and Whitney hooking up—Paz had insisted Whitney had thrown herself at him and he was trying to escape.

It was okay to think the worst of Whitney, but Lettie felt bad for thinking—even for a second—the worst of her brother.

"So what if he's buying his wife jewelry?" Daniel interrupted her thoughts. "I don't get it."

"Well, the president hasn't been seen wearing any of it."

"Oh. Then he's giving it to a girlfriend? That guy wouldn't know the meaning of the word commitment if it was tattooed on his forehead."

"Speaking of commitment, I forgot to tell you. Tracey also claimed that Jackie's mom and the vice president are dating."

"Wow! You think it's true?"

"It's not. Jackie said President Price is so mad about all the publicity Mrs. Ballou and Senator Ives are getting, she wants her mom and Ike Sawyer to act like there's something going on so the media chase them, too."

"Only in D.C.," Daniel said wryly.

Lettie shivered out loud as a blast of arctic air ripped through her parka.

"Where are you?" He sounded concerned.

"Walking to the metro. I just spent an hour at the Library of Congress and I think the temperature dropped fifteen degrees while I was in there."

"You need me there to keep you warm."

Lettie blushed at the thought of the last time they were together. At least Whitney had kept her mouth shut because no one at school had said anything.

"Lettie, I can tell you're blushing," Daniel teased. His voice got serious. "I meant it, you know, what I said after Whitney burst in on us."

After Whitney had retreated, they'd tried to pick up where they'd left off. But the moment had been ruined. They'd ended up climbing on her bed, but just to kiss and snuggle, and joke about the interruption.

"It takes a lot to shock Whitney. I never thought it would be us putting that look on her face, Lettie." Daniel laughed.

A cute little wrinkle appeared in the middle of his forehead, the way it did whenever he was worried.

"We don't need to rush anything, you know," he said, kissing my cheek.

It was amazing how patient he was. He'd been telling me that since our first date.

"I know. Slow is good for me," I told him, tracing the wrinkle with my finger. "But not too slow."

She smiled at the memory.

Her face grew red again and she hurriedly switched topics.

"Next time I go to the Library of Congress, *you* are coming with me."

It was one of her favorite places in the entire world and she was dying to show it to him. The ornate Reading Room, the elaborately painted vaulted ceilings. The painting on the dome of the woman representing "human understanding." Lettie loved that.

The temperature continued to drop and she quickened her pace along First Street, not stopping to stare at the majestic marble-and-sandstone Capitol Building, the way she usually did. She'd recently pasted an article in her journal about how slaves had been forced to help build it.

The view was spoiled a little by the ugly cement antiterrorist barricades, but that was the price of living in D.C.

"Want me to come over when you get home? I can warm you up," Daniel whispered temptingly.

The next shiver that slid down her spine had nothing to do with weather.

"Let me think about that." She deliberately paused for a second. "Okay!" They both laughed. "You can help me make the sign."

"What sign?"

"The sign for my bedroom door. When we lock it."

"I'm leaving now!"

Lettie sighed. "I'm bummed but it's not going to work. I have to finish my history paper."

"Way to let a guy down hard," he joked, then paused as if reading his messages. "Hey, I better go. Sam keeps texting me to call him. Can I call you back?"

"I'm heading into the metro, anyway," Lettie told him. "I'll call you when I get home."

Lettie let herself into the apartment. "Hello? Anybody home?"

No answer. She was standing at the coat closet, peeling off her parka, hat, and gloves when her cell rang again. *Daniel.* She dug around in her coat pockets until she found it, and read the screen with a pang of disappointment.

"Lettie! Are you alone? I need to tell you something." Laura Beth sounded distraught.

"Hang on, Laura Beth. I just walked in the door," Lettie answered, heading for her bedroom. She shut the door, flopped on the bed, and put the iPhone on speaker.

Laura Beth talked nonstop for several minutes, her words gushing out of her mouth like a jet of water.

Stuff about a hated half sister and her mother lying to her. At first Lettie thought it had something to do with Dina's candy trick.

"Not Dina!" Laura Beth snapped impatiently. "Arden."

"Slow down, Laura Beth, I'm not following you," Lettie said, trying not to snap back.

Laura Beth repeated her story, her agitated voice rising with each sentence. She ended with a sob and a honk—not her usual delicate sniff—as she blew her nose. For a second Lettie wondered if Laura Beth had lost her grip on reality. It sounded more like an episode of a soap opera.

Lettie leaned against the headboard and stared at the phone

lying by her side. "Oh my God, Laura Beth, you must be in shock," she said finally. "I can't believe it."

She took a deep breath. She knew her friends depended on her for sensible, no-nonsense advice. But they didn't always want to hear it right away, and Lettie wasn't too good at all that touchy-feely stuff that led up to the straight talk.

"What if it's a great experience? Maybe you'll love Arden," she said slowly, testing the Laura Beth waters before plunging ahead.

She was in midsentence when Laura Beth hung up on her.

In hindsight, Lettie regretted rushing into a resounding defense of Mrs. Ballou's adoption plans. She should have waited a few days until Laura Beth calmed down.

Thank goodness she hung up before I got to the part about how lucky she was to have a sister to take care of when I'd do anything to see mine right now.

At some point, Laura Beth *would* have to put aside her selfishness and realize the world did not revolve around only her. Arden was an orphan who needed a home. A loving home. Sooner rather than later.

Lettie's stomach growled. It was almost dinnertime but no one was home. *I guess that means dinner's up to me. I wonder if I should make enough for Whitney, too,* she thought as she wandered down the hall toward the kitchen. She picked up her iPhone and hit Whitney's number. To her surprise, she heard the familiar ringtone—"*I'm too sexy for my love, I'm too sexy for my shirt . . .*"—coming from Whitney's room.

Oh, she's home. She hung up and banged on the door.

"Whitney! I'm gonna make some pasta. Want some?"

Silence. Lettie knocked again and walked in. The bathroom door was ajar and Whitney was bending over the toilet bowl, her finger down her throat, forcing herself to throw up.

Shit. It's true.

Lettie had suspected for months that Whitney might be bulimic or anorexic or both—her dramatic weight loss, erratic eating, the breath freshener she was constantly squirting in her mouth . . . It all added up.

She remembered the first time she laid eyes on Whitney. It was at Mrs. Ballou's tea party for "the new girl." She'd been breathtakingly beautiful with a flawless caramel complexion that glowed with good health. Since then, her skin and hair had turned dull and her wrists were no bigger than Christa's.

Lettie tiptoed out of the room and quietly shut the door. She'd been keeping Whitney at arm's length ever since Taylor's memorial. Avoiding her as much as two people under the same roof could avoid each other.

That was impossible now. As much as she hated getting involved, she knew she had to do something. She just wasn't sure what or how.

Daniel was just about to give up trying to call Sam when he finally picked up his phone.

"Yo, Daniel. Wazzup?" he answered, his voice a little slurred.

"What do you mean what's up? You were trying to reach me," Daniel said impatiently. It sounded like Sam was either stoned or drunk.

"Come on, little bro. Does your big brother need a reason to call?"

You do. Cuz you never want to talk. You didn't even bother when we both were living in the same city.

Sam had had much more contact with Taylor. "Close" wasn't

the right word. They'd had this crazy relationship in which they were fierce rivals, constantly butting heads, each bent on outdoing the other's outrageous behavior. And from reading between the lines when Daniel talked to Taylor about it, their antagonism had become a lot more intense in the weeks before she died. *That's gotta make him feel guilty as hell.*

He heard Sam take a sip of a drink and picked up his own can of Coke from the kitchen table.

"So, how's it going with your luscious señorita?" Sam asked, drunkenly mangling the last word. "You two getting it on?"

"If you mean Lettie, I'm not about to discuss our relationship with you," Daniel answered hotly. "Especially when you're drunk."

"I take that as a 'no.'" Sam laughed at his own joke.

"Look, unless there's something important you want to discuss, I'm hanging up."

"You need to chill, dude," he slurred. "I just wanna give you some brotherly advice—"

"You need to sober up—"

Sam ignored him. "Take it from me, always keep a roofie or two in your wallet, right next to your condoms."

"What the hell are you talking about?"

Sam laughed again. "You give 'em just enough to relax 'em, man, that's all."

Daniel's mouth went dry, his heart stopped midbeat.

"Jeezus, Sam. You better be joking. We're talking about date *rape.* That is absolutely disgusting and completely illegal . . ."

There was a pause as Sam took another slug of whatever it was he was drinking.

"You're as bad as Taylor," he mumbled.

Daniel shivered. "What do you mean?"

Sam made a couple more loud slurping noises before answering.

"Taylor found out in high school I used roofies to get girls. She threatened to tell Mom and go to the cops unless I stopped. Can you believe it? Miss Wild Child Party Girl herself getting all holier than thou. She had no right to judge me. No right."

My family's imploding, Daniel thought. *Taylor's dead and now Sam's telling me he assaulted girls.*

"No right to judge you? You're a fucking rapist," Daniel said. He wanted to throw up.

"That's crazy talk. I never raped anyone. I told you, I just get 'em to relax. Get 'em interested. That's all."

Pain shot through Daniel's clenched jaw. What if there was even more to the story? He took a guess.

"Did Taylor catch you again? Discover that you were still doing it?"

There was no answer. *Did that son of a bitch just hang up on me?* Then he heard noises, almost like an animal whimpering.

"Shit, Daniel. She made me so angry. And now she's dead, man, and it's all my fucking fault."

Daniel slammed his fist on the table.

"What the *fuck* are you saying?"

Sam started crying, all his cockiness dissolved into drunken hiccups. Daniel heard him taking deep breaths as if trying to force himself back in control.

"Remember when we both came home for Thanksgiving? It was not long before the accident. We were all at Cottie's party."

Daniel remembered. He'd spent most of the night looking at Lettie, trying not to drool. But he hadn't done anything about it because he'd soon be back at boarding school in L.A.

"Jackie was there, looking incredibly hot," Sam said between sobs. "Like she was the only girl in the room."

"Slow down. I can hardly understand you," Daniel interrupted.

"I was pissed because Jackie never thought I was good enough for her. Never gave me the time of day. So I made my move. I fixed her a drink. But Taylor caught me spiking it. She dragged me outside . . . She was screaming like a crazy person . . . I told her it wasn't much . . . not enough to put a kitten to sleep.

"But she didn't believe me," he blubbered.

"Pull yourself together," Daniel snarled. He felt no sympathy for his brother. Just disgust. And despair.

"Taylor made me so mad, acting so sanctimonious, calling me a liar." Sam whimpered. "I lost it. I just wanted to screw with her. I told her some stuff that I shouldn't have . . ."

"What kind of stuff?"

"Stuff to hurt her. I shouldn't have done it. It messed her up real bad."

Sam paused as if waiting for Daniel to offer him some words of sympathy.

"What. Did. You. Say. To. Taylor?"

"I can't tell you. I'll never tell you. But she never got over it. I'm sorry. I'm sorry. I'm sorry."

The line went dead.

Lettie stared at the boiling pot of cheese tortellini, her appetite vanishing as her stomach twisted into knots over the scene in Whitney's bathroom. Her cell vibrated next to the stove.

"Lettie," Daniel said abruptly when she answered. "I've made a huge mistake."

The oxygen rushed from the room. Just when she thought she couldn't handle anything more . . .

He's breaking up with me!

All she could manage was a bewildered, "What do you mean?"

"Taylor's accident. It wasn't Andrew's fault. It was Sam's."

She could breathe again. He wasn't making much sense but whatever it was, at least it wasn't about *them*.

"I'm listening," she said quietly, turning off the pasta and sitting on one of the stools at the island.

She heard him out until his words dried up. The only interruption was the mystery woman's voice mail fading in and out of her head: *"Don't tell Daniel."*

Her heart pounded.

Guilt weighed down on Lettie's shoulders. She should tell Daniel everything she knew about Taylor's cell. But she wasn't sure how much more *he* could take, either.

Jackie and Andrew and Taylor. Laura Beth and Arden. Whitney's eating disorder. Her separation from her family. And now Daniel.

It seemed like everything the Capital Girls touched was turning to crap.

EIGHTEEN

It was already ten fifteen, but the three girls had agreed to meet at Laura Beth's. The three-story Federal-style mansion was big enough to hide an army squadron. Or avoid running into Libby Ballou, who thought they were working on their senior projects.

Sitting cross-legged on a canopied antique bed in one of the third-floor guest rooms, they passed around a hip flask filled with vodka and a plate of fiery Southern cheese straws.

Jackie expected Lettie to speak first. After all, she'd called them together. But Laura Beth immediately started talking about Arden.

"Just remember, Lettie and I are always here for you. Always," Jackie said soothingly.

Laura Beth smiled at her gratefully, shooting a look at Lettie.

"Lettie thinks I'm being selfish, not wanting us to take in Arden," she said, taking a ladylike sip of vodka.

You kind of are. But Jackie knew better than to say it.

"Lettie loves you," Jackie said. "But she has a different perspective on it. She's speaking as a big sister. And I'm sure the first thing she thought of when you told her was about Christa and Maribel and how much she misses and loves them."

At the mention of her little sisters, tears trickled down Lettie's cheeks, although she didn't speak.

Shame flooded through Jackie. She and Laura Beth had so much to be thankful for and took it all for granted. Lettie had so little, yet soaked it up as though she were steeped in riches.

"Of course you did," Laura Beth said, reaching over to rub Lettie's back. "Silly me, I didn't even think of that. I keep forgettin' you're practically an orphan now, with your mama and daddy gone and all."

Way to go. Foot-in-mouth disease again.

"What Laura Beth means is you're just temporarily separated from your family right now," Jackie jumped in. "And she didn't take that into consideration when she unloaded about Arden."

"Yes, that's exactly right." Laura Beth nodded. She shot Jackie a grateful look for turning her faux pas into the comforting words she'd meant to say.

"It won't be like that forever. Right, Lettie?" Jackie continued.

"I can't let myself think that." Lettie tried to smile. "I hope it's not wishful thinking, but there *are* signs that things are settling down a bit in Paraguay."

"Really?" Jackie exclaimed.

"Well, I got a letter from my aunt and uncle in California. They say the government might actually be ready to make some concessions."

"I can't imagine what it would be like living under a dictator like all those South American countries." Laura Beth shook her head.

"That's a stereotype that's so not true!" Lettie snapped. "Paraguay has held democratic elections since 1992! Sometimes it just takes democracies a while to get fully established."

Laura Beth chewed her lip in embarrassment.

"You're right," she said. "You'll be reunited with your family before you know it. And I can't wait to throw a big party to celebrate. And in the meantime you have us. We're your family, too."

She handed Lettie a tissue to wipe her eyes and ran her fingers through her curls. "Just one more thing about Arden, okay? It's about Mama. It hurts so much that she bald-faced lied to me for years. I don't think I'll ever be able to forgive her."

"I'm sure she thought she was doing the right thing, even though it wasn't," Jackie said.

Like Mom and Aunt Deborah not telling Andrew and me for almost a year that they knew he was driving the night Taylor died.

Jackie understood that they were trying to shield her and Andrew, while also protecting their own political futures. But it still hurt whenever she thought about it.

"What does Sol say you should do?" Jackie asked, steering the conversation away from lying mothers.

Laura Beth shook her head.

"It's not something I want to tell him over the phone. But he knows I'm really upset about something." Her face brightened a little. "He's catching the train down on Friday. We're gonna meet at his parents' pied-à-terre. Before Whitney's Valentine's party."

"At least that's one thing in your life that's going great. I'm so happy for you," Jackie said, determined not to show how envious she was.

"If Sol wasn't around, I don't know what I'd do!" Laura Beth said. "I'm already a bundle of nerves. What with havin' to watch my back whenever I see Dina. And I'm fit to be tied over Juilliard, not hearing a word yet."

She picked up a cheese straw and bit it in half. "I can't believe everything that's happening to me lately."

"To all of us," Jackie reminded her.

Lettie spoke up.

"Well, brace yourselves, there's more," she warned. "It's why I called us together."

She wiped the crumbs off her lips on a starched linen napkin before continuing slowly and deliberatively.

"I'm not sure where to start. I've found out something really unbelievably horrible about Sam Cane and I think it might explain Taylor's bizarre behavior just before she died."

All Jackie and Laura Beth could do was stare, slack-jawed, as Lettie told them about Sam and the roofies, the spiked drink at Thanksgiving, and his ugly fight with Taylor that spiraled out of control.

"But what do you think Sam told her that was even worse than that?" Jackie asked. "What could possibly be any worse?"

Lettie just shook her head.

"Jackie, you could've been raped," Laura Beth gasped, rocking back and forth, hugging one of the lacy pillows on the bed.

"I know, Laura Beth. Fortunately I wasn't. And he told Daniel it wasn't enough to do that."

She shuddered as she recalled Sam constantly touching her at Taylor's memorial and texting her about getting together.

Asshole.

"Think about what Taylor must have been going through,"

Lettie said. "It's so sad she couldn't confide in us. She was probably too ashamed."

Jackie realized she was shaking—shock, fear, and a thousand other emotions swirled through her mind. And in there, somewhere, was a little spark of gratitude. For Taylor. For saving Jackie from her sicko brother.

For the first time in a long time, she could think Taylor's name without feeling angry.

Yet even though the revelations about Sam helped explain Taylor's behavior, it didn't explain everything. And it certainly didn't explain Andrew's. *Unlike Taylor, he had no excuse for what he did.*

Jackie sat silently as Laura Beth and Lettie talked back and forth.

"How horrible for Daniel," Laura Beth said. "He must be beside himself."

Lettie nodded. "You have no idea."

"So, what do we do next?"

Lettie frowned and rubbed her arms nervously.

"We'll never have all the answers. But we have all the answers we *need*," she answered.

You might, Jackie thought, *but I don't.* It was as if Laura Beth and Lettie had forgotten what else happened that night. The sex.

"It's obvious the roofie thing is what the mystery voice mails were about," Lettie continued. "That woman must have wanted to protect Daniel from the terrible truth about his brother."

"That would be enough to push Taylor over the edge. It would be for me," Laura Beth said.

"I think so, too. And now the three of us need to let go so we can all move on and—" Lettie added quickly.

"Yes, but Sam's still out there, running around," Laura Beth interjected. "He could still go after Jackie."

"Daniel says his mom will deal with Sam. If anyone can put a stop to it, she can."

"But . . ." Laura Beth started to protest.

A plan started forming in Jackie's head.

"I agree with Lettie," she announced, breaking her silence. "Our top priority now is helping Daniel—and ourselves—to heal."

Laura Beth nodded. "I suppose you're right. What's important is that we can forgive Taylor and put all this behind us. Starting right now."

The girls put their arms around each other, as though scared they might lose one another if there was any distance left between them.

But Jackie had no intention of telling Lettie and Laura Beth what else she was thinking. That she wouldn't be dropping the puzzle. That there were still too many missing pieces to ignore. She didn't know the identity of the mystery woman. And she wasn't convinced that Sam's roofie use was the only secret Taylor was so desperate to keep from Daniel.

She was determined to figure it out. All of it. Whatever the cost.

NINETEEN

The crimson envelope was lying on the floor by the front door mail slot. It was embossed with shiny, gold hearts and addressed to Jackie in gold ink, with lots of curlicues and flourishes.

Obviously a Valentine's Day card.

Jackie dumped her heavy tote, filled with all the homework she'd been assigned that day, and slit open the envelope with one of her keys. Her pulse raced, half in anticipation and half with dread.

If it was from Scott, how was she supposed to react?

If Andrew had sent it, what was it supposed to mean?

She pulled out a white card decorated with a hand-drawn heart pierced by an arrow. Inside was a computer-printed poem made to look as though it was handwritten.

Roses are red
Violets are blue

When Andrew is dead
I'll be with you

She dropped it in horror. The floor moved like a wave and she grabbed the stair railing to steady herself, then sank to the bottom step. The ringing in her head was so jarring she clapped her hands over her ears.

Her mind spun with a jumble of questions.

How did it get past all the layers of security?

Why won't the stalker leave me alone?

When is this ever going to end?

Jackie moaned at the next thought. The other threats had been creepy. This was an actual death threat. And this time, she was the bait and Andrew was the target. Her heart twisted at the thought of anyone trying to hurt him.

She knew what she had to do. She picked up the envelope and card, grabbed her purse and keys, and ran out to the street where the Secret Service car was parked.

She pounded on the tinted window until the agent—someone she didn't recognize—rolled it down.

"You're supposed to be protecting me!" she screamed, waving the stalker's latest message. "How did this get past the mail check?"

Without waiting for an answer, she jumped in the front seat.

"Take me to the White House. I need to see my mother."

It was only a few short blocks away, but it seemed to take forever, giving Jackie too much time to think.

The first name to pop into her head was Sam's. Could Sam Cane be the stalker? He had wanted to have sex with her, enough to try to spike her drink. He was all over her at Taylor's memorial party and then kept sending her texts about getting together.

But obsessed with her? That was a stretch. Aside from the Thanksgiving party, they'd had no contact for years. And Lettie said she saw him leave Taylor's memorial with Frances Ives. Besides, he wasn't even in D.C. over winter break, so he couldn't have put the scary note on the White House Christmas tree: *You look so sexy in blood red.*

I suppose he could have bribed a White House employee. But that seemed far-fetched. Moreover, the Valentine's card was postmarked in D.C., and Sam was back in L.A.

What if it was somebody entirely different? Someone totally above suspicion, like a Secret Service agent? *Like Andrew's agent, Mark Davenport.* He'd covered up the fact that Andrew had been driving Taylor's car the night of the accident, but Jackie wasn't sure whether it was to protect Andrew or to have something on Andrew. Yet Andrew always insisted he'd trust Mark with his life.

The more she thought about it, the less likely it seemed that Sam would have paid someone to stick the note on the Christmas tree.

Yes, Sam should be locked up. But probably not for stalking.

By the time the car pulled up to the White House, she'd decided not to mention his name to her mom. But was it because she truly believed Sam wasn't the stalker? Or because she didn't want to cross Jennifer Cane?

Tracey Mills was hunched over her glass-topped desk when Whitney draped her arms over her mother's shoulders.

"Thank you so much for letting me have this Valentine's party tonight," she said, kissing the back of her mom's head.

"Yes, well, pull up a seat and let's finish up this to-do list so I can get back to work," she said curtly, picking up her notebook and pen.

I guess hug time's over.

She slid a chair over and sat down as her mother read out the list.

"Soft drinks. Check."

Angie—vodka. Check.

"Catered appetizers. Check. Monica O'Connor arranged for sushi, mini Thai spring rolls, and chicken satay."

Franklin—weed. Check.

"I know how hungry you kids get, so I've doubled the order," her mom said.

Yeah, it's called the munchies.

"Dessert. Check. Baked & Wired's delivering heart-shaped Valentine's pastries in about an hour."

Whitney—cinnamon-flavored condoms. Check.

"Deejay. Check. I've hired him for three hours, starting at nine."

Sex at midnight with Franklin. Check. Or sex with Paz. Double check.

Her mother threw down the list and pushed her glasses down her nose.

"I can't believe I agreed to such an elaborate Valentine's Day party," she said, rolling her eyes.

"Yeah, Mom. I really appreciate it."

Her mother pursed her lips and Whitney waited for the inevitable "I'm doing this for you, but what have you done for me lately?"

Go on, say it. You know you want to.

"I want you to have fun at this party, but it goes without saying . . ."

Don't say it, then.

". . . you need to keep your eyes and . . ."

Whitney finished the sentence for her: ". . . ears open. I know, I know."

She suppressed a smile.

Her mom would kill her if she knew the truth. Knew that Whitney was holding back. Sensibly and carefully planning how, where, and when to reveal her secret.

It could be some of Lettie's common sense is rubbing off on me. Here I am, actually thinking about the consequences of my actions, about who it'll hurt and who it'll help.

She knew that her secret, if revealed, would blow D.C. to bits. It was a scoop so big Tracey Mills would be crowned the queen of gossip, forever in Whitney's debt.

But unless she handled it exactly right, there'd be a lot of broken hearts, including her own.

TWENTY

Andrew was sitting alone at a table by a huge window overlooking the Potomac River. He watched Daniel, skateboard under his arm, making his way over as he dodged all the Georgetown students juggling their dinner trays and vying for seats.

Andrew had no clue as to why Daniel wanted to see him. The call came out of the blue and all he said was they needed to talk and no, it couldn't be postponed.

Andrew had suggested they meet at the Leo O'Donovan dining hall in case Daniel tried to make a scene. It was so noisy that no one would hear if either lost their temper and he could always disappear quickly without anyone noticing.

"Thanks for the heads-up on your red jacket," Daniel said, sitting down and shoving the board under the table. "Otherwise, I'd never have found you. It would have been like trying to spot a blind date in a nightclub."

What's going on here? He just gave me what passes for a friendly smile.

"What did you want to see me about?" Andrew asked cautiously. He pushed away his half-eaten slice of pizza and stirred sugar into his coffee. He usually didn't drink it sweet, but he wanted something to do with his hands and eyes.

The next words out of Daniel's mouth stunned him.

"I want to apologize," Daniel said bluntly. "I owe you a big one."

Andrew looked up from his mug.

"Which incident are you referring to? The one where you dissed me at Jackie's birthday dinner? Or the fistfight at Homecoming?"

"Listen, dude, you were the one who started that fight!" Daniel shot back, his eyes blazing.

Andrew held up his hands in surrender. "True. But it wouldn't have happened if you hadn't spent months telling everyone we know that it was my fault Taylor died."

"My behavior stank." He sounded calm again. "I know that now."

"What do you know?" Andrew asked, his voice dripping with sarcasm. "That I'm *not* a murderer after all? What, did you hold a secret trial and acquit me?" He gulped down most of his coffee to quell his growing rage.

"Andrew, I don't blame you for being angry," Daniel said quietly. "But I came here to tell you I'm really sorry for what I put you through." He wrung his hands. "I blamed you for my sister's accident and I was wrong. I know now who was at fault. It was Sam."

"Sam?" The word came out as a whisper.

Daniel's voice broke. "He messed with her head. I mean, really messed with her. You just happened to be there when she fell apart."

Finally, after all these months, Andrew had an answer to the questions that had hounded him. For a second, he pictured holding Jackie in his arms, her forgiving him, erasing all the pain he'd caused. But then it hit him. Even if Jackie could forgive him, nothing would erase all the guilt he felt. For betraying her, for losing control of the car, and for all the lies he'd told later. He'd have to live with that forever.

"You okay?" Daniel asked.

"Yeah. Are you?"

Taylor's brother nodded.

"Can I ask you a few more questions?" Andrew asked hesitantly.

Daniel nodded again.

"What did Taylor and Sam fight about?"

"I can't tell you that," he answered quickly.

Don't you think I have a right to know?

As if reading his mind, Daniel added, "I don't know the full story myself."

Maybe it didn't matter. Whatever went down between her and Sam, it apparently explained her out-of-control behavior with him that night and her crazy ranting about lies and cover-ups as they drove back to the party.

Daniel stood up, pushed back the chair so he could reach for his skateboard, and stuck out his free hand. "Please accept my apology, Andrew. I hope we can be friends again. At some point, anyway."

Without hesitating, Andrew shook his hand. "It's in the past," he said.

He stared as Daniel walked away, a distinctive figure in one of his funky plaid Goodwill coats and his top-of-the-line black-and-red Supra Society skateboard high-tops. He thought of all the death-defying tricks Daniel had been performing on his skateboard ever since fourth grade.

On the surface, Daniel and Taylor didn't seem to share many traits. But the extroverted wild child and the high-flying boarder with the quiet demeanor were both risk takers in their own way. Perhaps that was one reason he could forgive Daniel so easily. He was so like Taylor.

The cab pulled up outside the luxurious Newseum Residences on Pennsylvania Avenue. Laura Beth hadn't used her own gray BMW or the Ballous' car service, not wanting her mother to find out she was meeting Sol alone at his parents' apartment.

She hardly ever took a taxi and she'd forgotten how gross it could be—murky windows, stained seats, and a driver who barely knew his way around downtown.

She climbed out of the cab and went straight to the concierge. To her delight, he welcomed her by name. "Miss Ballou, Mr. Molla is waiting for you in penthouse three. Have a pleasant evening."

Riding up in the elevator, she was a muddle of emotions. She and Sol were going to be alone in the apartment for the first time ever.

But instead of making love—the way she'd dreamed about— she'd be pouring out the whole sordid Arden story.

Instead of looking gorgeous, beckoning to him as she lay on his bed in a sexy gossamer silk negligee, she'd be howling on the sofa, her skin blotchy with tears and mascara, her eyes puffy and bloodshot.

The good news was she knew Sol would take her in his arms and comfort her. That he'd say exactly the right thing. That he wouldn't care if she wasn't looking her peachy-pretty self. *All he'll care about is making me feel better.*

Outside his door, she put down the Louis Vuitton travel bag holding her outfit for Whitney's costume party and took a couple of cleansing breaths. *Try to be poised, Laura Beth. Remember what Mama says. Men don't like hysterics.*

She rang the buzzer and within seconds, Sol opened the door.

Before he could utter her name, she flung herself into his arms with a strangled cry.

He led her to the soft, buttery leather sofa warmed by the fire, and nestled close, one hand on her shoulder, the other holding hers.

"It's okay, Laura Beth. Whatever it is, we'll work it out," he whispered into her hair, his thumb rhythmically, soothingly rubbing the back of her hand.

She told him everything, her tears falling harder with every sentence.

"This has been an incredible shock for you," he said, untangling himself just long enough to grab a box of tissues on the coffee table.

"I knew you'd understand," she said, dabbing her eyes.

"It seems insurmountable now, because you haven't had long enough to absorb everything and I haven't been here to help you." She nodded.

"It has to be pretty hurtful discovering your parents lied to you."

He sees it the way I do. I knew he'd take my side.

But what he said next threw her off balance.

"But how sad for that little girl, who just lost her mother, babe." He turned her to face him and took both her hands in his. "She's lost everything."

"She's not a little girl. She's thirteen, for goodness sake," she said defensively.

"Yes, but she's still a child compared to you and she's all alone. Think how you'd feel if you were forced to leave Jackie and Lettie. If Libby died and you had no family."

"That would never happen!"

"That's probably what she thought, too. And now she's learned she's moving away from her home to live with strangers."

"I'm not a stranger! That sounds so cold," Laura Beth protested.

"You're exactly right. You're a wonderful, warm person who cares about people, who's unbelievably kind and does everything possible to make people feel welcome and comfortable."

"Yes, like with Lettie," she broke in. "I taught her how to fit in at Excelsior and how to dress and everything. I even wanted her to come live with me after her parents were deported. Why she'd choose Whitney is beyond me, but that's not my fault. I offered."

"Yes, sort of like that," Sol said hesitantly. He squeezed her hands again.

"Look, Laura Beth, Arden *is* your sister and she *is* coming to live with you. You can't change that. But think how much people will admire the generous Ballou women for opening their hearts to a homeless orphan."

Laura Beth was starting to feel a tiny bit better. Sol was so right.

"You've given me a lot to think about," she said, snuggling into his chest. "I knew it would help talking it through with you, Sol."

"And we'll continue talking about it as long as you need to."

She kissed him gratefully. And then passionately.

She ran her tongue across his even white teeth. His face had the clean, fresh smell of Dial soap, as if he'd just stepped out of the shower. His breath smelled both minty and uniquely, sweetly, his own.

She slipped her hands under his pale blue chambray shirt and ran them over his taut chest.

He groaned her name, caressing her thighs. Up and down. Slowly. Firmly. It made her crazy, in a way she never wanted to end. Her skin came alive under his touch. As if his fingertips were dipped in fire and ice.

"Don't stop," she heard herself say.

But a few minutes later, it was she who pulled away. She needed a moment to think. And she couldn't think if he continued touching her like that.

She stood up, smoothing down her dress and patting her wild curls.

Sol sat up, looking confused.

"Laura Beth, are you all right? Do you want to stop?"

"No. I just realized I must look a sight! Point me to the ladies' room and I'll freshen up and be right back."

Sol stood up, running his hands through his thick, black hair. His shirt was untucked and his face was flushed.

"You can use the one off my bedroom. Second door on the left. But you don't need to go anywhere," he said, holding out his arms to grab her. "You look incredibly sexy right now, with your hair all wild."

Laura Beth giggled and skipped out of reach.

She opened the door to Sol's bedroom and it was just as she imagined it would be. One wall was all glass, overlooking the Capitol and the roofs of the museums along the tree-lined Mall.

The other three walls were lacquered charcoal-gray and the king-size bed seemed to float above the floor.

She slipped into the bathroom, shut the door, and turned on the faucet to splash her face. She wiped off the smudged makeup with a tissue and brushed her teeth with his toothbrush.

This is it, she thought. She wasn't expecting it to happen tonight but it felt right. Completely right.

"I always thought it would be you, Andrew," she whispered into the mirror. Then she heard Sol calling her name and that sounded right, too. Completely right.

TWENTY-ONE

By the time Jackie talked herself out of, then into, going to Whitney's, the party was well under way.

The deejay was spinning drum and bass for several dozen kids who were either dancing to the music or sprawled on the white suede sofa that ran the length of the living room.

If Taylor were here, she'd be up on the glass coffee table, grinding away for the hottest guys in the room.

The rest of the party had moved to the balcony, which was strung with dozens of twinkling lights. The view of the Potomac was stunning, the river winding past the soaring spirals of the Georgetown campus. Not that anyone seemed to notice. Groups of teens were sneaking joints and chugging vodka-spiked Sprite, while others made out on the cushioned patio furniture.

Most of the guests had peeled off their costumes and scattered them all over the apartment's marble floors. Jackie felt totally absurd in her she-devil tail and horns.

"I'll be right over here," said one of her two Secret Service escorts. He pointed to two other agents standing against the wall.

The four of them, dressed in identical dark suits and white shirts, could have been guests in costume except they were at least twenty years older and they were the only ones not drinking.

Jackie knew the agents had been in the apartment all afternoon doing a security sweep.

Whitney called sounding furious. "What the fuck is up with these two creeps going through all my stuff?" she'd raged. "You need to tell them to get out. Now."

No way was I going to tell her about the death threat from the stalker and that both Andrew and I were under extra-tight security.

"If you want queen bees at your party," I told her, before hanging up, "you've got to put up with the worker bees buzzing around in your business."

To her relief, neither Whitney nor Tracey Mills were anywhere in sight. But neither were Laura Beth or Lettie.

Jackie headed for the powder room so she could ditch her costume.

She stood in front of the oversized mirror, surprised she didn't look the way she felt—emotionally drained, scared, and vulnerable. The person staring back at her was the It Girl. A poised, self-confident blonde in a sexy low-cut red satin dress that hugged every inch of her body and ended midthigh.

I look hot. So how come nobody loves me the way I want to be loved?

Someone must have told the deejay to turn up the music, because the walls started pulsing and her head throbbed.

Why did I even bother coming? I'm going home.

She dropped the horns and the tail in the trash can and unlocked the door as she checked the hem of her dress.

"This is the only way I can get you alone?" a male voice asked huskily. He pushed his way through the door and wrapped her in his arms.

His lips and his skin smelled so warm and familiar, she instantly responded. She was pulled in to him. One hand was on her butt and the other entangled in her hair. Instead of freaked, she felt safe.

She wanted to dissolve into the embrace and he moved even closer as if knowing it. He gently opened her mouth with his tongue, nibbling her bottom lip, and she ground against him urgently, her hands gripping his back.

Her eyes still shut tight, she was vaguely aware of the music stopping.

Suddenly her body vanished and it was Taylor making wild, angry, passionate, guilty love with Andrew. Was this how they were that night? Reckless, out of control, unstoppable? The way she felt now?

Somebody, a girl, giggled nearby.

Startled, she opened her eyes and met Scott's, the want in his eyes already melting away. They jumped apart as Dina, holding an iPhone, stood in the doorway with Angie.

"Having trouble telling one brother from the other?" Angie scoffed.

"We thought you guys were never coming up for breath," Dina smirked. "We got at least a dozen great shots."

"And don't bother asking us to delete them," Angie added. "Surprise! The answer's no."

Scott made a grab for Dina's cell, dropped it on the marble floor, and stomped hard. Bits of glass, metal, and computer guts flew across the hallway. The two girls just gaped.

"Now get lost," he told them coldly, and they fled.

"Problem solved," he said to Jackie.

She had to stop from flinging herself back into his arms again, even if this time it would be more out of gratitude than passion.

"I'm sorry those two idiots caught us. But I'm not sorry I hijacked you in the first place," Scott added. "Because I think you just made up your mind."

The way she'd responded to his kisses, she could hardly deny it.

But if Ankie's over and I'm in love with Scott, why do I feel bad?

Lettie and Daniel, their Che Guevara masks pushed off their faces and perched on their heads, walked into the kitchen. Paz was pinned up against the pantry doors by Whitney, who was dressed in a cowgirl outfit that barely covered her ass. She'd put her Stetson on his head and was waving a lasso.

"I can't wait to tie you up later," she said in a slurred stage whisper for everyone to hear.

Peering over her shoulder and spotting Lettie, Paz mouthed a desperate, "Help!"

Instant replay of the White House Christmas party.

She signaled Daniel with her eyes and they made a beeline for Paz.

"Hey, cowgirl, I think your boyfriend's in the other room, threatening a stampede unless you go lasso him," Daniel joked.

Whitney spun around, staggering a little in her high-heeled cowgirl boots, and leered at Daniel. "It takes at least three for a stampede. Wanna join us?"

Daniel grinned and draped his arm around Lettie. "That lasso's not long enough to rope me in." He nuzzled Lettie's neck, whispering just to her, "And I'm totally caught already."

"Good, because I don't want her getting her spurs into you," she whispered back. Daniel laughed.

Wow, that was actually funny. For me.

Despite being totally into Daniel, Lettie realized here was her chance to talk to Paz, who she hadn't seen for ages. There was something on her mind and she needed to clear the air.

She lifted her lips to Daniel's ear. "Help me out. I bet Whitney hasn't eaten all day. Can you take her over to the food, so I can talk to Paz alone for a minute?"

Daniel nodded and turned to grab Whitney by the hand. "Come on, cowgirl, let's pony up to the feed trough."

"Change your mind already?" Whitney giggled as he led her out of the room.

God, she's so thin she looks like she could break.

"Thanks, *mi hermana*," Paz said, taking a sip of his beer. "That girl never gives up. She's always texting me and calling me."

Lettie's heart sank. "Paz, you know who Whitney's mother is, right?"

"Of course."

She took a deep breath.

"Well, Whitney's a party girl, you already know that. But I'm worried that she's playing you. I mean, Tracey Mills pays her to feed her gossip tips."

Paz scowled. "What are you saying, Lettie? That I'd give

Whitney information about you and your friends for money? I'd never do that to you."

Her brother had always been quick to anger. *I'm not handling this well.* She tried again. "No! But you might not realize—"

He slammed his beer on the counter.

"Don't you get it?" he growled. "I'm straightening out my life here. I'm not going to blow a college degree and my job just to get in Whitney's pants."

Lettie blushed scarlet but Paz didn't seem to notice or care.

"Mamá and Papá never had much faith in me, but I thought you did."

"Of course I believe in you," she answered. "That's not what I mean—"

"Then what *do* you mean?" He sounded so angry. Lettie was starting to get mad herself.

"I'll tell you, if you'll let me finish a sentence! What I was about to say was . . . You might not realize when Whitney's using you. The other day, Tracey had an item hinting that President Price's husband was buying expensive jewelry for other women."

"First I heard of it. What's that got to do with me?"

"Some people might jump to conclusions and think it came from you."

"Well it didn't."

"I know that." No way would she tell him she'd been worried sick he *had* been the leak.

"The problem is, you're in the White House, including the family quarters, and your sister lives with the gossip columnist's daughter. I'm just trying to warn you how it looks."

He started to calm down.

"Okay, I get it now. Consider me warned."

He gave her one of his irresistible smiles. Lettie knew the effect it had on a lot of girls, not just Whitney.

"Sorry I flew off the handle. You're just trying to protect me. As usual."

He picked up his beer. "Let's go back to the party."

"You go. I'm going to wait for Daniel to come back."

"Okay. I love you, *mi hermana*."

Just before he headed for the crowded dance floor, he added, "You know, Lettie, I'm kind of surprised. You usually defend Whitney as a misunderstood misfit with a soft heart."

He was right. In trying to protect her brother, she'd trashed Whitney in the worst way. *Just like the mean girls at school, who live to put you down.* Worse, she'd done it knowing Whitney had deep, unresolved issues that were beyond her control.

Lettie looked down at her thrift store guerrilla fatigues and pushed away the strands of hair that had escaped from her messy ponytail.

I don't look like an Excelsior girl. But I hope I'm not starting to sound like one.

She sat down at the kitchen island to wait for Daniel. She could hear Whitney berating someone in the other room.

"Why didn't you bring more vodka?" she was complaining.

The kitchen door swung open and Whitney appeared, trailed by Angie and Dina.

"I brought an entire case, for God's sake," Angie snapped.

"Yeah, well, lucky for you, my dad always keeps some emergency whiskey under the sink."

"It's not smart to mix your poisons," Lettie told them, trying not to sound too preachy. "Be careful!"

The three girls rolled their eyes.

Whitney sidled up and grabbed the glass in front of Lettie. She took a big swig and spat it right out.

"Water!" she said in disgust. "I thought it was vodka!"

"It's Lame Lettie, whaddya expect?" Angie scoffed.

Lettie looked at the doorway, willing Daniel to come back.

"Where's your *boyfriend,* Lettie?" Dina mocked. "I wouldn't let him out of my sight if I were you. There're plenty of girls out there dying to give him what he's obviously not getting from you."

Whitney wagged her finger drunkenly in Dina's face.

"I got news for you, Dina. Lettie's keeping her man *real* happy."

"Whitney, that's enough!" Lettie snapped, her cheeks burning. "Stop it!"

Whitney shrugged and weaved her way over to the sink and got down on her hands and knees to look for the liquor.

Dina giggled. "I bet she says that to Daniel all the time. 'Stop it, Daniel, ooh, stop it!'" She swayed as she tried to straighten the wings on her Victoria's Secret angel costume.

Angie pretended to grope Dina, who shrieked and slapped at her hands. "Let me go, Daniel! This is wrong! I could get deported for this!"

Lettie was used to ignorant people making snide cracks about illegal immigrants. But it was usually strangers, not anyone she knew.

"You two are pathetic," she said.

She was sorry she spoke. It just seemed to egg them on.

"What are you *wearing,* anyway?" Angie asked. "Way to go sexy, Lettie." She ran her hands up and down her own costume, a skimpy French maid minidress, minus the apron, the cap, and the top four buttons.

Whitney got up from the cupboard, holding two bottles.

"Yeah," she said, squinting at Lettie. "Baggy army uniform. Big mistake, Lets."

This is only going to get uglier. Time to go.

Lettie got off her stool and moved toward the door but Angie blocked her.

"She obviously dressed in camouflage in case Immigration raids the party," Dina hooted. "She'll be all ready to crawl across the border and go back to where she came from."

"You mean, go back to where she belongs," Angie said.

Now Lettie was shocked. *They're not just ignorant, they're racist.*

Whitney put the whiskey on the counter and scowled at the two girls. "That's just mean!" she said, shaking her head. Angie and Dina ignored her.

"We know she *lives* here but she doesn't really *belong* here," Angie said. "She doesn't *belong* at Excelsior, either."

"Let's face it, Lettie's not one of us and never will be," Dina added.

Thank God I'm not.

To her surprise, Whitney turned on them.

"I told you before to quit picking on Lettie. You two wouldn't be anything, either, if it wasn't for me! Without me, you've got no hope of toppling Jackie Whitman or Laura Beth Ballou!"

"And you think you do?" Angie yelled back. "You have to bribe your own mother to spend any time with you."

Lettie watched Whitney's face change from anger to anguish in a blink.

"Yeah, I bet she likes Lettie better than you," Dina said, sneering. "That's why she let her move in. So she could pretend she had a *real* daughter!"

Whitney reeled back, as if she'd been punched in the stomach.

Lettie couldn't stand it anymore. "Are you guys even human? Do you have any feelings at all?"

She didn't know how they'd react, but she didn't expect them to burst out laughing.

They brushed past her and Whitney, still laughing, and grabbed one of the whiskey bottles. "Let's get back to the party. You two are real downers," Angie said.

Lettie felt overcome with pity for Whitney. "You can't believe anything those two say," she said, walking to Whitney's side. "They just wanted to hurt you."

But Whitney avoided Lettie's eyes. She unscrewed the cap on the whiskey and raised the bottle in the air. "I'll drink to that!"

TWENTY-TWO

Andrew was waiting for Jackie in the study off his White House bedroom, bent over a textbook, headphones on, tapping his foot.

He must have sensed her presence because he raised his head as she hovered silently in the doorway.

"Hi," he said, removing his headphones.

"Hi," she answered. "Sorry I'm late. Traffic."

He stood up as if to hug her, but she avoided it by grabbing a chair and pulling it next to his. She didn't want the distraction of his electric touch.

They both sat down.

"What did you want to see me about, Jackie?" he asked politely.

Her mouth was so dry her voice came out thick and sticky. Deciding to make a clean break was one thing. Actually doing it was something else.

"Us," she said, swallowing. "After what we said at the VRAG fund-raiser, we need to make our break official. Public."

Andrew's face was unreadable. "Yes, it's stupid to keep on pretending."

"It is."

He was making it easier than she expected. But she couldn't help but wonder once more . . . *Why isn't he fighting for me?*

And then she thought: *Why do I keep craving that? When I don't even want him anymore?*

It must be my ego. She was so used to everyone clamoring for the It Girl. Rejection was not in her playbook. But that was too strong a word for how Andrew was acting. He seemed indifferent.

Andrew picked up a pen, twirling it between his thumb and his forefinger. He seemed to be deciding whether or not to say something else.

When he did, it threw her off-balance.

"Is Scott a factor in this?"

He must have heard about them making out at Whitney's party.

"This has nothing to do with Scott. This is just about us," she answered, her cheeks burning.

He smiled wryly. "You think I haven't noticed you two flirting every time you're in the same room?"

"I know we have and I'm sorry I hurt you. I really am," she said. "But this is not about me choosing between brothers. You know what this is about. It's about betrayal. And not mine. Yours."

She made a point of keeping her voice neutral, without any hint of bitterness or accusation.

His indifference vanished.

"I know," he said, his voice choking. "I screwed up everything.

I wish I could take it back, but I can't. I wish you could forgive me." He leaned forward, staring into her eyes.

Maybe he is going to try to win me back. Blame Sam for all the craziness the night of the accident.

"But you can't, and there's nothing I can do to change your mind . . ." His voice trailed away and he broke their eye lock.

What they'd had together had been so great, and he'd trashed it. Taylor popped into her head. Not Taylor the traitor, but Taylor the friend.

"I could be hit by a truck tomorrow, so why would I wanna waste time?" Taylor asked, after I teased her for hitting on three (three!) guys at our very first Excelsior–St. Thomas mixer.

For a second she got serious.

"Everybody's looking for that total connection. Even me! Big shock, huh? We all want that guy whose mind is as hot as his body. You know, someone you get off on just by talking.

"In the meantime, the search goes on!" She roared with laughter.

Andrew had been Jackie's "total connection." Until the accident.

She was tired of talking. Tired of thinking. She just wanted to curl up in a ball and sleep without dreams.

"I'm sorry," she told Andrew. "I'm going to tell Mom now. That there'll be no more Ankie. You should do the same. They'll need a heads-up when the press figures out it's over."

"At least we both know where we stand," he said, running his hand through his hair.

He smiled tenderly. They both stood up and she let him hold

her for a second. This time she didn't resist. It felt comforting and kind. Just what she needed.

As she left the study, he called out to her. "What about you and Scott?"

She kept walking.

Jackie waited outside her mom's office, her nerves jangling, just like earlier in the week when she'd handed her mother the deadly Valentine's card.

She would have preferred to do this in private, but her mom had been hard to catch lately. Leaving extra early and coming home late, on weekends, too.

It'll be easier breaking the news to Mom, Jackie reassured herself. *It won't be a total shock. She pretty much already gave me permission to break up with Andrew.*

She replayed the scene at home, before Christmas, when she told her that she and Andrew were having a rough time and even hinted something about another girl . . .

"Don't ever feel like you have to stay with someone. Not for me. Not for anyone," Mom had said.

Jackie squirmed in her chair and glanced at her two Secret Service agents standing a discreet distance down the hall.

Come on, Mom. The longer she hung out in the hallway, the more chances of running into Aunt Deborah, whose office was just around the corner. And she *definitely* wasn't up for that.

"Yankee Doodle Dandy" started playing on her iPhone. Laura Beth.

"Jackie, I did it!"

"What are you talking about?"

"I *did* it," she repeated. "You know, Sol and I . . ."

Laura Beth's timing couldn't have been worse.

". . . had sex!" Laura Beth squealed into the phone. "But it was so much more than that. It. Was. Incredible. You have no idea. That's why we never showed up at Whitney's last night. We couldn't tear ourselves away."

Jackie thought she'd throw up if she had to listen any longer.

"I never thought I'd be the first one to have a real boyfriend, someone who wanted you as much as you wanted him." Laura Beth giggled into the phone. "I always thought that would be you and Andrew."

Jackie fought the urge to hurl the phone across the hall. Was Laura Beth deliberately trying to hurt her or was she just oblivious?

The door opened and her mother appeared with the vice president.

"I gotta go. My mom just showed up," Jackie said abruptly, but added, "I'm happy for you, Laura Beth. I really am."

"Okay, but I can't wait to tell you *everything*," Laura Beth burbled. "As soon as I get back from New York . . . Oh, forgot to tell you, Sol and I took the train up this morning . . . Mama thinks I'm doing a weekend stay-over at Juilliard."

"Have fun." Jackie hit end, shoved her cell back in her purse, and stood up.

"Hi, Jackie," Ike Sawyer said, shaking her hand. "Nice to see you. Congratulations on Yale. It's actually my alma mater."

Distracted by Laura Beth's call, she was only half-listening.

"Oh? Cool," she said vaguely.

She thought about making a joke about Carolike, but before she could think of anything, he'd limped away.

Poor guy. *He lost part of his leg fighting in Vietnam and we're still bring-ing home wounded soldiers,* she thought. Like Tanya and Vic.

"Nice to see you!" she shouted at his back. He waved without turning around.

Jackie hugged her mom, holding on to her a little longer than usual, inhaling her scent. *She must have changed her perfume.* It re-minded her of her dad's Old Spice.

"Sorry, Jackie, but I only have fifteen, twenty minutes. I have to get to a G8 planning meeting." She smiled at her daughter. "You okay? You look a little out of sorts."

Jackie shrugged. "Oh, it's just Laura Beth. She can really get on my nerves sometimes."

"Like mother like daughter." She laughed. "Libby's a handful, too. But if it's any comfort, our friendship's lasted a long time and yours will, too." *Almost word-for-word what Aunt Deborah said.*

Her mother led her to the overstuffed brocade sofa in a far corner of the office.

"I can tell there's something important on your mind. So spill."

Jackie decided to just come right out and say it. There was no way to soften the blow.

"I can't do Ankie anymore," she said simply. "Andrew and I are over, unofficially and officially. I'm sorry, but I can't keep pre-tending just for the sake of Aunt Deborah's campaign."

She felt the sobs rising in her chest out of nowhere and fell into her mom's arms. She realized she had to purge herself of everything that had been killing her inside. How she and An-drew had been torn apart by lies and betrayal. She needed her mom the way she'd needed her as a little girl, to chase away the monsters under her bed.

She pulled away a little, staring at her hands. "There's something else that hurts so bad," she mumbled.

She took a deep breath, wiped away the tears, and gathered her courage. "Remember when I told you a while back that Andrew and I were not in a good place?"

"Of course, I remember. You hinted that there had been some other girl—"

"Not some other girl, Mom. Taylor. He cheated on me with Taylor."

Her mother gasped, but Jackie continued without pause. She just wanted to get the words out and over with. "They had sex just before the car crashed. My boyfriend and my best friend."

"Oh, Jackie. I can't believe it. Andrew and Taylor!" Her mother shook her head in shock. "Why didn't you break it off right when you found out?"

Is that a serious question?

"Because of Ankie."

"Well, of course, Ankie was a gift to the administration," her mom said defensively. "But this is *your* life, Jackie, not mine or Aunt Deborah's. I *never* wanted you to go against your own heart. I told you that."

Jackie didn't want to argue about it, but there was no question her mom was sugarcoating reality. She and Andrew had been convenient pawns in the president's public relations strategy to win the hearts and minds of voters. And they'd milked it for everything.

"I'm not looking for sympathy," Jackie said evenly. "I just want you to know why I can't continue this charade."

"Of course not! But how did Taylor and Andrew even—"

Jackie held up her hand to hush her.

"Mom, I don't want to rehash it. I never want to talk about it again. I just need you to support my decision and make it okay with Aunt Deborah. Without telling her about Andrew and Taylor."

Her mother grabbed her hand midair and held it between her two.

"I'll fix it with Deborah and I'll be discreet."

She gave Jackie a reassuring smile, but her eyes were filled with maternal worry and her face seemed to sag.

"I feel I've let you down, Jackie," she said softly. "Not just about this. But about hiding the fact that Deborah and I knew Andrew was driving the car when Taylor died." Her voice was heavy with sadness.

"There's not a day goes by I don't regret not telling you the truth. I wanted to protect you from more hurt. But I was wrong to lie to you."

Her mother frowned. "I also made a political decision to cover it up to protect Andrew and Deborah. And I'm so sorry. Please forgive me."

Jackie appreciated her mom's honesty but she would never fully understand the "how." *How could you lie like that to your own daughter?*

She thought back over the past year.

If she was really honest with herself, she'd betrayed her mother's trust, too. By stealing secret information from her mother's desk and giving it to Senator Griffin so he'd destroy the photos of her and Eric.

My motives were no better or worse than Mom's. Yeah, I wanted to protect her and Aunt Deborah's careers, but I also wanted to save myself from total humiliation.

Jackie's head was spinning from the emotional overload.

"I understand, Mom. It's okay," Jackie said, just wanting to drop it.

She squeezed her mother's hand.

"It's not easy living in a political fishbowl. I don't think they have any parenting books on that," Jackie said with a little laugh. "Don't worry, Mom. I love you so much. And I feel so much better now that Ankie's done. It's a total relief to finally make the decision. I'm just sorry you're stuck with Carolike."

Her mom laughed, her eyes lighting up.

It wasn't that funny.

"I have to tell you something." She leaned in to Jackie and held her gaze. "Jackie, you know you're the most precious and important person in my life and that will never change."

What's she trying to say? Jackie wasn't sure she could take any more true confessions.

"Yeah, I know that . . ."

"I've been single for so long. It's been lonely sometimes and . . ."

"Oh my God, Mom. You had a date? That's great! Who with? When was this?"

Her mom's smile stretched even wider.

"It's been going on since before Christmas. I didn't want to tell you because of everything happening in your life and I wanted to make sure this was serious."

Jackie remembered something Scott had said at the White House Christmas party. She'd forgotten about it until now.

"When did your mom and Ike start dating?" Scott asked after we walked away from two of Aunt Deborah's most trusted advisers.

"What?!"

"C'mon. You couldn't see how into each other they were?"

"Is it Ike?"

Her mother blushed. Jackie had never seen her do *that* before.

"He's a wonderful man, Jackie, a truly good person, and I can't wait for both of you to get to know each other better."

Jackie was consumed by a mix of jealousy, resentment, and fury that her mother had kept yet *another* life-altering secret from her. She was paralyzed, unable to speak. She thought they knew each other so well, were so attuned to each other's moods and aspirations. *How could she have fallen madly in love without telling me or me noticing?*

But perhaps it was no different from Jackie's own situation. *Mom didn't see that I'd fallen out of love with Andrew and I never sought her advice. Or maybe it was more that each of us chose to ignore all the signs.*

"Have you told Dad yet?" she asked numbly.

How's he gonna take it? He was acting kind of jealous when he called me.

Her mom shook her head. "Only what he's read in the gossip columns about Carolike. He doesn't tell me whom he's dating— even if he could remember their names—and Ike's my first serious boyfriend. That's such a silly word for people our age."

What would you prefer, my lover? How about my hookup? Or my man toy? Yuck.

Jackie pondered, again, this sick city they lived in, where everyone had secrets and pretended to be things they weren't. Where your friends—or even members of your own family—could turn fake before you realized.

"I'm happy for you, Mom," she said. She only wished it were 100 percent true.

TWENTY-THREE

It was amazing how one little Bliss massage—okay, one seventy-five minute head-to-toe work over—could be as good as sex. Better than sex, if it was Franklin. *But if you're talking Paz ... I'll have to find out.*

Whitney got into her mom's black vintage Beemer and picked a sticky white shred out of her hair, a remnant from the ginger rub that supposedly detoxified your skin.

"We both smell of ginger." She giggled. *It almost makes me hungry.*

Her mother turned on the ignition and smiled. She looked so relaxed, her cat claws retracted for once. *She's gonna start purring any second.*

Everything was going according to plan.

Step one was to get her mom alone.

Angie's words at the party still stung. But just because she was totally right about their so-called mother-daughter relationship—or lack of—didn't give her any right to say it. And definitely not at her own party. *The bitch.*

Fortunately, step one literally fell into Whitney's lap.

"I got this from a grateful lobbyist who liked what I wrote about him," her mother said, tossing a coupon for two free massages at the Bliss Spa in the W Hotel. "I was going to take Brenda—she's my new personal shopper at Saks? But she just called to cancel. Do you want to come with me? We leave in a half hour."

Step two: Get her declawed and caged. Done, with a little help from the masseuse.

Her mother pulled into the traffic on F Street.

Now for step three: Pounce.

"Mom, I got the scoop of a lifetime for you—"

"That's what you always say, Whitney!" her mom interrupted, sounding uncharacteristically lighthearted. "Let's just relax and not talk shop."

Whitney never thought she'd live to see it, but her mom was almost *too* chill.

"No, seriously, Mom, this will make you the number one, go-to columnist in the entire country."

"Whitney, are you short of money again?"

"Mom, will you please just listen to what I gotta tell you? And make sure you have both hands on the wheel cuz you're gonna freak when you hear this."

"Oh, for heaven's sake, you're ruining my Zen. Just tell me."

Oops, here come the claws. I better hurry.

"Okay, okay. Libby-Ballou's-husband-had-a-love-child-and-the-kid's-coming-to-live-with-them-and-the-senator's-gonna-adopt-it. I-mean-her."

She ran out of breath.

"Holy shit!" Her mom spun the wheel so sharply the tires slammed into the curb. She turned off the motor. "Oh my God, I'm gonna be on the *Today* show!" she shouted, holding her arms out in front of her as if framing her name in lights. "And Jay Leno and Letterman and Jimmy Fallon!" She didn't even give Whitney a passing glance. Let alone a thank you.

Whitney rolled her eyes. *You're welcome.*

She finally turned to her daughter.

"Who's your source?" she asked abruptly. "You've been wrong before. Like the fake Ankie engagement. Remember that one?"

How could I forget when you're always reminding me? It was torture, but Whitney forced herself to eat the retort. "I got it firsthand. I stood outside Lettie's bedroom door and heard her talking to Laura Beth on speakerphone."

"Yes!" Her mom thumped the steering wheel triumphantly.

"There's just one catch, Mom. You gotta write it so you don't hurt the girl. Arden."

"Bah!" Her mother waved dismissively. "The girl's not the point! It's about sleazy, two-timing Preston Ballou—the dirty trickster himself pulling the dirtiest trick of all. It's not the crime, it's the cover-up, as we say in Washington."

Her mom's imagination was running wild.

"Him and Libby Ballou covering it up! I bet they paid off the woman. Maybe she was a hooker. That'd be perfect!"

Tears welled in Whitney's eyes but, of course, her mother wasn't looking at *her*. She was preening her hair in the visor mirror like she was already in the greenroom prepping for Anderson Cooper.

"And Jeffrey Ives! He was terrified it was going to come out during the campaign and kill his candidacy. That's why he's agreed to adopt the girl. To make him and Libby look good. It's so obviously a preemptive strike! Soon as the campaign's over, they'll ship that kid off to some boarding school in Europe and you'll never hear from her again."

"Stop!"

Her mother turned to her, shocked. "What are you crying about?"

"You! I'm crying about you!" Whitney shouted. "All you ever think about is yourself! I told you that you can't write it that way."

"Why on earth not?"

Whitney wiped away her angry tears. "Why do you think? You of all people should understand."

She ignored her mom's hostile look of warning.

"If you trash her new parents, you're going to ruin Arden's life. Whichever way you write the story, it's going to be huge. You're going to be huge. So why not write it without wrecking the kid's life?"

Her mom glared. "Since when did you become so sensitive?"

"Don't you get it, Mom? Mara. Think about Mara. My sister. Your other daughter."

Her mom pursed her lips. "We don't talk about her."

Yeah, that's the problem. You and Dad never dealt with the guilt that no one was watching her in the pool. You just buried yourselves in your jobs and forgot about me.

Whitney barely remembered the drowning itself and was never told the details. She was only five at the time and was on a playdate at her best friend's house. Mara was seven—old enough, her parents must have thought, to let her swim alone in their backyard pool. When she sank below the surface it was like she disappeared, not just from their lives, but from her mom's and dad's memories. Even the framed photos of Mara scattered around the living room mysteriously vanished.

At first Whitney was happy to have her parents all to herself. They'd told her Mara had gone to heaven and she assumed it was only for a visit. But instead of lavishing her with attention, her mom and dad left her with babysitters most of the time. They never mentioned Mara's name and eventually Whitney realized Mara wasn't coming back. Whenever she uttered Mara's name, they changed the subject, and eventually she stopped talking about her sister. Just like them. Pretending Mara had never existed.

The problem is, they act like I don't exist, either.

It was Lettie moving in that had stirred up all of Whitney's memories of having a sister.

"It's been thirteen years, Mom, and *I* want to talk about her," Whitney shot back.

Her mom stared stonily ahead, though her clasped hands were trembling slightly.

"Doesn't having Lettie living with us make you think about how you used to have two daughters? When I just told you about Arden, didn't that make you think of Mara?"

Her mother still wouldn't look at her. Whitney was used to yelling at her whenever she checked out like this. But on this topic, she had to tread carefully if she was to reach her mother's soft spot. Hopefully she had one.

"What if the media had blamed you and Dad when Mara drowned?" Whitney asked. "How would that have made me feel, knowing everyone thought my parents were bad or screwed up or didn't really want me?"

She searched her mother's face. But there was no clue as to what she was thinking.

If she ever had a soft spot, it looks like it's turned to stone.

"I can't think straight right now," her mom said in a monotone. She revved the motor and peeled out into the traffic. "We need to go home."

Okay. But when we get home we're gonna talk some more. Like it or not.

"I wish it came in red, cuz I surely don't need white anymore." Laura Beth held up a sheer white nightie with a ruffled butt and garters and gave her two friends an exaggerated wink. "What do you think?" she asked. *More importantly, what will Sol think? As if I can't guess.*

"I think you're jumping the gun. It's called a bridal garter," Jackie cracked, reading the label. "But you could buy one for your mother."

"Ewwww." Laura Beth looked revolted. "Thanks for ruining it, Jackie." She didn't put it back, though.

Lettie moved to a nearby rack of pretty, old-fashioned baby-doll pajamas.

"And you should get a pair of these for Arden. Maribel and Christa would die for something like this," she suggested.

"I'm still trying to come to terms with her living with Mama and me, thank you very much, Lettie. I'm way off from taking her shopping for intimate apparel. And I'm starting to regret inviting you two along."

She laughed to show she was joking. *Fancy that, I actually mentioned Arden without feeling angry.*

"I got what I came for," Lettie said. "Sorry, but I've got to go. I'm supposed to hang with Tanya."

"What you really mean is ... this is not your kind of scene," Jackie teased.

Not yours, either, now you're officially single. Jackie had told both her and Lettie what had happened, calling them as soon she'd left the White House.

"But I do like their blue lace bras!" Lettie smirked, holding up her shopping bag as she made for the door.

"Do you think she and Daniel have done it yet?" Laura Beth whispered.

"If she's suddenly ditching her cotton bras for sheer and sexy, they're doing more than holding hands," Jackie guessed.

"Gosh, Jackie, what if Lettie has sex before you, too? You could knock me over with a feather."

Jackie's smile froze and Laura Beth could have kicked herself for being so insensitive. She nervously fingered the small solitaire diamond on the fine gold chain around her neck, figuring an apology would just make it worse.

"What happened to your bigger-is-better rule?" Jackie asked, a trace of bitchy in her voice as she eyed the new necklace.

"Sol gave it to me. To symbolize our first time together. But he didn't want it so big and flashy that Mama would get suspicious," she whispered. "Not like that tacky diamond tennis bracelet that Frances Ives claims she got from a secret admirer."

Laura Beth had her suspicions as to who it was: Bob Price.

She never shuts up about how brilliant he is and how she loves working with him. And since Tracey Mills got ahold of those Tiffany receipts, we all know he's been buyin' out the store for someone other than his wife ...

Jackie grabbed her by the arm and shook it.

"My goodness, Jackie, what are you doing?" Laura Beth didn't want to make a fuss in public, but if Jackie didn't let go, she was going to leave a bruise. And how would that look with her bridal garter?

She saw Jackie look around as if checking to see whether anyone was nearby. A couple of customers were paying at the cash register and her two Secret Service agents were totally preoccupied with the rack of teddies on the far side of the store.

Laura Beth had to lean in close to hear what she said next.

"I think you know as well as I do who Frances's so-called secret admirer is," Jackie hissed in her ear.

They both mouthed the words together: "Bob Price!"

Jackie pulled her into a changing room and told her about Deborah Price finding what she assumed was her "surprise" Valentine's gift from Bob.

"But he never gave it to her. Because Mom told me later that Aunt Deborah was really upset that he'd forgotten Valentine's Day."

They couldn't hear anyone else in the changing area, but they still kept their voices low.

"I bet Frances was the one who leaked the Tiffany receipts to make more trouble between the Prices," Jackie added. "Scott says she's always hanging around the family quarters."

"That stupid girl thinks she can break up his marriage and that he'll marry her?" Laura Beth sniffed.

It was a familiar story in Washington. A beautiful young woman falls in love with a powerful, older, married man. Problem was, without his wife, Bob Price was a powerless nobody.

"I can't wait! This will bring her down! And take her bratty sister down a peg or two as well!" Laura Beth was ecstatic.

"Yeah, well, it could take us down, too," Jackie warned. "Having a secret affair is one thing. But if Frances is determined to break up the Prices and the press learns about it . . ."

". . . Neither of us will be moving into the White House after Election Day," Laura Beth finished the sentence.

Jackie nodded. "A scandal like that will wreck both the campaigns and we can say hello to President Hampton Griffin." She made a gagging sound on the last three words. "You and I *have* to work this out. Together."

Laura Beth didn't answer right away. As much as she despised Frances, it was hard to believe she'd be selfish enough to ruin her own father's presidential dreams.

"Well?" Jackie asked impatiently.

"You're right." Laura Beth nodded, smiling. "We can actually do something that will help *both* campaigns. It's brilliant."

And there's lots in it for me: The campaign will owe me big-time. And I get rid of at least one of the ugly stepsisters.

TWENTY-FOUR

Tanya had her back to the door when Lettie screamed.

"Oh my God, Tanya! You're standing!"

Tanya slammed the filing cabinet shut and turned around slowly, a wide grin spread across her face to hide her disappointment. She'd planned to be waiting in her wheelchair in the hospital lobby and stand up at the last moment, just as Lettie reached her.

Oh, well, it doesn't matter. I still surprised her.

"I bet you thought you'd never see me back on my own two feet." Tanya laughed. She lifted the left leg of her gray sweats to show her the metal prosthetic lower leg that disappeared into her sneaker. "Well, sort of on my own two feet. Only one of them's original. I'll be running and dancing before you know it."

Vic Hazelton, working quietly at his desk, looked up from his computer screen.

"Hello, Lettie," he said in his understated way.

"Hi, Vic."

Tanya expected him to ask about Jackie. She knew he missed her a lot, although they spoke on the phone now and then.

But all he said was, "Tanya's doing great, isn't she?"

"Yes, I can't believe it!" Lettie rushed over to hug her friend. "This is the best news ever!" She stepped back to admire Tanya's steady stance.

"You're early! I had this big surprise planned for you in the lobby," Tanya said, reaching out to brush a strand of hair off Lettie's face. She fingered the soft, black hair before tucking it behind Lettie's ear. "Your hair's so beautiful, Lettie. You should let me put it up for you for Prom. And do your eyes." *They're so trusting and honest.*

Lettie blushed. "Okay, that would be nice."

"Let me give you my walking demonstration. I can only do back and forth a couple of times across the room," she explained. "But when I get used to it, will you take me shopping so I can buy some more flattering pants than these ugly sweats?"

"You look great in those sweats. But sure." Lettie smiled. "It'll be fun. I can even ask Laura Beth to come with us. She's my personal stylist. At least, she thinks she is."

"No . . . I just want it to be you and me." *You won't act weird about the way I walk and you won't make a big fuss if I fall.*

When Tanya found out she was getting a volunteer SAT tutor, she'd been suspicious and resentful, figuring Lettie would be one of those privileged private school seniors, a spoiled little rich girl who'd treat her as a charity case and only be there to fulfill her graduation requirements.

But she quickly discovered that Lettie was nothing like she

expected. They had become so close, Tanya looked forward to their sessions, which grew longer with each visit as they got to know each other.

"It'll be my first outing without the wheelchair," she told Lettie. "We could even get lunch somewhere nice. My treat, now that I'm a working woman!"

Tired, she lowered herself into her wheelchair and Lettie pulled up a chair.

"It's a date." Lettie grinned.

Cool.

"So, how's the job going?" Lettie asked, looking around the office and the desks piled with papers.

"Great."

"Is Dr. Rosen treating you okay, Vic?" she asked him. "I mean, after you sent him that note . . ."

Vic shrugged. "He understood I was just defending my friend."

Lettie fished around in her backpack.

"Gosh, I almost forgot. Jackie gave me your passes to the White House Easter Egg Roll." She handed one to him and one to Tanya.

Vic put the ticket in his shirt pocket, looking disappointed. "I thought I was going with Jackie."

"No, she's arranged for a cab to pick both of you up at the hospital front doors. So you two need to be out there by eight o'clock. It says on the ticket which gate to go to. And make sure you bring your ID."

The Easter celebration was one of those rare public events at the White House. Tens of thousands of parents and kids had free run of the South Lawn, where celebrities, top officials, including the president and her husband, musicians, and clowns all entertained the children. The highlight was the egg roll itself, a race that involved little kids pushing along an egg with a spoon.

"You don't want to be late for the breakfast beforehand, okay?" Lettie smiled.

"I definitely won't be late. I have a big surprise for Jackie," Vic said with a shy smile.

"What are you planning?" Tanya asked, curious. This was the first time he'd mentioned it. "Did you write her something special?"

She'd once seen a book of love poems on his desk. When she'd asked him about it, he'd confided that he was teaching himself to write poetry.

"I've been working on it a long time," he said, his face turning pink.

"I bet she'll love it," Lettie said. "I know she enjoys your journal entries. Not that she shares them with anyone," she added quickly.

"Tell Jackie thank you so much for the tickets. I can't wait," Tanya said.

She was beyond excited at the prospect of visiting the White House again. It had been like a dream when a fellow African-American, Barack Obama, was elected president. But never in her wildest dreams had she imagined she would one day be a *guest* at the White House. And never, ever, *twice*. First the Christmas party and now this!

"Vic, did you get that letter off to Senator Griffin this morning?" Dr. Rosen was suddenly in the room.

"Why, hello, Lettie," he said, walking over to shake her hand. "What good timing! We just found out the fund-raiser cleared even more than we thought. Three hundred and fifty thousand

dollars. Which shows what an invaluable asset Jackie is. Perhaps you can let her know."

Lettie nodded. "Sure."

"Hopefully, she'll realize that it's all about helping soldiers like Vic and Tanya here and change her mind," he continued. "It's not about personalities and politics. It's far more important than that."

"Uh huh," Lettie said in a neutral tone.

Tanya was incredibly grateful to Dr. Rosen for hiring her but sometimes she wanted to strangle him. Like right now when he sounded like a pompous, conniving ass. *And he shouldn't be trying to use Lettie to get to Jackie.*

She turned her wheelchair toward the door.

"Dr. Rosen, Lettie and I were just leaving," she said, cutting him off. "We need to go over my SAT practice tests."

Lettie pushed her chair into the corridor.

"See you both tomorrow morning!" Tanya called out.

"Yeah, bye!" Lettie sounded relieved.

They both rolled their eyes.

"He can be real pushy, can't he?" Tanya joked, as they waited for the elevator. Lettie looked too worried to laugh.

"Do you think I should talk to Jackie like he wants me to?" she asked. "I don't want him taking it out on you if I don't."

She's such a sweetheart.

"Don't sweat it," Tanya said reassuringly. "He won't. Just forget about it."

Lettie pushed Tanya down the path that wound between Dr. Rosen's rented office and the veterans' rehab hospital. The

late-winter sun took the chill off the air and tiny pink buds were starting to appear on the cherry trees. Lettie stopped the wheelchair at a park bench.

"Let's sit here for a minute," Lettie said, helping Tanya out of her chair. "I have some good news to tell you, now. But don't get too excited. It's nowhere near as great as yours."

"Is it good news from home?"

Lettie felt a familiar stab of pain shoot through her heart. It was always there, lurking. Anything could trigger it. The smell of freshly chopped cilantro or a slice of ripe mango. Little girls giggling in a playground. Jackie's or Laura Beth's mom giving her daughter a spontaneous hug. Tracey Mills wasn't a hugger, not even with Whitney, and that made Lettie ache for her mamá, too.

She shook her head.

"No, nothing like that. Though I just got a letter from Papá. They're still living with my grandparents. But it's really cramped, even more than our old apartment here. Mamá and Papá have to sleep in the front room so it's hard for them to get any rest."

"What about your sisters?"

"They're still having a hard time adjusting. Remember, I told you at first they were excited? It was like they were on vacation. Especially when they saw the hens and the pig out back. My *abuelos* gave them the job right away of feeding the chickens and collecting the eggs."

"Yeah, I thought that was really smart, giving them an important role in the household," Tanya said.

Lettie nodded and smiled.

"Yes, they loved that. But the novelty's worn off. They miss their friends and there's no Internet or anything like that, not that they have a computer, anyway. Papá says now they cry them-

selves to sleep almost every night, asking when they're coming home and when I'm coming to see them."

"Why don't you contact their friends' parents and ask them to write to the girls?"

Lettie shook her head.

"The problem is the mail's hopeless. The only way I'm able to hear from Papá is through diplomatic pouches."

"I'm sorry, Lettie. It must be so hard on you," Tanya said. "Do you want to talk about something else to get your mind off it? You said you had something to tell me. Is it something about Daniel?"

As much as Lettie trusted Tanya and would have liked her advice about Daniel and Sam and Taylor's voice mail messages, she couldn't share those secrets with anyone outside the Capital Girls.

"No, it's something else."

"Come on, tell me!"

"I got rejected by Princeton!" Lettie said excitedly and broke into peals of laughter.

"I don't get what's funny. That's horrible news, isn't it?"

"Not when Yale not only wants me, but is offering me a full ride!"

Tanya screamed and threw her arms around Lettie.

"Lettie," she murmured in her ear. "Congratulations! They are so lucky to have you."

Tanya leaned even closer and kissed her on the cheek. Her lips lingered there, as gently as a butterfly alighting on a rose petal, then slowly moved to Lettie's mouth.

Lettie felt a warmth and tenderness seeping through her body. She closed her eyes and parted her lips a little, caught up in the delicious moment.

Then she broke away. Her face, which a second ago had grown hot with unexpected desire, now burned from embarrassment and confusion.

What's going on? Tanya just kissed me. And I just kissed her back.

"Lettie, I'm sorry. I didn't mean . . ." Tanya whispered.

"Tanya, I'm with Daniel. I don't . . ." Her voice died away. She locked eyes with her friend, who looked stricken.

"We just got carried away by my news and your news," Lettie said firmly, trying to sound casual. "It's fine. Let's just forget about it."

Pretend it never happened and nothing's changed.

TWENTY-FIVE

"I'm hittin' the full-screen button so I can see your yummy buff chest up close," Laura Beth told Sol. "'Course, it would be better if you were on a 3-D TV so I could see you life-size, especially if you're not going to wear a shirt when I'm Skypeing you."

Sol laughed. He was sitting cross-legged on the queen-size bed in the Upper West Side luxury apartment that they jokingly called his "dorm room."

She paused, obviously waiting for him to return the compliment. He loved that she blatantly devoured every inch of his muscular thighs in the Under Armour Boxer Jocks that fit like a second skin.

"I don't need 3-D to see how unbelievably sexy and beautiful you are," he answered.

Only my Laura Beth would put on that sexy, see-through whatever it is and drape herself across the bed like Cleopatra.

As if reading his mind, she flipped over to show him the flirty ruffles on her shapely dancer's butt. "You haven't said anything about my new Victoria's Secret lingerie," she said, winking at him over her shoulder before rolling over on her stomach to give him a full view of her cleavage.

"Are you deliberately trying to torture me?" he teased. "I think I'm going to have to impose a dress code from now on. So I can survive these nightly conversations."

Laura Beth was just as rich, socially connected, and driven as all the other girls he'd dated. But they were all so predictable—headed for a Wall Street career and a traditional life. Laura Beth was one of a kind, with her magnetic Southern belle spark and her bright-light Broadway dreams.

Hard to believe he wasn't even interested when Andrew first suggested they meet.

"Get real, Andrew. Have you forgotten I'm Iranian and a Muslim? What would I have in common with a spoiled little Southern belle?"

Andrew grinned. "You'd be surprised. You've never met anyone like Laura Beth. You'll see."

He'd agreed to spend the weekend in Washington and go to Aamina's party, but he'd had no intention of spending more than a polite couple of minutes with Andrew's fix-up. And he'd almost blown it, going off with Whitney for a stupid, fifteen-minute hookup. Fortunately, Laura Beth had forgiven him.

What was I thinking? He knew the answer. He'd never tell Laura Beth, but in some ways she and Whitney were alike. Both were outrageous, gorgeous, and unpredictable. And irresistible. The difference was Whitney didn't have Laura Beth's heart.

"Laura Beth, you are over-the-top unbelievable." He laughed again. "That's why I adore you."

"Okay, we gotta get serious now, Sol," she said, sitting up straight.

"Serious about what . . . other than you?"

She giggled.

"Stop teasin'."

She must want to talk about Arden again. Ever since she first told him, they'd spent hours discussing it. *I think I'm slowly getting through to her but—*

"Earth to Sol!" Laura Beth snapped her fingers. "We need to discuss this college stuff. I've been thinkin', ever since you got your acceptance letter from Georgetown . . . How are we gonna continue our relationship with me movin' to New York and you movin' here?"

"We already live in separate cities, Laura Beth. Nothing's changed, we're just switching places."

He was transferring to Georgetown to study international relations, but looking at her now, all he could think about was *relations* with her.

She pretended to pout. "But there'll be all those hot Georgetown girls trying to get your attention." She waited, obviously wanting him to deny it.

I should tease her, make her squirm. But he couldn't do it.

"Laura Beth, you have all my attention. One hundred percent. I love you."

"I love you, too," she answered. "Oh, I forgot to tell you. I got my first college acceptance."

He knew it couldn't be Juilliard because she'd be bouncing off the walls with excitement. So it had to be one of her safety schools. Sarah Lawrence College or the Tisch School of the Arts at NYU.

"I got in to Tisch!"

"That's fantastic!"

She shrugged. "It isn't Juilliard. That's where I'm goin'."

Okay, how am I gonna handle this? I don't think I can put it off any longer.

Sol had been wracking his brain to think of some way to tactfully prepare Laura Beth for a possible letdown. He was worried how she'd take it on top of the shock about Arden.

As much as he was into her, he also knew how much she liked getting her way, how she expected and demanded it.

"Laura Beth, you know I think you're unbelievably talented," Sol said, choosing his words carefully. "But Juilliard is harder to get into than the Ivies. Something like less than eight percent of applicants get accepted."

She wrinkled her nose as if a bad smell had invaded her bedroom.

"Are you sayin' I'm not gonna get in?" Her voice was tinged with resentment.

"I'm saying you *deserve* to get in," he said. *But that doesn't guarantee you will.* "I'm just trying to prepare you in case things don't go the way you're planning. Getting in to any college is so arbitrary. It's a crapshoot."

"Crapshoot?!" Laura Beth visibly bristled. "I know you're just trying to protect me. But how can it be a crapshoot when I'm offering them real talent and great grades? I need you to stay *positive*, not go all negative on me."

"Laura Beth, I'm your biggest fan. But Tisch would be incredible, too. People like Elizabeth Olsen, Alec Baldwin, Lady Gaga, they all went there."

Her reaction was totally in character, but at least he'd planted the seed. Now he just had to sit back and hope it would take root.

TWENTY-SIX

Lettie and Whitney were on the path hugging the Potomac River as it snaked past the Watergate. It was one of those fresh, sunny afternoons that heralded the invasion of tens of thousands of tourists whose vacations revolved around cherry blossom season.

There was so much Lettie needed to get out in the open.

Not just Whitney's eating problems. Her lousy choice of friends, for one thing. Why she hung with two girls who were so vicious they'd make racist jokes and attack their best friend at her own Valentine's party and think it was all so funny.

Lettie could still see the pain in Whitney's eyes when she had chugged from the whiskey bottle, trying to pretend she didn't care. That was when Lettie knew she couldn't put it off any longer.

When she suggested they take a walk after school, Whitney looked at her incredulously. "Why would I wanna walk when I can go guy-watching with Angie and Dina at the St. Thomas lacrosse game? That's how I get *my* workout."

"Well, I want to talk to you," Lettie persisted. "Can we at least get together after the game?"

Whitney shot her a puzzled look. Then, to Lettie's surprise, she caved. "Okay, I'll go with you now. Whatever."

But they'd only walked a couple of blocks from the Watergate, when Whitney slowed down.

"Let's sit here," she said, pulling Lettie down with her onto the grass.

"That's your idea of a walk?" Lettie joked. She looked at Whitney and got worried. "Are you okay? You don't look so great."

"Gee, thanks, Lettie," she said, batting her eyelids and making a goofy air-kiss. "That's not what all the guys say. Except for *your* Daniel."

Lettie flushed.

"Speaking of sex, how is it with you and Daniel?" Whitney asked mischievously.

"Whitney!" Lettie's face got redder.

"What? You two are into each other, right? And you're exclusive, right? If there's no one else, what's the big deal?"

"You know I don't like talking about this stuff," Lettie answered. "I really appreciate that you haven't told anyone about that day you walked in on . . ."

"Your beginners' session?" Whitney scoffed. "What's to tell? That was Sex 101. All the rest of us have advanced to AP."

"Okay, that's enough," Lettie said, but she couldn't help laughing.

Whitney rubbed her head as if she had a headache.

"Did you eat today?" Lettie asked.

Whitney shrugged one shoulder. "I guess not. I was gonna get lunch with Angie but I got busy."

"I don't get why you hang out with Angie and Dina," Lettie said, seizing the chance. "They're so mean to everyone. Not just me. But you, too. Like what they said at Valentine's."

"Yeah, well, I set them straight the next day," Whitney snapped.

She lay back on the grass and closed her eyes. Finally she opened them. "Listen, Lettie. I need to tell you something. But you gotta promise not to freak."

She's going to tell me about her bulimia. I can't believe this was so easy.

"I sort of overheard you at home the other day, talking on your cell to LB about her new baby sister."

Oh. My. God.

A hard rock of dread formed in Lettie's stomach and tentacles of panic threatened to squeeze the breath out of her lungs.

"Whitney, what have you done? You didn't tell anyone, did you? Tell me you didn't tell your mother."

She already knew the answer without even waiting for it.

How could I have been so dumb, putting the conversation on speaker? I've ruined everything. How am I going to explain this to Laura Beth? She's never going to talk to me again. What's the media going to say about Arden? I've wrecked her life, too.

"Yeah, I did tell Mom," Whitney answered, adding quickly, "but don't lose your shit, Lettie. I planned it all out. Nothing bad's gonna happen. I fixed it. Really. Mom's writing a *positive* story."

Lettie was frantic. "Are you totally delusional? Your mother's a *gossip* columnist! And you've just given her the biggest scoop of her life!"

Whitney gave an exasperated sigh. "I *told* you, it's gonna be okay. She's already interviewed Libby Ballou and Senator Who-ever."

Lettie let out a gasp of horror. All the outrageous stuff Whitney had done in the past, all the spying and lying, was *nothing* compared to this.

"Trust me," Whitney said. "She's gonna spin it to make them look great! How they're, like, opening their arms to this little orphan so she can live happily ever after!"

"She's going to spin it, is she?" Lettie fumed. "What, the same way she spun that 'nice' story she wrote about *me* when I came to live with you?"

That was one article Lettie hadn't pasted in her scrapbook. Under the headline "How Opening Our Home Opened Our Hearts," Tracey Mills had humiliated Lettie, portraying her as an abandoned, needy foreigner and the Remicks as the "guardian angels" who would give her the chance to live the American Dream. Tracey had even compared herself to Angelina Jolie.

"Chill, Lettie. She's gonna do what I told her this time. I can't tell you why she will. But just trust me."

That word again. "Whenever I start to trust you, you screw me over. Why would I trust you again?"

Instead of shouting back as she expected her to, tears formed in Whitney's eyes and her shoulders slumped. She shut her eyes and sat silently for a few seconds.

"Because of Mara," she whispered.

"Who?" Lettie snapped. She was so sick of Whitney playing games with the truth.

"Mara was my sister," Whitney said.

Lettie's immediate reaction was . . . *one more trick*. But the look on Whitney's face erased her doubts. "Go on."

Whitney spoke gingerly, as if picking her way through her words.

"She died when I was five and she was seven, so I don't remember a whole lot, except that we were like a *real* family then. Not like how it is now."

Lettie was filled with such deep and instant sorrow and pity for Whitney, there was no room left for any anger. Poor thing. Every time you peeled away one messed up layer, there was another one under it. She shook her head, unable to come up with any words.

"Believe it or not, Mom was always hanging with us, taking us on picnics and stuff," Whitney continued. "And she and Dad would play Go Fish with us every night after dinner. We always had family dinners. The four of us."

Lettie couldn't imagine Tracey as warm and fuzzy. She wondered if Whitney was embellishing a little. But that was okay. Good memories were what comforted Lettie when she was overwhelmed by longing for her family.

"Mara and I were best friends. She even made Mom buy us matching outfits and she taught me stuff, like how to tie my shoes and make a daisy chain . . . I remember that."

"How come you never talked about her before?" Lettie asked. "There aren't even any photos of her at your house."

"We're not allowed to."

Whitney explained how after Mara accidently drowned, her parents sold the house, moved to a different neighborhood, and enrolled her in a new school.

She described the frustrating conversation in the car with her mother and the one she forced on both her parents that evening when her dad got home.

"Good thing you were making out with Daniel at the movies, cuz it wasn't pretty," she joked weakly.

She said she practically had to tie them to the sofa to get their attention. But eventually, they opened up like they never had before.

"We must have talked for over an hour. It's the longest time they've spent in the room with me since Mara died."

Her parents had told her they'd blamed themselves for Mara's death and that's why they'd shut down. Put on protective coats of armor, was how they put it.

"They even admitted what shitty parents they've been to me. Although I think the words they used were 'low key.'" Whitney rolled her eyes. "They promised to do better. The article about Arden is the first step."

Lettie put her arm around Whitney's shoulders and squeezed. "I'm so sorry, Whitney. How awful to have to keep all that locked up inside without being able to talk about it."

Whitney squirmed out of Lettie's hug.

"Yeah, whatever," she said gruffly. "Anyway, Mom promised to treat Arden the way she'd have wanted Mara and me treated. To write it as a kind of tribute to Mara and to prove to me that she really is trying to do better. And Dad's proofreading it to make sure."

"You could make your own tribute to Mara," Lettie suggested.

"What do you mean?"

"From what you've told me about Mara, I don't think she'd like you hanging with girls like Angie and Dina. She'd have wanted something better for you, don't you think?"

Whitney frowned. "My friends are none of your business, Lettie."

"I know that. But let me ask you something. Do you think of me as your friend, too?"

"Duh. Yeah. I just told you the biggest secret in my life."

"Will you be telling Angie and Dina, too?"

"What are you smoking?" Whitney retorted. "I'd *never* tell them about Mara. They'd treat it like some big joke."

"Exactly."

"I don't need you as my big sister stand-in, Lettie."

"No, of course not."

Whitney smirked. "Not unless you're offering something more . . . and Daniel makes it a threesome."

Lettie, remembering Tanya's kiss, blushed.

"Chill. I'm joking."

"Ha ha. You don't say." She took a couple of deep breaths. "I'm serious. I feel like we're actually starting to become real friends. And real friends tell each other when something's wrong."

"What's up now?" Whitney sighed.

"You. You don't take good care of yourself. For one thing, you take too many pills."

Whitney snorted. "You were popping pills for a while, remember?"

When she'd been so stressed about school and Paz joining the Paraguayan army, Lettie had grabbed a handful of Whitney's pills to help her sleep. But she hadn't abused them the way Whitney did.

"It's not just the pills. You don't eat properly. You're endangering your health."

Please. Just admit it. Don't make me say it.

"Who are you? Dr. Oz?" Whitney stood up, swaying slightly. "I knew I should've gone to the lacrosse game."

Lettie tugged on her skirt.

"Please sit down. I think you know what I'm trying to say. I know you have an eating disorder and I want to help you—"

"You're freakin' crazy!" Whitney shouted. "You don't know what you're talking about!"

Before Lettie could stop her, Whitney pulled out of her grasp and headed for the sidewalk.

"Whitney, wait! Please."

"Fuck you!" Whitney yelled over her shoulder.

Lettie knew she'd blown it. *I need help,* she thought. *Whitney claims Tracey and William have promised to be better parents. I guess we'll find out.* She picked up her cell and made the call.

TWENTY-SEVEN

"You are so lucky, Carolyn." Deborah Price sighed, pouring herself a cup from the silver Tiffany coffeepot. "It's what every woman dreams about. Having a man who makes you feel desirable and special." *Bob hasn't done that in years.*

"Thanks to you," Carolyn answered, setting a plate of biscotti on the coffee table. "You're the one who helped get Ike and me together."

"I just wish Andrew and Jackie had worked out, too . . . For their sakes, not just for the publicity. They had such chemistry."

"FYI, I've told both of them—not that they really need telling— not to comment to reporters when the media finally catches on," Carolyn said.

"Good, thanks," Deborah said. She wasn't one for regrets or dwelling on what-might-have-beens—no politician has that luxury. But as a mother, she couldn't help wondering . . .

"Were we wrong to turn them into Ankie?" she said aloud.

"I've thought about that a lot lately," Carolyn said, nodding. "It's not like we forced them together. They really *were* in love. But we certainly milked it for our benefit. And we definitely turned a blind eye when their relationship soured."

"Andrew's been a mess ever since the accident, that's for sure, though he seems to be pulling himself together at last," Deborah said, opening a packet of artificial sweetener and shaking it into her cup.

"I'm starting to second-guess myself on how we handled that, too," Carolyn answered. "Whether we should have just come right out and admitted he was driving."

"We had no choice!" Deborah said sharply. "We've gone over this! If we'd told the truth, it would have followed Andrew his whole life. It would be stamped on his permanent record."

Like Ted Kennedy and Chappaquiddick. He might have followed in JFK's footsteps, won the White House, if he hadn't driven off that bridge and let that poor girl drown.

Deborah stirred her coffee around and around, hardly aware of what she was doing.

"You're right. And don't forget Jennifer Cane, too," Carolyn said, nibbling the end of her biscotti. "She'd never forgive Andrew and she'd do everything in her power to ruin him." She checked her watch. "It's ten after two. I wonder if Libby's deliberately being late to put us off balance?"

Deborah just shrugged. She was still focused on her family. After sneaking out of the White House to spend an hour at Carolyn's town house, this was her chance to let off steam without fear of being overheard.

"Bob and Scott are no help with Andrew," she said. "My two sons act as though they're archrivals. Bob, of course, is too busy with his 'extracurricular activities'"—she made quote marks with her fingers—"to know or care about what's going. That's the way he's always been. But you know that."

The perfect First Family, what a joke. More like the fucked-up First Family and their screwed-up values.

She couldn't seem to stop her stream of consciousness.

"Maybe it's all my fault," she said, holding up her hand when Carolyn seemed about to come to her defense. "No, it's true. Maybe I'd have had a normal life—a good marriage and happy kids—if I'd never gotten into politics. I could have been working on my family's problems instead of taking on the country's."

She felt tears welling behind her eyes.

"You know, Carolyn, I should be used to his cheating by now. But when I saw that diamond bracelet, I really thought he was trying to turn things around. Inject some romance back into our marriage. What a fool I was."

Carolyn shook her head. "You're no fool. It's what you said earlier. We all crave love but sometimes that yearning blinds us to reality."

The doorbell rang and they looked at each other.

"I hope we don't have to 'persuade' her to cooperate," Carolyn said.

"She has to. What choice do any of us have?" Deborah replied, hearing one of her Secret Service agents open the front door.

Libby Ballou didn't just walk into the living room, she burst in. She was wearing one of her Republican-red power suits under a mink coat and five-inch heels that ensured Deborah wasn't towering over her when they hugged.

223

ella monroe

The three women exchanged kisses and sat down.

Carolyn handed her a coffee and passed her the plate of biscotti.

"No, thank you, darlin'. This bride-to-be needs to be watchin' her weight," she said, slipping her arms out of the mink. Her signature Ann Hand jeweled flag pin sparkled on her lapel.

She'll be flashing that patriotic pin on every outfit from now to Election Day. But I bet we won't be seeing that extravagant little animal skin on the campaign trail.

"My two dear friends, we've known each so long . . . Can you believe our little ones are about to graduate and go off to college?" Libby said, taking a dainty sip of coffee. "Now, where was I? Oh yes. I feel we can dispense with small talk."

Deborah's body stiffened. *She* was president. *She* was in charge here, not Libby.

Libby leaned over and put her hand on Deborah's arm.

"Oh, Deborah, honey, I'm so sorry this had to happen. Again. And that business with the tennis bracelet? Why that was just heartbreakin'," she added, playing with the huge diamond engagement ring on the chain around her neck. "You must want to skin Bob alive."

Deborah gritted her teeth.

"Libby, I'm sorry to interrupt, but we're on a tight schedule," Carolyn interjected. "We're all here because . . . ."

Libby finished the sentence. ". . . Because we know what this would do to both our campaigns if this unpleasantness ever got out."

So it's "our" campaigns? What are you running for, Libby?

Her tone was so sickly sweet, it took all of Deborah's famous

224

self-discipline not to shake off Libby's hand and order her out of the room the way she did with uncooperative lawmakers.

"Carolyn and I have a plan already in place, Libby," Deborah said firmly. "There's an immediate opening, based in London, with the Agency for International Development. It's for an expert to head a new education program. Lots of travel all through eastern Europe."

Carolyn added, "Frances is eminently qualified. It's a great career move."

And there'll be no career if she doesn't take it.

"Europe?" Libby mulled it over. "Aren't there a lot of royal families over there? Why, that's sheer genius. There's nothing like a romance with a prince to cure a broken heart. She'd be plumb crazy not to grab it!"

Deborah rolled her eyes at her chief of staff. "So it's settled then. Jeffrey needs to make it clear to her that she has no choice."

Libby raised her eyebrows.

"Jeffrey? Oh no. I'll handle Frances. This whole sordid matter is just between us girls. That way, if it ever gets out—not that it will, mind—but if it does, my Jeffrey has complete deniability. Those media vultures won't be able to touch him."

Yes, but they could destroy me. It looks like the Velvet Steamroller is back with a vengeance. Conniving little bitch.

The last person Carolyn spoke to before she finally got to bed that night was Libby.

"It's all done, Carolyn," Libby said. "It wasn't even a hard sell.

Not a word of protest about breakin' up with Bob. I believe she's happy as a clam. She's leavin' with a diamond bracelet and a job to die for. Oh, and I promised to upgrade her flight to first class."

One crisis averted. Let's see what tomorrow brings.

TWENTY-EIGHT

Jackie and Scott had been secretly hanging out since she killed off Ankie. They'd stolen brief moments after school, finding empty rooms for their hidden trysts at Excelsior and St. Thomas.

Sometimes they had so much homework, that's all they did. Now that Frances had stopped tutoring Scott—he told Jackie she'd gotten this great job offer overseas; he obviously had no idea how or why—Jackie was helping him with physics.

Other times, between classes, they snuck into the empty gym and made out behind the bleachers, hot and heavy and frantic.

It was so different from ninth grade, when they'd spent a lot of time together doing fun things like jumping into the Potomac from the rope swing and ice-skating at the Sculpture Garden on the Mall. When they were on the campaign trail with Aunt Deborah they'd sneak off for burgers in whatever town they were stuck in. They'd sometimes held hands and there *had been* a few kisses but that was about it.

In some ways it had been more fun than now, with Jackie constantly looking over her shoulder.

This afternoon they were in the Excelsior gardener's shed, a quaint stone cottage originally built as a gatehouse when the property was a fancy estate.

Jackie loved the earthy smell of the seedlings sprouting in the rows and rows of little pots. The air was warm and moist and sensual.

She and Scott were sitting on a worn sofa that sank in the middle, throwing them together. As if they needed an excuse. Jackie opened the physics book on her lap.

"When's your quiz, Scott?" she said, trying to concentrate.

"Right now," he joked, putting his hand on her knee. "The first question concerns matter and motion, energy and force."

He kissed her hard. Her lips burned with pleasure as his tongue sought hers. "How's that for energy?" he asked, breaking off for a second. He moved his hand under her skirt and up her thigh with firm, hard strokes that sent fiery jolts through her entire body.

"And I think I've got a handle on the motion stuff." He grinned as she moaned.

There was a loud thud and she leapt away from him.

"What's wrong?" he asked.

"I thought I heard someone," she said nervously.

"It was just the textbook. It fell on the floor," he told her.

"Oh. Okay."

"Jackie, when are we going to quit with all this cloak-and-dagger stuff?" he asked gently.

"I know. I know," Jackie said, straightening her skirt. "But it's still too soon. Can you imagine the media circus if word leaked out now? Every time your mom held a news conference, that's all they would ask her about."

"Yeah, it would be like Kate Middleton dumping William for Harry." Scott laughed.

"But most of all, I don't want to hurt your brother," she said, resenting how callous he sounded.

Scott's good mood vanished.

"So Andrew gets to screw me over one more time?"

Jackie was taken aback by his tone. "What do you mean? What did Andrew do to you?"

Scott laughed bitterly.

"What, Number One Perfect Son didn't tell you? Where'd you like me to start?"

His voice was annoyingly whiny. But she desperately needed to know what he meant so she bit her lip and waited for him to explain.

"Andrew *knew* I was smoking way too much weed, starting at the end of eighth grade. And he did nothing."

Jackie frowned. "I don't think that's right, Scott. I don't think *any* of us knew back then. I was hanging with you all the time in ninth grade and I didn't know, so why would Andrew?"

Scott shrugged. "Well, if he didn't know then, he sure knew when I got caught. He was the first person I called. To get me out of it."

"Huh?"

"Yeah. When the cop stopped me for having a busted taillight and found Taylor's weed, Andrew refused to intervene with the police for me. You know, get them to drop it."

"But Andrew was just a kid, too, back then. Why would you think he could pull strings with the police?"

He ignored her question. "Instead he gave me this big fucking lecture about being irresponsible and crap about consequences." He picked the physics book up off the floor and threw it across the room. "He sounded just like Mom."

He got up and paced back and forth in front of her.

"Scott, didn't you know?" she asked. "It was Andrew who went to your mom and dad and convinced them to talk to the police. Get the charges dropped in exchange for you going to reform school."

He stopped pacing and looked at her in surprise.

"Andrew's the reason all hell didn't break loose," she continued.

He shook his head as if to deny it.

"Who fed you that line? Wouldn't be Andrew, would it?"

Jackie felt like slapping him. "As a matter of fact, no, it wasn't. My mom told me."

He practically pouted. "Then why didn't he tell me he was going to help? Instead of lecturing me like he was better than me."

"I don't know. Maybe he was trying to put the fear of God in you to be more careful," Jackie suggested.

Scott sat back down next to her.

Jackie was struck by a sudden revelation.

"Is that why this stupid rivalry thing between you and Andrew got so intense?" she exclaimed.

"Even if what you said is true . . . What about the fact that as soon as my back was turned, the second I was sent away, he started dating *my* girlfriend?" Scott shot back.

Oh my God. He's trying to blame Andrew for everything.

"For one thing, I wasn't your girlfriend," she said, irritated.

"Not officially. Secondly, Andrew and I didn't get together until much, much later. And third, if you resented Andrew, why didn't you resent me, too?"

"You're making me feel like a jerk," Scott said, giving her a lopsided little-boy smile.

He leaned over, his anger dissipating, and they kissed softly. His kiss got more urgent and he pressed into her.

Jackie kissed him back, feeling the passion instinctively sweep up her body. But her mind was distracted. *I just told you you've been blaming your brother all this time for no reason and your reaction is to make out with me?*

He's immature, she thought. She wondered why she'd never noticed it until now. It wasn't surprising, really, since—if you didn't count the flirting and the kissing—they hadn't spent all that much time reconnecting in any meaningful way.

She tried to imagine him being her "total connection" the way Andrew had been. *Will we grow into it?* she wondered. *Do I want to even try? And if I'm so uncertain, is it worth hurting Andrew so badly on the off chance that Scott and I might connect?*

She slowly pulled her mouth from Scott's and gently pushed him away.

"Don't you find this really upsetting? Knowing now that the whole rivalry thing with Andrew was based on a series of misunderstandings?" Jackie asked.

"It's not just that, Jackie," Scott answered with a shrug. "Andrew and I just don't get along. If it wasn't that stuff, it would be something else . . ."

Jackie was disgusted.

"That's a ridiculous thing to say," she said hotly. "Genetically, there's no one closer to you than your brother. There's a biological bond there, whether you like it or not, and you owe it to him and yourself to sit down and work it out. Or at least try."

He threw her a puzzled look, which she ignored.

"But I don't think you and Andrew can do that if you and I are together. It would just end up being about me instead of what it's really about. Which is the two of you."

It took him a moment to realize what she was really saying. "You're dumping me?" he asked, shocked.

"I'm not dumping you, Scott," she said gently. "Our relationship never really got off the ground. It was mostly just flirting and sneaking around and making out."

And she had to admit she found him unbelievably hot and probably always would. But it wasn't enough.

Finally, she was making a decision.

"Don't you see?" she said. "We just can't be."

TWENTY-NINE

"'Who said all politicians are hypocrites? Not presidential hopeful Jeffrey Ives. He doesn't just talk family values, he lives them.'"

Libby Ballou was making Laura Beth read Tracey Mills's blog out loud to her, insisting she was too nervous to read it herself.

"That's nice, giving Jeffrey credit right off the top," her mother interrupted.

Laura Beth nodded, though she thought she and her mama were the ones who deserved all the credit. After all, they were the ones making the big sacrifice, not Jeffrey.

If only Mama had let me be included in the interview, I could have spun it my way. But her mother had insisted that she and Jeffrey go alone because "we're used to handling untrustworthy journalists like Tracey Mills."

Laura Beth forced herself to read on.

"'Here's my superexclusive scoop: Senator Ives and his fiancée,

Republican socialite Libby Ballou, are adopting an orphaned teenaged girl! Even though the thirteen-year-old was fathered out of wedlock by Mrs. Ballou's late husband, political consultant Preston Ballou!'"

Laura Beth stumbled over the last painful sentence. *It's official. Now everyone knows Daddy cheated on Mama and me.*

"Why did she have to say that?" she asked.

Her mama looked at her in disbelief.

"It was not an immaculate conception, darlin'. She said it as politely as one can. There are much more unpleasant ways she could have put it."

That's fine for you to say, Laura Beth thought. *You don't have to face the kids at school tomorrow.*

Her mother nudged her. "Go on. Keep readin'."

"'After learning of the child's existence just weeks ago—following the death of the young girl's mother—they immediately came to her rescue. All they saw was a child in need of a home and loving parents.'"

Despite the article's obvious flaws—no mention yet of her own sacrifice, for one thing—Laura Beth had to admit that Lettie was right. All in all, Whitney's mom had written a "positive" story.

Laura Beth had been furious when Lettie fessed up about Whitney overhearing their phone call.

Even after all these years of living in D.C. and learning everything Laura Beth and Jackie had tried to teach her, Lettie was still incredibly naïve. *Fancy her putting any calls on speaker when that two-faced sneak, Whitney, and her shameless mother were within spyin' distance.*

Laura Beth focused again on the computer screen. What she read next started making her mad all over again.

She was almost at the end and yet there was still no word about *her*, Laura Beth. *After all,* I'm *the new big sister.*

When she finally got around to seeing her name, Mrs. Mills had the audacity to put the two ugly stepsisters in the very same sentence. Referring to *"the wonderful, blended family-to-be with three—and now—four daughters, Laura Beth Ballou, Frances and Dina Ives, and Arden Oliver."*

"Why is she lumpin' me in with Frances and Dina? I'm the blood relative here," Laura Beth demanded to know. "I'm the one who's gonna be saddled with all the responsibility."

"Laura Beth, are you forgettin'? You're goin' to be away at college in the fall. If you're at Juilliard, you'll be so busy you won't even have much time for visits home."

"I will too, Mama. Sol will be at Georgetown. I'll be here a lot."

It was as if she hadn't spoken.

"Dina will be the one showin' Arden around, introducin' her to new little friends," her mother continued. "Takin' her shoppin' and all."

Not if I can help it. No way is that heinous female gonna get her fangs into that innocent girl. Even if it means playing protective big sister.

Carolyn Shaw couldn't believe the garbage she was reading. She was shocked, although she shouldn't have been. Preston Ballou had been a first-class sleaze. But a thirteen-year cover-up? It had Jennifer Cane's fingerprints all over it. And so did the leak with its positive, pro-family spin.

She forced herself to read the rest of the nauseatingly gushy blog. Including how Tracey Mills had been given exclusive access to follow the family throughout the campaign.

Carolyn felt a headache coming on. She grabbed her iPhone and hit the third person—after Deborah and Jackie—on her favorites list.

"Ike? Got any kids I don't know about? Who might be available for adoption?" she joked weakly.

Her next thought was like a blow to the stomach. *I wonder how many kids Bob Price has fathered? Let's hope we never find out.*

THIRTY

Whitney burst into Lettie's room without knocking. "I told you! I told you it would be okay, Lets!" she yelped, grabbing Lettie's hands and jumping up and down like a little kid. She was so close Lettie could smell the minty spray on her breath.

"Yeah, I just read it," Lettie answered. "Your mom really is trying to do the right thing."

Whitney plopped down on the bed.

"Plus, my little insurance policy didn't give her any choice."

"Your what?"

"Let's just say I have a little something on Mom that she knew I'd use if she didn't come through." Whitney giggled, practically giddy with excitement at what she'd pulled off. "Aren't you proud of me, Lets? I'm finally learning how this town operates. And you know me, I'm a big operator."

Lettie shook her head and nervously chewed on a fingernail.

She sat down on the bed next to Whitney and braced for what was coming.

Somebody knocked on the door and Lettie's palms instantly got sweaty as Tracey and William walked into the bedroom. *Right on time.*

"What are you guys doing home?" Whitney asked, looking puzzled.

Her father closed the door behind him and her mother, her eyes red, sat on the end of the bed.

"What's wrong?" Whitney asked, concerned. Then the worried look on her face turned angry as if she suddenly understood why they were there.

"What the fuck?" she screamed, turning on Lettie. "What have you done, you meddling little bitch?"

The look on her face was murderous, her mouth twisted into an ugly, agonized sneer. Lettie's skin burned as Whitney's eyes bore into her like red-hot lasers.

Before she could say anything, Tracey reached for her daughter's hand.

"Whitney, we haven't been very good at showing it, but we do love you with all our hearts," Tracey said.

"You are more precious to us than anything," her dad added.

He reached out to stroke Whitney's hair but she jerked away and wrenched her hand from her mom's.

Lettie forced herself to meet Whitney's eyes.

"I know it's scary, Whitney. Really scary," she said. "But we're doing this because we care about what happens to you."

"You don't know anything about how I feel!"

Whitney leaped off the bed and tried to open the door. It was locked. She whirled around. "Give me the fucking key. I'm so outta here."

Her parents shook their heads in unison.

"We have to talk about this—" her father started to stay.

"About what? How you treated me like I was as dead as Mara all these years? Except when Mom needed me for her lame column to make her look good?" She turned her back and pulled furiously at the door handle.

"Whitney, we're sorry. We wish we could change the past, but—" her mother pleaded.

"The past? What about the present? It all sucks." The handle rattled and the door shook but didn't give way.

"We know you're hurting," Tracey murmured. "We want to change that. We know you have an eating disorder and it's destroying you. We are going to help you beat it. We don't want to lose you."

"You're wrong. I. Do. Not. Have. An. Eating. Disorder," Whitney said defiantly, grabbing the handle with both hands. Finally, giving up, she sank to the floor, her back against the locked door.

Lettie got off the bed and sat down next to her, trying to hide how scared she felt. "I don't want to lose you, either, Whitney," she told her softly, her voice trembling a little. "You're my friend and I'm not going to let you down."

Whitney stared stonily ahead. "I. Do. Not. Have. An. Eating. Disorder," she repeated, hugging her knees and rocking as if to comfort herself.

Tracey and William joined them on the floor.

Lettie had spent several days reading up on interventions. She knew this could go on for hours. *But even if that's what it takes, I'm staying.*

THIRTY-ONE

Andrew paused just outside the Blue Room.

He'd been stressed all week at the thought of facing his friends.

It should have been fun. His oldest friends getting together for breakfast in one of the most breathtaking rooms in the White House. And later, all of them joining the crowds outside to celebrate the Easter Egg Roll.

Yet he felt like an outsider.

It would be the first time he'd seen Daniel since Taylor's twin had apologized. *Should I shake his hand or hug him?*

A *hug,* he decided. Because Daniel had done more than just apologize. He'd made it possible for Andrew to think positively about his future.

He hadn't seen Jackie, either. Not since their talk in his bedroom. He longed to see her, yet he cringed at the thought of it.

While he'd felt a wave of relief that all the pretending was over, it was still a fresh wound in his gut. Not that he wasn't expecting it and not that he could blame her. God knows he'd been a jerk, drinking too much, slacking off in his studies, acting belligerent around Jackie when he intended to be anything but.

He rubbed the empty spot on his finger where he used to wear the abstinence ring. He'd thrown it away after one of his lowest points, the public fistfight with Daniel outside the Homecoming dance. Wearing or not wearing the ring was irrelevant. He and Jackie hadn't—and now they never would—made love.

They came so close, even after Taylor. He could taste her on his lips. Feel her hands, tender yet scorching . . .

He forced himself to stop the fantasy. Because that's all it was.

Instead, he thought about Laura Beth and Lettie. Laura Beth, who used to practically swoon whenever he was near. And Lettie, always so reluctant to judge, who saw the good in everyone. But even she had almost believed Daniel's worst suspicions about him. *Will they snub me, knowing every shitty thing I've said and done?*

And then there was Scott, who turned everything into a competition. Including their quest for Jackie. *How do I make that right?* It was too late for Sam and Taylor, but perhaps not for him and Scott.

There was so much at stake today. *This is my chance to start turning everything around.*

He squared his shoulders and walked in.

The round mahogany table was set for nine, and everyone was there except Andrew.

Number One Perfect Son must be stalling so he can make his grand entrance, Scott thought grumpily.

He'd been looking forward to this day as his chance to get Jackie alone and persuade her to change her mind. Starting with sitting next to her at breakfast.

But his mother, her usual bossy self, had taken charge of the seating and ordered place cards for the table. She'd put him next to Laura Beth and Sol. Vic Hazelton, wearing his dress uniform, was on one side of Jackie. The other empty chair was reserved for his effing brother.

Jackie was pointing out the various historic paintings on the wall to Vic, who looked fascinated. Which made Scott wonder if the soldier was all worked up about art or having the undivided attention of the sexiest girl in the room. The cliché about girls falling for strong, silent types and guys in uniform made his chest burn with jealousy.

Laura Beth, even more animated than usual, had spent the first five minutes gushing over the oval-shaped parlor, the gilded wood-and-crystal chandelier that hung from the center of the room, and the panoramic view of the South Lawn. Crowds of children were already squealing and chasing White House aides dressed as giant Easter "rabbits."

Now Laura Beth was yammering on about the china.

"Oh look, it has a butterfly and a dragonfly and a cute little ladybug. There's even a snail," she burbled, examining one of the plates from the Bushes' private dinner setting. When the plate started to slip out of her hands, Scott reached over and took it.

"Oh, Scott, thank you, thank you!" she said effusively. He noticed the linen napkin in her lap was twisted into a tight ball.

Usually he found her hilarious, but right now she was driving him nuts. *How does Sol stand it 24/7?*

But Sol definitely seemed to be into it. He was grinning at

Daniel and shaking his head good-naturedly. "Hey, Daniel, con-gratulations on Penn," he said. "And Scott, I heard you got into Johns Hopkins. Way to go."

Scott grunted. "Yeah, thanks."

Lettie, with Daniel and Tanya on either side of her, was up-dating them on Paraguay. Something about a possible agreement between the government and the protesters over there. Bor-r-ing. Though the news apparently excited Tanya so much, she grabbed Lettie's arm and clung to it. He noticed Daniel throw them a quizzical look.

"I thought you said Andrew was coming?" he heard Vic ask Jackie.

"He'll be here. He's the star of the show," Scott butted in.

"Oh, okay. I just wanted to make sure," Vic said, glancing at his watch.

Looks like the favorite son has another adoring fan.

One of the six doors opened and Andrew ambled into the room, smiling.

Scott wished he didn't feel so much anger toward his brother. Jackie was right when she said they needed to sit down and hash it out. He just couldn't face it yet. Not until he tried one last time to get her back.

He watched his older brother pull out the chair next to Jackie. Even though they didn't touch, he could almost see the heat com-ing off their bodies. Jealousy prickled under his skin.

Why do I want her so much? Because of our history together? Because she's playing hard to get? Because she's the irresistible It Girl? Because Andrew took her away from me? He wasn't sure he knew the answer. Maybe all those reasons.

Instead of sitting down, Andrew stayed standing.

"Hey guys," Andrew said loudly. "This is going to sound corny but it's important I say it."

Everyone, even Laura Beth, stopped talking.

Andrew cleared his throat. "Tanya, Vic, at the risk of sounding like my mother, what I'm about to say is off the record, okay?" He laughed, but waited for their nods. "You guys are my oldest and closest friends, and Scott, it goes without saying, I love you, bro."

We just don't like each other very much.

"This has been a tough year for all of us and I've let all of you down when I should have been there for you. I just want you to know that I'm truly sorry and I'm determined to make a fresh start."

There was a stunned silence. Scott looked at Jackie, whose eyes were wet, but she was smiling and staring up at Andrew. Everyone seemed to be waiting for him, Scott, to say something. But his mind was a blank. Fortunately, Sol jumped in.

"That's the best news we've had in months," Sol said. "We love you, too, Andrew, and we're here to help you any way we can." He grinned. "Now can you please sit down and shut up? We're all starving."

Everybody else had gone to the Easter Egg Roll, leaving Laura Beth alone with Sol.

"I thought they'd never leave! I was about fit to bust over breakfast!" Laura Beth exclaimed.

"I thought you seemed a little hyper," Sol said. "What's going on?"

She opened her pocketbook and pulled out an envelope, waving it under his nose.

"You heard from Juilliard?" Sol asked instantly. "What did they say?"

"It just came in the mail as I was leavin'. I wanted you to be with me when I opened it."

She took a long, deep breath and ripped it open. Then let out a shrill and completely defeated cry. She dropped the letter on the table, where they were still sitting, and slumped against Sol's chest.

It must be a mistake.

Sol picked up the letter and read it.

"Oh, Laura Beth. I'm really, really sorry," he murmured, folding her into his arms.

Mama lied to me. She lied to me again. Just like she lied about Arden.

"Mama said she was going to pull strings for me. I bet she never even tried. She thinks she can force me to go to Sewanee, her precious little alma mater. Well, she's wrong!"

Sol handed her the glass of water in front of her. She waved it away.

"Laura Beth, your mother wouldn't do that," Sol ventured, rubbing her back. "I'm pretty certain having connections doesn't make any difference at Juilliard."

She sat back and glared at him, shaking off his touch and crossing her arms.

"So what you're saying is, I'm not good enough."

"No, not at all, Laura Beth. We talked about this, remember? It's so incredibly hard to get in there. It doesn't mean you don't deserve to. You're unbelievably talented."

She began to cry. She'd never in her whole life felt so desperate or disappointed. Learning about her daddy and Arden was *nothing* compared to this.

"What am I gonna do, Sol? All my dreams are gone."

She let Sol take her in his arms again. But she barely listened to what he was saying. Something about those other schools in New York.

"Sol, take me out of here. I can't bear to face anyone," she pleaded.

"Do you want me to take you home?"

"No. That's the last place I want to be."

Jackie was reading *Bailey Bilby Saves the Easter Bunny*, a sweet picture book about a furry little Australian animal. A group of first graders were sitting enthralled at her feet. But she was having trouble focusing, her mind still reeling from Andrew's unexpected and heartfelt apology.

Members of the public swarmed all over the South Lawn. Aunt Deborah was at the actual egg-and-spoon race, posing with an angelic-looking toddler in a frilly pink dress as camera shutters clicked wildly.

Jackie and her friends were assigned to different reading groups. Nearby, Andrew and Scott were taking turns reading *Peter Rabbit* to a huddle of rapt kids. She wondered if they had sorted out their differences yet. She doubted it from the way Scott had been giving Andrew jealous looks at breakfast and his silence after Andrew's apology. *It's not your business anymore, Jackie.*

She held up the illustrated page for the children to see.

"'When the little girl grabbed the bilby by her ears to hug her, she gave a tiny squeal. "I don't want to hurt you. I love you," the little girl cried,'" Jackie read.

Watch out, kids, love can really hurt, she wanted to warn them.

Her throat was sore from trying to be heard above the happy

noise of excited children. As she bent down to pick up her Nalgene, a different kind of scream pierced the air.

"No!!"

The sound came from the direction of Andrew's reading group. It was followed by more screams and the noise of children crying. She jumped up, knocking over her chair, and without even thinking, she ran toward the commotion.

She pushed her way through the crowd and reached a circle of uniformed Secret Service agents who'd been roaming the grounds.

"I'm Jackie Whitman! Let me through," she cried. From behind her, a couple of medics pushed her aside. She grabbed the rear guy's coat and forced her way through.

Andrew was collapsed in his chair, blood seeping through his shirt. His face was deathly white and his eyes were closed as the medics hovered over him. His breath came out in strangled rasps.

Less than a foot away, a tangle of bodies writhed on the ground. A male figure in a shirt and khakis staggered to his feet, a bloody knife in his hand.

Scott. He looked dazed, his empty eyes staring straight through her.

Oh God. Oh no. Scott's stabbed Andrew and it's all my fault!

She heard her own voice pleading at the agents on the ground: "Get up! Take the knife from Scott! Someone stop him!"

Why was no one listening? It was as if she wasn't there.

It's up to me, she realized.

Scott was almost close enough to touch. She leapt in front of him and made a grab for the knife—just as two of the agents stood up, holding on to a slumped figure, his hands cuffed. He was wearing some kind of army uniform. Several brass buttons were missing and the pants were caked in mud.

The young man raised his head and looked right at Jackie. A gash on his forehead dripped blood down his cheek. A sad smile of recognition spread across his face.

"Surprise! I did it for you, Jackie. So we can be together," he whispered.

It was Private Vic Hazelton. Her stalker. Andrew's attacker.

THIRTY-TWO

As Jackie turned the corner onto Twenty-third Street, a black Lincoln Town Car pulled up to the curb outside George Washington University Hospital. Within seconds, a woman wrapped in a camel-hair coat emerged from the hospital entranceway, walked briskly to the car, and slid inside.

Jackie ducked behind a vendor's street cart.

What's Jennifer Cane doing here?

She watched the car disappear and entered the hospital lobby, immediately spotting Secret Service Agent Mark Davenport who would escort her up to Andrew's private room.

"How's he doing, Mark?" she asked.

"Much better this morning," the agent answered, smiling. He turned somber. "I feel . . . I just . . . Why wasn't I there to prevent the attack?"

"It wasn't your fault," Jackie said, seeing the agent flustered and emotional for the first time ever.

She didn't say anything more. She still wasn't sure whether to trust him, whether he had actual feelings or not. He'd helped cover up the truth about Andrew driving Taylor's car, but was loyalty his motivation or possible blackmail?

They walked past the security detail stationed in the hall and he left her outside Andrew's room, where two more Secret Service agents were standing guard.

Jackie tiptoed into the room, which was filled with flowers and balloons.

She pulled up a chair next to Andrew's sleeping face. An enormous bouquet of brilliantly colored peonies sat on his bedside table along with a basket filled with oversized rainbow Whirly Pops from Dylan's Candy Bar in New York.

She studied his features, all so familiar. The brown stubble on his cheeks that used to tickle so enticingly when he nuzzled her neck. The hair that always looked sexily mussed no matter how many times he combed it. The soft lips that could kiss so hard.

Stop it. It's over, remember? You decided no Andrew, no Ankie, no Scott.

There was no trace of bitterness or self-destructive anger on his face. He looked more rested and peaceful than he had in over a year.

She didn't want to wake him yet. It had been only a week since the stabbing and he still needed to rest.

Her eyes wandered around the room, taking in all the state-of-the-art equipment. Andrew was getting the best medical care that the Prices' money could buy.

Perhaps if Vic Hazelton had gotten better taxpayer-funded care for his brain injury, Andrew might not even be here.

As much as she despised Dr. Rosen for using her, she still believed in his cause. The nation was willing to send young men and women like Vic off to war, but was unwilling to properly care for them when they came home physically and mentally damaged.

To her, Vic was almost as much a victim as Andrew.

Although Vic had confessed to writing the stalker's notes and making all the threatening calls, he denied ever wanting to physically hurt Jackie. He insisted he merely wanted to protect her from Andrew. So she could fall in love with him. Even if that meant kidnapping her or killing Andrew to make it happen.

He was still being psychologically and medically evaluated and it was unclear if he would ever stand trial or what his future held.

Andrew opened his eyes, smiling slowly when he saw Jackie sitting beside him. "I must have fallen asleep. I'm glad you're here instead of The Fixer."

Jackie gave a start. "She was here to see you?"

He nodded and struggled to sit up, wincing in pain. His PJ top was unbuttoned, revealing a large bandage on his chest. The knife had missed his heart but it had punctured a lung.

"For a knife wound that wasn't life-threatening, this sure hurts like hell," he grumbled. He smacked his lips. "My mouth's dry. Can you a hand me a lollipop, please?"

She peeled off the cellophane wrapping and handed him one. "Who sent you these?"

He grinned. "Who else? Laura Beth. She sent the peonies, too. Don't tell her, but the smell's overwhelming. But she'll be upset if she sees they're not front and center."

"Has she been in?"

Andrew shook his head. "No. I'm surprised."

"She's going through a lot right now. In addition to Arden, she got rejected by Juilliard."

"Shit. Poor Laura Beth."

"I know. It's awful."

"How's she handling it?"

The way she handles all drama. Loudly.

"It takes a stabbing to take her off the front page," Jackie joked.

Laura Beth had called her as soon as Andrew's condition was upgraded, and Jackie had rushed over to the house right away.

"You're one of the most resilient people I know, Laura Beth," I told her. "Look at everything you've had to cope with. Losing your father. Your mother trying to break up you and Sol. This new information about Arden. And now Juilliard."

Laura Beth nodded, sniffling.

"If anyone can turn lemons into lemonade, it's you," I said.

"How much lemonade can a girl consume?" she said, allowing herself a tiny smile. Good, she can joke about it, sort of.

"Look at Arden," I said. "You're starting to accept her. You told me the other day that you were going to take her shopping, teach her all about D.C., who to hang with, who to avoid—"

"Yes, well, that's because I don't want Dina influencing her."

"Yes, but that shows you're starting to accept the reality of the situation."

"I suppose," Laura Beth said reluctantly. "But Juilliard. That's different. That was my entire future. All my Broadway dreams."

"Since when has 'no' ever stopped you?"

"Well, I can hardly sit on Juilliard's doorstep till they let me in, now can I, Jackie?"

"You'd do it in a second if you thought it would work," I teased. "But who says Juilliard is your only ticket to Broadway? Tisch and Sarah Lawrence are fantastic opportunities." And she'd been accepted at both.

"Yes, but it's not Juilliard," she insisted.

"Well, maybe Juilliard wasn't meant to be."

"What do you mean?"

"You have so much more to offer, Laura Beth," I said, really laying it on thick. "Juilliard would suck up every waking moment. You'd never get to see Sol. And I know how much you're looking forward to traveling with the campaign."

I saw a little flicker of light in her eyes.

Damn. I'm gonna regret that last remark. The last thing I should be doing is encouraging her about the presidential race.

Laura Beth gave one of her dramatic sighs. "I don't know, Jackie. My mind's a jumble."

Jackie smiled at Andrew. "Between Sol, Lettie, and me I think we can convince her that not getting into Juilliard does not herald the Apocalypse."

They both laughed.

"I can talk to her, too, when I see her," Andrew offered.

"That'd be great."

She remembered that she'd started to ask him about his visit from The Fixer.

"Andrew, what did Jennifer Cane want?"

"I guess, to forgive me. She said . . ."

Jackie's stomach somersaulted. "Forgive you?" She lowered her voice to a whisper. "Did she find out you were driving?"

He shook his head. "No! God! She said she wanted to tell me

not to blame myself for Taylor. She didn't mention Sam by name, of course, but she said Taylor was going through some hard stuff right before the accident and had been acting erratically."

It confirmed what Jackie suspected. Jennifer Cane knew what had freaked out Taylor. But she'd never tell Jackie. And Jackie knew better than to ask. Her only hope was the mystery woman on Taylor's phone, and she hadn't tried to reach her since before the stabbing.

I've got to keep trying. I'll call again as soon as I get home.

"And get this," Andrew continued. "She said she was sorry she hadn't come to me after it first happened. She must have just discovered she has maternal instincts after all."

He grinned. "Maybe I oughta get stabbed more often. Not only has Jennifer Cane changed her stripes, but Scott turns out to be a hero."

Jackie's face burned over how she'd thought *Scott,* his own brother, had stabbed Andrew. When he'd actually saved Andrew's life by wrestling Vic to the ground and getting the knife. A table knife Vic had swiped from their breakfast in the Blue Room.

"Yes, he is." She nodded. "Now would be a good time for you two to end your feud."

"Yeah, I know. The morning of the breakfast, I was thinking that we needed to sit down and talk. I'm the big brother. I should've taken the initiative as soon as he moved back home."

Jackie decided to tell him the reason for Scott's anger. How Scott thought Andrew had abandoned him when he asked for help with the police.

"But I didn't!" Andrew exclaimed when she finished.

"I know that. But Scott didn't."

Guys could be so dumb sometimes. If the two brothers had

just communicated with each other, they could have avoided all this wasted hurt and resentment.

"Don't worry, I'll fix it with Scott," Andrew said, reaching for her hand. "At least you and I aren't fighting. We're talking like friends."

"Like we used to be," she reminded him.

She gently extracted her hand, even though seeing him like this—sweet, sensitive, positive—reminded her of why she first fell in love with him.

It almost made her want to climb into his arms. Forget that the last fifteen months of hell had ever happened.

Whitney was hanging with Lettie in the seniors' lounge during midmorning break. She'd kicked off her shoes and put her feet up on the coffee table, nibbling on a protein bar and watching Lettie's fingers race across her iPhone screen.

Fortunately the other *Crapital* Girls were somewhere else. Jackie was supposedly playing nurse with Andrew. And Laura Beth had a makeup test or make-out session or something.

"It's break time, Lettie. You better be sexting Daniel," Whitney joked.

Lettie shook her head, still tapping. "No. I'm setting up a time to meet with my history professor to go over my paper."

And I'm the one who needs therapy?

Now that she'd admitted she had an eating disorder—it was a miracle her mother hadn't insisted on taping the three-hour intervention as an episode for *Celebrity Rehab with Dr. Drew*—she'd started regular therapy . . . before she lost motivation and her parents lost interest.

"Maybe I should drop out of school now and check myself into inpatient treatment," she said casually, almost to herself.

Lettie didn't seem to be listening.

"Since I dumped Franklin. And Paz turned me down for Prom . . ." Whitney poked Lettie with her foot. "By the way, thanks for all your help with that, Lets. Not. I could spend Prom night in a clinic, getting 'examined' by a hot intern instead."

Lettie looked up, frowning. "Did you say something about dropping out?"

Whitney shrugged. "Yeah. I think I'll drop school so I can jump-start my comeback."

Lettie plunked down the iPhone and faced Whitney. "That's crazy talk!" she said, exasperated. "You're *not* dropping out. There's absolutely no reason why you can't continue your outpatient treatment and stay in school and graduate with our class. Then you can concentrate all summer on getting better and be ready to start college in the fall."

Whitney looked sheepish. "Um. Yeah. About college . . ."

"I don't understand why you still haven't heard from anyone."

Shit. I guess I better tell her.

"Put it this way. I haven't heard any yeses and I haven't heard any nos." She grimaced. *"Comprendo?"*

Lettie's face turned dark red as if she were trying to stop the top of her head from exploding.

"You didn't apply anywhere?" Her voice was incredulous. "What were you thinking?! Do your parents know?"

"Get real, Lettie. You know them. They thought I was applying but they never bothered asking to see the applications."

"So why was I working with you all year to keep your grades

up? There are plenty of places you could have applied to. Or do you have some grand plan?"

"Uh, I dunno. Go to surf school? I'm not big on planning ahead, other than making sure I got a couple of condoms in my wallet."

It was just a joke but Lettie looked like she was about to gag. "Puhleeze," she said.

Even to Whitney's own ears, it sounded lame. What *had* she been thinking? Other than about heading back to Cali and her old friends. Not that she kept in touch with them all that much anymore.

Just one more thing to talk to the shrink about.

Angie burst into the lounge, Dina in tow. Lettie sat back silently, watching to see how things would play out.

"Yo, Whitney!" Angie exclaimed. Her eyes darted over Lettie as though she wasn't even there. "We've been looking for you everywhere. This little study corner is the last place I expected to find you!"

"Yeah, what's up with you?" Dina rolled her eyes. "We're bailing to go hang at the Tidal Basin. Some of the guys are renting paddleboats."

Lettie picked up her iPhone, pretending to study the screen. Out of the corner of her eye, she saw Whitney grimace.

"Paddleboats?" She snorted. "What are ya, six years old? I suppose after that, you're gonna ride the merry-go-round on the Mall?"

"Hey, we're gonna get stoned first," Angie said, ignoring her sarcasm.

Whitney seemed to be mulling it over. Lettie's heart sank. It was unrealistic to expect Whitney to suddenly drop the two mean girls but she'd still *hoped* it might happen.

Angie tapped her foot impatiently.

"What? You think hanging with Lame Lettie'll be more fun?" Dina spoke up. Both girls giggled.

"You know, I think I'll stay here," Whitney said slowly.

"Whatever," Angie said, shrugging. "Catch you later."

They slammed the door behind them.

"How come you're not going with them?" Lettie asked.

"I don't need the stress." Whitney wriggled her bare toes. "I decided there's already too much toxic stuff in my life. You know how you're all hung up on the *Butterfly Effect*?"

Lettie nodded.

"Well, I'm calling this the *Mara Effect*."

Lettie was amazed. "You're not gonna hang with Angie and Dina anymore?"

Whitney shrugged. "I didn't say that. It's more like I'm weaning myself off them. Without cutting off all my party options. You know?"

Lettie tried to hide her disappointment. For a second, she'd thought Whitney was going cold turkey. *At least it's a start.*

"Like you're weaning yourself off the pills?"

"Yeah."

"So, you want to do something later?"

Whitney grinned. "How about we ditch school and go get high and ride the paddleboats? I still got some Chronic left over from Franklin. Just you and me. You gotta admit, Angie and Dina had a great idea."

Lettie just laughed. "We're not skipping class, Whitney. But we can do it after school."

THIRTY-THREE

Jackie sat in her Prius, her fingers drumming on the steering wheel. She'd been studying the house across the street for at least fifteen minutes. Practicing what she was going to say.

The house looked deceptively normal—a typical Washington brick colonial with a white picket fence enclosing a manicured lawn and two flowering dogwoods. There was definitely someone at home. A beige sedan sat in the driveway and lace curtains fluttered in an open downstairs window.

As Laura Beth says, it's showtime.

Sucking in her breath, she willed herself out of the car, across the street, and through the front gate. Before she could change her mind, she walked quickly up the brick path to the red front door and rang the brass buzzer.

"Coming!" a woman's voice called from inside.

The butterflies in Jackie's stomach suddenly morphed into savage creatures fighting to get out.

You can't throw up. Do your breathing exercises.

The door opened.

"Hello, Mrs. Rogers," she said. Her voice came out more nervous than she'd like.

Get a grip. She cleared her throat and spoke louder. "I'm Jackie Whitman."

"I know who you are," Pamela Rogers answered, the smile vanishing. "I have nothing to say to you."

The woman started to close the door in Jackie's face. But Jackie was too quick. She pushed back with her foot and then her whole body. The door gave way and Jackie stumbled inside. Just like in the movies.

"I told you we have nothing to discuss," Mrs. Rogers insisted. But her voice shook.

"I know that's not true and I'm not leaving until I get the truth," Jackie answered, sounding way more confident than she felt.

She eased her way past Mrs. Rogers and kept walking down the hall.

"Where do you think you're going?" There was panic, now, in her voice.

"I'm looking for somewhere comfortable to sit while I'm waiting for answers." Jackie couldn't believe her own boldness, but she had no choice.

Two days earlier, someone had finally answered the mystery number she'd been dialing off and on since after Taylor's memorial. Not a woman. A man.

"Hello? My name's Jackie Whitman," I said as soon as he picked up.

"Oh, yes. Jackie," he cut in. "You were a friend of Taylor's. I'm Taylor's uncle, Michael Rogers. I think my wife, Pamela, and I met you at her grandparents' house one time."

I felt so stupid. How could I have forgotten that Jennifer Cane had a much younger sister? I could have saved myself weeks of stress and frustrating phone calls that always ended in a full mailbox.

Flustered, I tried to think of what to say next.

"Yes, we did. Uh, is your wife there by any chance?"

"Sure." I heard him put down the phone as a voice in the background asked, "How did she get our unlisted number?"

There was a muffled response and then Pamela Rogers picked up the receiver. "Hello, Jackie. What can I do for you, dear?"

My heart stopped. It was the voice. No question. I willed myself to be strong and not to cry.

"Mrs. Rogers, I've been trying to reach you for weeks."

"We were away. We just got back."

"I got your number from Taylor's cell, Mrs. Rogers." I heard Taylor's aunt gasp. "You left several scary voice mails just before she died."

There was a long silence.

"Mrs. Rogers?"

"It was just a little family misunderstanding. Nothing important, Jackie."

"Well, Taylor was acting really, really upset before the accident and your voice on the phone sounded frightened. Taylor was my best friend, Mrs. Rogers, and I need to understand what was going on in her life."

The aunt's voice turned icy. It freaked me out. It was like Jennifer Cane was on the other end.

"It was nothing. It's not relevant. I can't help you, I'm sorry." The line went dead.

The dark hallway led into what looked like a family room, with an overstuffed sofa and a side table displaying photos of Taylor and Daniel at different ages.

Jackie, with Pamela Rogers on her heels, sat down on the sofa and pulled Taylor's cell out of her purse.

Without a word, Jackie pushed the play button and put it on speaker. The anguished words bounced off the walls and the ceiling and echoed in her head. *"Please, please, don't tell Daniel."*

"I told you on the phone, Jackie, it was just a silly family fight that I didn't want Daniel dragged into," Mrs. Rogers said abruptly, standing over her.

Jackie ignored her and played the next message.

"Taylor, please call me, honey. Please, I'm begging you." Then the third, the scariest of all: *"We have to talk. This is not just about you, Taylor. This could be dangerous if they find out."*

Mrs. Rogers swayed and sat down at the far end of the sofa, staring into space as if dazed. Jackie knew she was close to solving the riddle. She was desperate to drag it out of this woman, yet terrified to learn whatever it was. She summoned all the courage she had left.

"Look, Mrs. Rogers, Taylor was my best friend in the entire world," she said emotionally. This was her plan—to appeal to Mrs. Rogers's caring side. She was counting on her to be a whole lot more sympathetic than her Fixer sister.

"We trusted each other. We told each other everything. But

the night she died, she did something horrible to me and completely out of character. And I need to know why."

Jackie's heart fell when Taylor's aunt didn't react.

Okay. Backup plan.

"I also know her brother, Sam, had something to do with it," she said.

Mrs. Rogers's head shot up at the mention of Taylor's older brother. But she still didn't speak.

"I know that Sam and Taylor had a huge fight and whatever it was he said to her drove her crazy." Jackie plunged on. "I need to know what Sam told her. Otherwise, I will never be able to forgive her for what she did to me and I will never be able to get over it."

Jackie paused.

Taylor's aunt stared at her for what seemed like minutes. Then she took a deep breath as if she'd made a decision.

"Obviously this means a lot to you, Jackie," she said, pausing. "And it sounds as though Taylor and you had a very special friendship. I'm going to take a huge chance here and put my trust in you."

Jackie's heart skipped a beat. *Here it comes.*

THIRTY-FOUR

"But first," Mrs. Rogers said, "you have to promise that what I tell you stays between us. No one else must know."

Jackie nodded. She would have promised anything to get the truth.

Mrs. Rogers turned her head and stared at a fixed spot on the opposite wall as if reading a teleprompter.

"When I was eighteen, I fell desperately in love with a married man," she said. "I was incredibly naïve. I thought he'd leave his wife and marry me. But then I got pregnant and he wanted nothing to do with me."

Jackie wasn't sure whether to murmur sympathetically or let her go on. *Don't interrupt,* she decided.

"I was too young to cope with being a single mother, so I put the baby up for adoption and tried to get on with my life as if

267

none of it ever happened," Mrs. Rogers said, still not looking at Jackie.

Where is she going with this?

"But apparently Sam found out and he told Taylor," she added, shaking her head.

Jackie waited for her to continue. *Hurry up!*

Mrs. Rogers dragged her eyes away from the wall and met Jackie's. Her eyes were the same piercing blue as Jennifer Cane's.

"And that's it," she said firmly, adding, "You can understand how incredibly painful it is . . . dredging it all up."

Jackie frowned, confused. *I don't get it. So what if Taylor's aunt had a baby out of wedlock? Why would Taylor care?*

As if reading her mind, Mrs. Rogers dropped her gaze and started talking again.

"When Taylor called me to ask if it was true, I lied and told her I had no idea what she was talking about. Taylor was furious with her brother, saying something about him lying to her and that she'd never forgive him."

Jackie saw the woman gripping her hands in her lap so tightly they were turning white. *There's more she's not telling me.* Somehow, she had to draw her out.

"I can see that. Taylor and Sam were always at each other's throats. It drove her crazy." Jackie nodded, feigning understanding. "By the way, how did Sam find out?" she asked, keeping her voice casual.

Mrs. Rogers hesitated.

"Sam's no good," she said finally. "Even when he was little, he'd steal money from his mother's purse. When he was a teenager, he got more daring. He broke into the Canes' house safe, looking for cash, and found the adoption papers."

Jackie wasn't surprised. She could just imagine Sam doing something sly like that.

"Jennifer made him promise to keep it a secret. But every time he needed money he threatened to tell."

The more details Mrs. Rogers gave her, the less sense it made. *Why would Jennifer Cane have her sister's baby's adoption papers? And why was she so desperate to keep it from Daniel? And what was so dangerous about any of this?*

"You're not telling me everything," Jackie said, shaking her head. "Or else you're lying."

She didn't give Mrs. Rogers time to deny it.

"I'm calling Sam Cane. Right now," Jackie threatened. "I bet he'll talk."

Mrs. Rogers gave an agonized cry. "No! You can't do that!"

"Would you prefer I call your sister Jennifer?"

Now Taylor's aunt sounded hysterical. "You can't! Jennifer saved my life! She made it possible for me to see my baby grow up!"

What?! Panic rose in Jackie's throat, threatening to strangle her.

Mrs. Rogers must have realized she'd said too much—without meaning to—because she clapped her hand over her mouth. Then she put her head in her hands and wept softly.

She only raised her head when Jackie picked up her iPhone. Mrs. Rogers put out her hand to stop her.

"This must never go beyond this room," she said, her eyes suddenly as icy as Jennifer Cane's. Jackie suppressed a shudder. "Promise me again."

"I promise." *We'll see.*

"What I'm about to tell you is exactly what I told Taylor. It's the whole story." Mrs. Rogers fixed on Jackie this time, instead of the wall. "I happened to get pregnant at the same time my sister Jennifer was expecting twins. You probably find it hard to believe, but back then, unwed mothers were stigmatized."

"Uh huh."

"So I decided to spend my pregnancy hiding at our family's beach house in Florida and have the baby adopted down there. Jennifer joined me during her last trimester so we could be together when we each gave birth."

Jackie clenched her jaw to stop from shouting at the top of her lungs, *Get to the point!*

"While we were down there, a terrible thing happened. One of Jennifer's twins died in utero, before the pregnancy was full term."

For a second, Mrs. Rogers seemed lost in thought. The only sound in the room was Jackie's heart violently pounding through her entire body.

Oh my God. Is she saying . . .

"So Jennifer secretly adopted *my* baby . . . and pretended she'd given birth to two healthy children," Mrs. Rogers began again. "Twins. Taylor and Daniel."

Jackie was stunned into silence. Of all the scenarios she'd imagined, nothing came close to this. *I must be hallucinating.*

Somehow she found her voice.

"You're telling me that Taylor and Daniel aren't twins at all? They're cousins? They were really *your* baby and *Jennifer's* surviving baby?" *Say no. Say no. Say no.*

But Mrs. Rogers nodded, letting tears trickle down her cheeks, not seeming to notice them.

"Don't you see?" she pleaded. "It made perfect sense. I was heartbroken at the idea of never seeing my baby again. And everyone expected Jennifer to arrive back in Washington with twins, anyway. It allowed me to be a part of my child's life, even if it was just as an aunt."

Jackie's head was spinning around and around, and her heart was breaking into thousands of painful, pointed shards. She couldn't bear to think of Taylor dealing with this all alone.

First Taylor discovered her older brother, Sam, was still using date-rape drugs. Then Sam got his revenge by telling her she was *adopted* and she wasn't a twin at all. Daniel was not even her brother. He and Sam were her *cousins*.

If only you'd told me. I would have kept your secret. I would have cried with you and shared your pain.

The word "dangerous" suddenly popped into her head. None of what she'd heard explained that part of the mystery.

"You warned Taylor on the phone that if anyone found out, it would be dangerous," Jackie said. "What you've just told me is unbelievably traumatic. But what's dangerous about it?"

When Mrs. Rogers didn't answer, Jackie replayed the events in her mind.

There *was* one key piece of the puzzle still missing. Taylor's aunt hadn't named the baby's father. If he was famous, he might go to any lengths to cover up the existence of an illegitimate child.

"Tell me who got you pregnant," Jackie demanded.

Mrs. Rogers looked cornered. Then her body sagged as if giving up.

"I was having an affair with Bob Price," she whispered.

Jackie couldn't breathe. The screams in her head were so loud she barely noticed Mrs. Rogers was still talking.

"When I told Bob I was carrying his baby, he was ruthless. Remember, back then, his wife was a senator who already had presidential aspirations. He called me a whore and denied he was the father. Then he accused me of trying to trap him. He tried to bribe me to have an abortion. When that didn't work, he threatened me. So I fled to Florida."

Jackie dreaded asking the next question but she had to know.

"Did Deborah Price know any of this?" *Did my mom know?*

Mrs. Rogers nodded. "Deborah knew he'd knocked up some unnamed teenager, but he told her he'd taken care of it," she said bitterly.

She must have noticed the anguish on Jackie's face, because she added, "Don't worry. I'm almost certain your mother didn't know anything about it."

After chasing the truth for so long, Jackie now wished that Andrew had never found Taylor's cell, that he'd never given it to her, that she'd never listened to the messages, and that she'd never dialed Pamela Rogers's number. Anything, even the agony of not knowing and the pain of not understanding, was better than the truth.

I was so stupid to think that finding out would make all the hurt go away. Why didn't I listen to Lettie and Laura Beth and just let it go?

But now that Mrs. Rogers had opened up, there was no shutting her up.

"Now, do you understand how dangerous this is?" she asked angrily, not waiting for Jackie's answer. "Do I need to spell it out?"

She got to her feet and paced the room.

"If it came out now, it would be the end of the Price administration. And it would throw the next election to the Republicans. The Democrats would do anything to keep this quiet. Anything."

"No, Aunt Deborah would never do anything bad . . ." Jackie began.

Mrs. Rogers wheeled around.

"Don't be such a little fool! It's not just the Prices. It's the whole political machine behind them. The Democratic kingmakers, the lobbyists, the companies, all the people who put her in the White House and profit from *their* president's policies."

Jackie closed her eyes.

No wonder Taylor couldn't handle it. I can't freakin' handle it.

The next thought made her want to vomit. Andrew and Taylor had slept together.

"Oh. God. Oh sweet Jesus. Andrew was Taylor's *half brother.*" Jackie moaned out loud.

"What? What did you say?" Pamela Rogers shook her arm roughly. "No! No, you misunderstood, Jackie."

She forced Jackie to look her in the eye as if to make sure there would be no confusion.

"It wasn't Taylor who was adopted," Mrs. Rogers said. "I had a *boy.* I gave birth to Daniel."

Leaving Pamela Rogers's house, Jackie ached as if she'd just finished a marathon. In a way she had. She fell into bed. But as soon as she climbed under the covers, all she did was toss and turn, going over everything she'd learned.

By dawn, she'd finally decided on the best of all her bad options. She would keep the truth from Daniel, Andrew, and Scott—shelter them from a heartbreak they might never recover from. Protect them. As Taylor had done.

She also knew she *had* to find a way to lock up the secret. Not allow it to poison her thoughts and distort her relationships—the way it had eaten away at Taylor.

You can do this, she told herself. *I'm not as close to this as Taylor was. They weren't my parents, Daniel's not my twin.*

Somehow she got through all her classes without anyone noticing she was totally distracted.

She tried to pay attention at lunchtime when Laura Beth talked nonstop—as she'd been doing every spare moment of every day—about what she was going to do about Arden and college. Fortunately, Lettie took the lead, pretty much making the same points Jackie had.

"I didn't get into my first choice. Princeton didn't want me," Lettie pointed out. "But what happened next was even better. A full scholarship at Yale."

"Yes, but Lettie, you'd be grateful for *anything,*" Laura Beth said tactlessly, apparently forgetting Jackie's advice to think before speaking.

Jackie rolled her eyes at Lettie, who shook her head in surrender.

At home after school, Jackie tossed her uniform in the bathroom hamper, showered, and picked out a floral-print dress from Ginger in Bethesda Row. *These spring colors will cheer up Andrew,* she thought as she stared in the mirror. Despite everything weighing on her mind and no sleep, and Taylor's dreadful secret that was now hers to keep, she had to admit she looked awesome. Her long blond hair fell on her shoulders in a lustrous cascade and the layers of mascara on her lashes made her blue eyes look enormous.

Andrew's doctors had discharged him the day before, so she was going to visit him at the White House.

Her stomach was churning. This would be her first test—to see if she could control Taylor's secret or if the secret would control her.

But that wasn't the only thing making her nervous.

Their hospital visits had gone well. They hadn't fought. And they hadn't rehashed any of the bad stuff. It was almost like they were back to being best friends. Except no matter how hard she tried, she couldn't shake the old memories of when handsome changed to hot. And friendly became passionate.

"God, Jackie," she said to her reflection. "What the hell's wrong with you? That's your hormones talking, not your head."

As she climbed the stairs to the First Family's quarters, the first person she ran into was Scott. He and Daniel had been close friends in middle school and she suddenly wondered if there'd been a subconscious brotherly connection. She forced herself not to go there. Not to stare at him, not to look for any similarities to Daniel.

"You coming to see Andrew?" he asked. She nodded. "Yeah, Andrew told me you've been visiting every day."

Her face grew hot.

"Scott . . . I—"

"It's okay, Jackie," he interrupted. "Nothing like a near-death experience to put things in perspective. I figured this might bring you and Andrew back together."

"We're not—"

He cut her off again. "Whatever it turns out to be, it's okay. Really." He grinned. "I'm off to Hopkins for accepted students' day. New scene. New girls. Though you set the bar high."

Jackie hugged him. "You'll be fighting them off, and even more so now that you're a national hero. Have fun."

She walked away from Scott and headed down the hall to the Queen's Bedroom.

Okay, you pulled it off with Scott. You can act natural with Andrew, too.

She felt the first ray of hope that with time and determination, Taylor's secret would end up in the same place as her parents' divorce—that corner of your heart reserved for devastating events that you eventually learn to live with.

Andrew was sitting up in bed, typing on his laptop. Leftie, lying next to the bed, raised his head. Recognizing Jackie, he thumped his tail loudly on the floor.

"Knock, knock," she said from the open doorway.

The rumpled sheets and the familiar smell of his bedroom—so different from the starched and sterile hospital room—were an unsettling reminder of all the times they'd come so close to making love.

"Hey!" He beamed. "Just what I need. An excuse to take a study break. These online lectures really suck."

"You must be feeling better if you're hitting the books," she said, walking over to the leather armchair by his bed. He smelled faintly of cologne and shampoo and she inhaled deeply.

"It's the only way to keep Mom out of my room." Andrew grinned and ran his hand through his hair. Funny how such a mundane gesture could be so sexy. "She's suddenly turned into a helicopter parent. It's a wonder the entire U.S. government hasn't ground to a halt."

"Her extremely talented chief of staff wouldn't let that happen," Jackie kidded.

"Oh yeah. What was I thinking?"

"Even Scott's been hanging around," Andrew added. "He and I have decided that as soon as I'm feeling stronger, we're going to spend a few days together at Camp David to see if we can go back to being brothers instead of rivals."

He closed the laptop, put it on his bedside table, and grimaced. He lifted up his tee to examine the raw, angry scar.

"Are you still in pain?" Jackie asked, concerned, though she couldn't help but stare at his bare, muscular chest. When she dragged her eyes back to his face, he was grinning at her. She rolled her eyes to cover up her embarrassment at having been caught.

"I can't tell if it's the knife wound or indigestion from all the cookies Dad's been baking and force-feeding me," Andrew said, pulling his shirt back down.

Bob must be bored. He obviously hasn't found a replacement for Frances yet.

"I haven't thanked you for spending so much time visiting me," Andrew said suddenly.

"As if I wouldn't, Andrew. We've practically spent our entire lives together."

He gave a rueful smile.

"It's ironic that as soon as we made a clean break from Ankie, we've been getting along better than we have in more than a year."

She avoided his gaze by bending down to pat Leftie's long silky fur.

"Jackie," Andrew said softly, forcing her to straighten up and meet his eyes. "It's almost like we used to be. Before I turned into an asshole."

You sure were.

But to be fair, Taylor's death had turned both of them into people they didn't want to be. Sad, angry, and self-absorbed, thinking mostly about themselves instead of the other person.

"It wasn't just you, Andrew." She surprised herself by admitting it out loud. "It was me, too. I felt so hurt and betrayed that I started acting like a pious bitch."

"What do you mean?"

She wasn't sure exactly. The words had spilled out of her mouth almost before she realized it. She replayed them in her mind. *I started acting like a pious bitch.*

Andrew was still staring at her. He started to say something, but she waved her hand to stop him.

"Wait. Just let me think this through."

Was what Andrew had done with Taylor all that much worse than her and Scott? Hadn't *she* been powerless to stop kissing Scott once they started? Even though she wasn't sure how she felt about him. And Eric! She'd forgotten all about Eric. *I was ready to give it up in my own mother's office! Five minutes after I met him!*

In some ways, she'd unfairly used Andrew as a scapegoat. He wouldn't have sex with her, so she two-timed him with Eric. He had sex with Taylor, so she went with Scott behind his back.

Yet she and Andrew and Taylor were like any other teens with raging, out-of-control hormones, trying to figure out the whole messy growing-up thing. Confusing physical desire with emotional commitment.

Yes, they'd both made stupid, hurtful mistakes. And the biggest one of all was throwing away that "total connection" Taylor had talked about.

A real relationship was built on so much more than sex. At the core was genuine friendship. And that meant trusting and talking and having patience and forgiveness.

"Jackie!" Andrew said impatiently. "Tell me what you're thinking."

"I think what I mean is," she began slowly, "I didn't, or I couldn't, distinguish between emotional and physical betrayal."

She took his hand.

"We've both been so stubborn and stupid. After Taylor died, we forgot how to talk. I mean *really* talk. So we could work on healing my hurt and your guilt instead of giving into it."

His fingers tightened around hers.

"Jackie, you are amazing."

She leaned forward and her mouth touched his lightly, lingering for a second before moving away. He tasted just the way she remembered. She licked her lips to seal in the moment. He looked surprised, then his face flushed with emotion. She couldn't tell if it was relief or hope or apprehension.

"Okay, let's start talking," he said. "And see what happens."

THIRTY-FIVE

Laura Beth gently placed a huge bouquet of multicolored parrot tulips on Taylor's grave.

It was the first time she'd visited the cemetery since Sol confessed to sleeping with Whitney.

Being here stirred up all the grief that had been slowly fading over the months. The horror of losing Taylor, not just as the brilliant spark who lit up their lives but as Laura Beth's closest confidante.

But I am surviving without her, she realized, *even with everything that's happened. I can still draw on Taylor's spirit. That will always be a part of me.*

And she had Jackie and Lettie to turn to as well. They were helping her sort out her feelings about Arden and where her own future lay. She was beginning to see Arden as a victim in need of rescue. And Tisch or Sarah Lawrence were certainly a means to still get everything she wanted—Broadway, Sol, and the role she deserved in Jeffrey's campaign. *I could make the difference between him winning and losing!* she thought.

Laura Beth had pretty much excused Taylor's betrayal once she'd learned about Sam's degenerate behavior. But she wondered if Jackie had. She found it hard to believe that Jackie had given up searching for all the answers. And if so, why hadn't she asked for her and Lettie's help? The only explanation was ... there was more to the story than Jackie had revealed. A cover-up like Uncle Ham suggested at his news conference? Something that would not only ruin Andrew's life but destroy the president, too?

In spite of a few rocky moments, her and Jackie's friendship was still intact. They'd worked together to get rid of Frances Ives and they'd promised each other to play fair as the campaign heated up. But how could she keep up her end of the bargain if she learned the whole truth about the night of the accident?

And then she realized, in a fleeting moment of maturity, *It's better if I never know.*

Lettie thought her bunch of yellow daisies looked like weeds next to Laura Beth's magnificent tulips. It reminded her, yet again, of how different they were and how amazing it was that the four of them ever became the Capital Girls. And not just that. Their special friendship had *lasted,* even without Taylor, who'd been the magnet.

For the first six months after Taylor's death, Lettie had visited the grave often and always brought daisies. The most recent time was last summer when Daniel had showed up.

———

"I always wondered who was leaving these," Daniel said. "I've seen them here a lot."

I remember thinking how cute he was. He had this beautiful white-blond hair and intelligent blue eyes. And he was so easy to talk to. Just like Taylor.

It was also the first time Daniel had claimed Andrew was hiding something about the accident.

She stared at Taylor's headstone. *Why didn't you tell us about the fight with Sam? You shouldn't have dealt with this alone. If you'd leaned on us, the accident might never have happened.*

She'd always been the one to lean on Taylor. *We all did.*

Now who did she have? Her family was still thousands of miles away and who knew when they'd all be reunited? Whitney's family rescued her with a place to live and food on the table. But those three were only just learning to be their own family. The intervention had been gut-wrenching—and right now, Whitney needed to lean on *her*. That was one reason Lettie had agreed to spend the summer with her in L.A., where Whitney was going to continue her eating disorder treatment.

"Dr. Whitney's already got a special treatment plan for you, Lettie. Surfing, chilling, and stargazing Hollywood style," Whitney had joked. *"By the time you get back to D.C., you're gonna be a genuine Valley Girl."*

Not likely. But she did hope that by the end of summer, she and Whitney would be even closer. They'd probably never be as tight as she was with Jackie and Laura Beth. But there were some things she didn't dare tell even them. Like about Tanya.

I'm all alone on that one.

Not even Taylor could have helped her. *How could I tell her that my feelings for Daniel—her own brother—are so confused, especially after Tanya kissed me?*

If only feelings could be stacked into tidy little piles, each with their own separate labels. The only hope she had of resolving her confusion, she knew, was to get away from both of them for a while.

Jackie was the last to place flowers on the grave—a large bunch of white gardenias—their heady perfume almost too much. Like Taylor.

She straightened up and the three of them put their arms around each other, heads bowed, each deep in thought.

She broke away from the others and sat down next to the grave. "Come sit with me," she said, patting the bright, spring-green grass.

They formed a circle.

"It's all going to be so different when I'm in New York and you two are at Yale," Laura Beth said tearfully.

"It seems so unreal," Jackie murmured. "Moving away from D.C. Not seeing each other every day. Leaving our families."

She could have bitten her tongue. Lettie's family was long gone. She took Lettie's hand and Lettie squeezed back to show it was okay.

"For the first time since Mamá and Papá left, I feel like everything's going to work out in Paraguay," Lettie whispered as if not to jinx it. "And when it does, I want you both to visit there with me. So I can show you all its beauty. Like Iguassu Falls, which are in the jungle with toucans and butterflies and rainbows, and the government palace in Asunción, which is almost two hundred years old."

"It sounds incredible," Jackie said. "I'd love to go."

"Me, too." Laura Beth nodded. Then she slapped her forehead in mock horror. "I can't believe it but we haven't given a second's thought to graduation. Or what we'll wear to Prom and all the parties. All the gifts . . ."

Jackie nudged her. *Shut up, Laura Beth.*

Lettie's face was a mask.

"Lettie, have you written your valedictorian speech yet?" Jackie asked quickly.

Her friend blushed. "Just the outline."

"Yeah, right. I bet it's written, polished, and memorized."

They all laughed.

"You should rehearse it with me so I can stage direct you," Laura Beth instructed. "You know, your enunciation, hand gestures, standing position . . ."

Jackie and Lettie exchanged looks.

Laura Beth's eyes filled with tears again. "I'm scared, guys," she admitted. "What if I end up the worst singer and dancer and actress in the entire department? Wherever I decide to go."

"Forget it," Jackie said. "You. Are. Brilliant. You're going to knock 'em dead."

"Laura Beth, you rock," Lettie added.

Laura Beth gave a weak smile. "You say that because you're my friends . . ."

"Yes, and friends don't lie!" Jackie shot back. "Now, quit fishing for compliments."

Change the subject.

"When's Arden coming?" Jackie asked. They needed to quit avoiding the topic of her arrival.

"Midsummer. A couple of days after you and I get back from our trip to Europe."

Laura Beth won't admit it but it's just a matter of time before she turns Arden into her mini-me. She could picture Laura Beth and Arden on the campaign trail in color-coordinated outfits.

"Have your mama and the senator set a wedding date yet?" Jackie asked.

Laura Beth shook her head. "They want to wait until Arden is living with Mama and me and has adjusted to her new school. Maybe sometime in the late fall or winter."

"I think that's really nice," Lettie said, "that they're putting her first. It's going to be hard for her, especially after losing her own mother."

"Well, I'm just glad they're not getting married during *my* graduation. I mean, we only graduate from high school once. Besides, we need plenty of time to plan the wedding."

"You mean *you* need plenty of time to plan the wedding," Jackie teased. "I bet you've already picked the bridesmaids' dresses."

Laura Beth smiled sheepishly. "Well, I have asked our personal shopper at Saks to keep an eye out for me."

"What about asking your friend Friedrick VonDrak?" Jackie joked. They all shuddered at the memory of the bizarre runway show in New York.

"How are your mom and Ike Sawyer getting along?" Lettie asked.

"No wedding bells, yet," Jackie said. "I just wish they'd go ahead and elope. I don't know how long I can put up with Mom giggling and acting like she's our age every time he calls. It's gross."

Jackie was learning to swallow her jealousy. Her mom and Ike were so happy around each other. Besides, she didn't want her mom to be lonely when she left for Yale.

Laura Beth frowned.

"Speaking of boyfriends, I'm nervous about Sol and me still being in different cities when we start college in the fall."

"Sol's not a player, Laura Beth," Jackie reminded her. "He told you about Whitney when he didn't have to . . ."

Laura Beth perked up and beamed, the tears miraculously vanishing.

"You're so right. I should be more trustin'. Like you are with Daniel, Lettie."

Lettie, turning red, didn't answer. But that didn't stop Laura Beth. "Come on, Lettie. We want details. Is he a good kisser?"

"Oh, Laura Beth, stop teasing," Jackie intervened. She added, joking, "Of course he's a good kisser. They're incredibly cute together and they're going to live happily ever after."

Lettie chewed on a blade of grass.

"Just like you and Andrew?" Laura Beth winked.

"We'll see."

But she couldn't hide her smile. They were still talking, talking, talking. And occasionally more than that.

Just thinking about their kiss last night gave her delicious goose bumps.

I'd just gotten up to leave when he pulled me onto his lap.

His mouth came down hard and his hands slipped under my shirt, caressing my back. At first, they were just gentle strokes but they got more urgent as our kiss got more passionate. It felt so familiar yet fresh and new and exciting.

I couldn't stop myself. I ran my hands along his muscular arms, then linked them behind his head, probing his mouth with my tongue, drinking him in.

He began to moan, breaking off the kiss.

"We've got to stop!" he said huskily.

"You're right. We need to take it slowly," I agreed and slid off his lap.

"No. I meant stop because my chest is killing me," he said, bracing his wound with his hands.

We both dissolved into fits of sheer happy, carefree laughter.

Jackie was aware of Laura Beth and Lettie staring at her, waiting for her to confide in them about her and Andrew.

But she wasn't ready to share. Not yet.

"You and Andrew are so perfect together," Laura Beth said, breaking the silence. Jackie gave her an appreciative smile. That was big, coming from someone who'd always dreamed of winning Andrew for herself.

But Jackie knew it was way more complicated than that. They could be *great* together. But was anything perfect?

If Taylor and this past lousy year have taught me anything it's that you don't have to have a perfect relationship in order to be in love. And you don't have to be perfect to be a good daughter. And true friends are not always perfect. But they are worth a second chance.

She now totally got it that Taylor, carrying such a monumental secret, had been out of her mind with anger, shock, and grief. Not only that she and Daniel weren't twins, but that Andrew and Scott were Daniel's half brothers. And that Bob Price had never wanted Daniel as his third son.

But why have sex with *Andrew*?

Was it revenge? Was Taylor hoping to get pregnant and destroy the Price family's reputation?

Or was it to get back at Sam by beating him at his own game? To show that, unlike him—the guy who thought he needed drugs to get girls—she, Taylor, was irresistible?

Or was Taylor so burdened by her secrets that she couldn't face a lifetime of lying to those she loved, starting with her best friends? To commit an act of betrayal so unforgivable—sleeping with *Andrew*—the Capital Girls would never ever have anything to do with her again?

Jackie would never know for sure. But she guessed it was the last reason. After all, Taylor prized loyalty and honesty above all else. In some sick way she must have thought that forcing the Capital Girls to cut her loose would somehow set her free.

Once again, Laura Beth dragged Jackie back to the present.

"So, have you two done it yet?" she asked Jackie, giggling.

"Laura Beth!" Lettie playfully shoved her backward onto the grass.

"Why, Laura Beth, ladies don't kiss and tell," Jackie said in a pathetic attempt at a Southern accent.

"'Course, there's that little matter of a knife wound in his chest and a punctured lung," Laura Beth added, picking grass out of her hair. "After waiting so long, you surely do need to make certain he's fully recovered . . . so you can truly appreciate what you've been missin'."

Lettie groaned and pushed her down again.

Jackie looked at her watch. "I need to go. I'm supposed to be at Founding Farmers at one o'clock."

"What's that?" Lettie asked.

"It's a restaurant near the White House. It's the latest in Mom's series of Jackie-and-Ike-getting-to-know-each-other lunches."

The girls stood up and gazed at each other.

"Look what the three of us have gone through . . . and survived," Jackie said.

"It just shows best friends can deal with anything." Laura Beth nodded.

Maybe even the campaign, Jackie thought.

"What about Whitney?" Lettie asked.

Jackie shrugged.

"Whitney? What she's got to do with *us*?" Laura Beth said scornfully.

"She needs our support, Laura Beth. I care what happens to her," Lettie said.

"I know you do. She's lucky to have you," Jackie said kindly. "And we're glad she's getting help, honestly."

We'll all be better off.

Lettie's face fell, as if she knew what was coming—a great, big b-u-t.

"But after everything she's done, I'll never be able to trust her," Jackie admitted.

"Not the way we trust each other," Laura Beth added. "She just doesn't know how to be a Capital Girl and never will."

Before the other two could answer, Laura Beth grabbed their hands.

"Jackie!" Lettie smiled. "You're wearing your bracelet again. And you added the infinity loop Laura Beth designed!"

Jackie nodded and jangled the Capital Girls charms.

"Let's make a Capital Girls pledge," Laura Beth announced. "No more secrets."

"Okay. No more secrets," Lettie said, nodding.

"No more secrets," Jackie repeated.

But even as she uttered the words, Jackie knew it was a promise she'd already broken.

But keeping *that* secret—Taylor's secret—was meant to protect. Not harm.

It suddenly occurred to her that Taylor had handed her a golden trump card. Not just a secret to hold close, but the chance to end Jennifer Cane's hold over Jackie. A way to force The Fixer—in exchange for silence—to put an end to Sam's disgusting behavior.

She could even use it, if she needed to, to make Bob Price a better father to Andrew and Scott, and a better husband to Aunt Deborah. *Was that how Jennifer Cane started out?* As a keeper of secrets to protect those she loved? Her sister, Pamela, and her adopted son, Daniel? And when did she realize that secrets were also powerful tools that could create fortunes, change votes, kill careers, destroy lives?

If Jennifer Cane can be The Fixer for bad, why can't I be The Fixer for good?

A silly childhood rhyme—a Capital Girls favorite—played in Jackie's head. *"Secrets, secrets are no fun. Secrets, secrets hurt someone."*

But I will never use secrets to hurt people, Jackie silently vowed. *Not unless I have to.*

ACKNOWLEDGMENTS

Thanks to Charley for all the cooking and encouragement. Thanks also to our literary agent, Joanna Volpe, and our St. Martin's editor, Sara Goodman, who made this series possible. And thanks to all our wonderful friends for their support.

IN THE NATION'S CAPITAL, EVERYTHING IS A POPULARITY CONTEST.

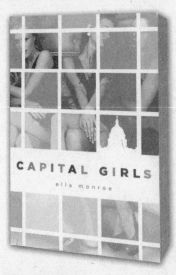

Check out the Capital Girls and Ella Monroe online

St. Martin's Griffin